Book # 2

D0187747

to WALK in his MOCCASINS

I hope you enjoy the sequel

Happy Reading,

Sharon Lewis Koho

10 – 17 – 07

a sequel to
The Painting on the Pond

SHARON LEWIS KOHO

Bonneville Books
Springville, Utah

© 2005 Sharon Lewis Koho

All rights reserved.

No part of this book may be reproduced in any form whatsoever, whether by graphic, visual, electronic, film, microfilm, tape recording, or any other means, without prior written permission of the publisher, except in the case of brief passages embodied in critical reviews and articles.

ISBN 13: 978-1-55517-878-9
ISBN 10: 1-55517-878-2

Published by Bonneville Books
an imprint of Cedar Fort, Inc.
2373 W. 700 S., Springville, UT, 84663
Distributed by Cedar Fort, Inc., www.cedarfort.com

Cover design by Nicole Williams
Cover design © 2005 by Lyle Mortimer

Printed in the United States of America

10 9 8 7 6 5 4 3

Printed on acid-free paper

To the memory of my husband, Bill.

ACKNOWLEDGMENTS

Special appreciation to my dear family and friends who believe in me, support me, and encourage me with their patience, kind words, and unconditional love. Special thanks to Leo and Bonnie Lewis, Dr. Betty Turner, and Kathleen M. Charlie. And with gratitude for sweet memories to Chyenne.

PROLOGUE

Late July

Jerry grinned as the two bicycles coasted down the hill toward the meadow.

"What a fabulous day! Just smell the pine trees and wild flow—"

"Last one to the creek does dishes," Roxanne called, crouching over her handlebars and peddling fast as she swept past Jerry.

"Hey," Jerry said as he leaned forward and increased speed with his powerful legs, but he couldn't catch her. She suddenly tipped the bike sideways, rolling across the thick meadow grass as her bike skidded to a stop on the creek bank. Jerry, coming up fast behind her, veered to the side, trying to miss her bike. His front tire struck a gopher hole and flipped him over the handlebars into the crystal clear creek. When she saw that he was all right, Roxanne curled her feet under her, sitting on them on the bank as she laughed. Jerry, gasping from the shock of frigid water, pulled himself up the bank, flopped down beside her and wrapped his dripping arms around her. She shrieked and tried to get away, but he held her tight, placing a soppy kiss on her lips. "You get the dishes," he mocked.

"Not so; I reached the bank before you did." She shivered and giggled, leaning against his cold wet shirt.

"You said creek, Roxy, not bank." He gathered her closer and muffled her argument with another kiss.

Later that night, Jerry sat on the braided rug in front of Roxanne's gas fireplace. She snuggled beside him, so warm, so precious, so real in his arms, her blond curls resting on his shoulder. Her hand was holding tightly to his as she caressed his fingers with her other hand, the one with the diamond ring he'd just given her. She looked into his eyes in the flickering firelight, her sweet face aglow with happiness as tears trickled down her cheeks. "This is for real, isn't it Jerry? You and me forever, forever."

CHAPTER ONE

Late August

Jerry Stone lay on the stretcher, watching the spinning helicopter blade above him as it cut through the twilight still hanging in the early morning Alaskan sky. He was dazed and chilled to the bone even though his wet clothes were removed and most of the black muck wiped from his body.

The shock of Eric and Roxanne's betrayal, the shattered betrothal, the grief-filled flight through the rugged terrain, and his terrifying plunge into the bog all seemed like a distant nightmare. Paralyzing numbness and the blackness of despair had replaced his senses as he sank deeper and deeper into the bog. He nearly died. He'd wanted to die, but David and Rachel would not let him die. Now, flying above the rugged wilderness that was almost his grave, numbness still engulfed him. Excruciating pain in his thigh seemed unreal, disconnected, part of that terrible dream. Piles of blankets covering him held no warmth. He only felt emptiness and cold as he slipped into unconsciousness.

Several hours later, in the surgical recovery unit of the Fairbanks hospital, pain was Jerry's only sensation. Starting at his foot, it wracked his leg from toe to hip and up his spine. Jerry groaned in agony. He felt warm blankets lifted from his hip and the sharp sting of a hypodermic needle as a faceless nurse injected morphine into his muscle. The pain gradually subsided, and he slept. He remained sedated and groggy most of the day.

Later that evening the taste of salt awakened Jerry as a tear trickled down his cheek and entered the corner of his mouth. He had been dreaming about Roxanne. Staring into dim light sifting through the drapes, he swallowed the salty taste and then wiped his eyes on his bed sheet, not wanting to think or feel or remember.

Shifting his focus upward, he looked at a pole extending from the head to the foot of his bed. Two pulleys supported a rope stretching from metal pins in his knee beyond his ankle and toes to a dangling sandbag. The weight of the sandbag tugging at his thigh suspended his left leg in a stirrup. "Well, this is a fine fix I've gotten myself into," he complained. A feeling of helplessness and despair washed over him. He moaned and laid his head on the pillow with a defeated sigh. *She's gone. Everything is gone. Where in the world do I go from here?*

A nurse entered and flipped on a light. "How are you feeling, Mr. Stone?"

Jerry's enormous heartache was his to bear alone, so he quickly buried his grief beneath a facade. The mood of the stocky nurse was cheery, so he gathered his wits and tried to play along. "Like a truck ran over me," he answered with a weak grin. "Did one?"

"Not likely—maybe a moose," she answered. He winced as she stuck a thermometer in his ear.

"I know this is a dumb question, but what did I do to myself?"

"You fractured your femur and have been suffering from severe hypothermia," she said, removing the thermometer when it beeped. "Your below-normal temperature has increased, but now you're running a slight fever." She removed a blanket.

"Hey, bring that back; I'm still cold," he protested.

"I know." She gave him some aspirin. "The chilling should stop soon. Too many blankets will spike your temperature."

Jerry swallowed the aspirin, chilled more by the apple juice that washed it down. "Brrr, where's the hot chocolate?"

"Sorry, you're on clear liquids until the doctor comes in. Would you like some warm broth?"

"Blah! Just nuke the juice next time and plop in a cinnamon stick?"

She smiled. "I can do warm juice. We're a little shy on cinnamon sticks. Want it now or later?"

"Later works. Can I get out of this contraption?"

"I'm afraid not; you have a lot of shattered bone in your thigh that needs to grow back together. Your fracture will require traction for a few weeks," she said as she took his blood pressure and counted his pulse. "Take big breaths and cough deeply. You need to clear your lungs so pneumonia doesn't set in. After all you've been through, that is a danger."

Gripping a trapeze bar above him, Jerry winced and groaned as he tried to shift his position. "This is the pits. I want out. I'll pay good if you'll help me escape."

"Not a chance," she chuckled. "I'm a nurse, as in helping people get well." She tried to make him more comfortable; nothing helped. "I'm sorry, but it's too soon for pain medicine. I'll help you work the pump when it's time."

"Hey, it's time! This blasted weight is pulling my leg off." Jerry grimaced, trying to shift again. "I just can't believe I was stupid enough to do this to myself. I must have taken idiot lessons from David."

"Who's David?"

"My best friend, he does dumb stuff like this all the time."

"Don't be too hard on yourself." She winked, pointing to the call button on his bed rail. "Try to get some rest. Call me if you get too uncomfortable."

"What do ya' mean if," he grumbled. She smiled and flipped off the light as she left the room.

Jerry moaned and took a deep breath, trying to relax. Finally he drifted off to sleep. Suddenly, he couldn't breathe. He gasped for air as the pull of the bog sucked him into its oozing belly. He

tried to scream, but the icy goo filled his mouth and throat. Jerry awakened with a sudden jerk and sat up abruptly, sending shooting pains through his thigh. He groaned and shuddered, pulling his sheet more tightly about him, realizing how close he had come to allowing his life to end. The smell of the bog was washed away, but the thick stench still permeated his nostrils. If David hadn't called him a coward, startling him with icy splashes of that hideous slime in his face and mouth, Jerry would have died like his father.

He could still see the terror on David's face as he heaved stone after stone into the putrid muck just inches from Jerry's head. David was relentless, taunting him, commanding him to grasp the branch Rachel Duncan had extended to him. Fueled by the sickening taste of the slime and David's cutting words, fierce anger surged through Jerry, burning like a fire into his nearly lifeless limbs. Suddenly, he wanted to live, to strike David, to lash back with all of the hurt, heartache, and anger he had ever endured. He had grasped the branch. David had saved his life. "Thank you, God," Jerry whispered. "Thank you for my friend." A tear squeezed past his eyelashes although he squinted hard to hold it back.

He also tried to hold back thoughts—unwelcome thoughts— but they forced a vision of Roxanne into his mind. Jerry gave a deep sigh. *We came here to help David and Kimberly save Eric and Rachel's father's claim. They knew the lost gold mine was somewhere on Sam Duncan's claim, but he had never found it. Sam's lost mine had belonged to Kimberly and Roxanne's great-grandfather until his disappearance nearly a century ago.* Jerry shook his head in dismay. *I can't believe this happened. While I was trying to help Eric Duncan find his father's treasure, he stole mine.* Jerry moaned and buried his face in his hands. *What commanding pull did Eric have to so easily destroy all that Roxanne and I had planned: our dream cottage, lots of babies, children gathered around us, a home filled with laughter and love, just growing old together and living happily ever after. We were so good for each other. How could she forget?*

Jerry took a deep breath and lowered his hands. Far greater

than his own suffering, he feared for Roxanne. They had only just met Eric. What kind of man was he, really? What were his true intentions? Was she safe? Jerry felt so helpless. He couldn't protect her. From earliest childhood he had been taught that God loves and protects his children. *Please, God, protect Roxanne. Bring her back to me.* Jerry's plea was more a thought than a prayer, but a serene feeling of comfort filled the silence of the hospital room. He sensed, however, that Roxanne would never be a part of that comfort. Her sweet pixie face framed by short golden curls, her dancing brown eyes, and her bright intoxicating smile, faded into the shadows of the dim room. Accepting the loneliness that was now his companion, Jerry let himself slip into the spirit of peace that surrounded him. He rested his head on the pillow. *Thy will be done*, he added to his silent prayer.

The following day, Jerry was more alert and the pain was more intense. His emotions were riding a roller coaster of grief, anger, despondency, and acceptance. The only thing that calmed him was acceptance. He tried to settle his mind there, but it was out of control. He preferred to sleep. He ached for sleep. When the morphine eased the pain enough that he could rest, he buried himself in sleep.

That night the phone in his room rang. He clumsily fumbled for the receiver and answered it.

"Hey, Bud, how are you? You hanging in there?" David's voice sounded worried and strained.

Wanting to reassure him, Jerry tried to be cheerful. "Well, my leg is anyway. Yeah, I'm okay. Thanks to you I'll have a lifetime to fish. I'm hurting pretty bad right now, but I could still cast a mean lure if they'd set my bed afloat."

David tried to chuckle. "Hey, I'm sorry I'm not there to do it for you. They say Alaskan fishing is the best. I uh . . ." There was a long pause. Then David cleared his throat. "I . . . I'm so sorry for all those things I yelled at you. I didn't mean . . ." He cleared his throat again. "Jerry, no hero has ever been more loyal or courageous than you." David's voice choked and fell silent.

"Ah, quit groveling, you punk. I yelled at you when you were being stupid. That's what friends and brothers do. Forget it."

Then followed a moment of silence—the comfortable silence that begets understanding. Finally, David spoke. "Kim and I wanted to fly to Fairbanks today. You'll never believe what happened, though. Kimberly saw the cave in a dream last night. We followed her premonition and found the lost mine. It's rich in gold, so Sam Duncan's claim is saved. More amazing than that, we found the skeleton of Nathan Demeron sitting against the cave wall. An earthquake trapped him, and his gold mine became his tomb.

"Kimberly's still a little shaken up, but finding her missing grandfather after all these years has given her a sense of peace. We've gotten permission from the coroner to fly Nathan's body back home with us. I have to build a makeshift coffin for transport from here, and then buy a casket in Fairbanks. I hate to put you off, Jerry, but I probably won't get to see you till tomorrow afternoon. I'm really sorry. I need to be there for you . . . now more than ever.

"The airline won't hold the body overnight, so one of us has to leave by tomorrow evening. Kim said she'd fly home with Nathan's remains, and then meet Mom when she arrives on Friday. That way I can stay until—"

"Are you cracked?" Jerry sputtered. "Send your wife home from her honeymoon alone with a dead grandpa? Not on my account! Kim needs you to see her through this. Besides, with burial arrangements to make for Nathan, you can use every spare minute you have to get ready for your mother. You've got to be there when Jan arrives. She's been waiting your whole life to see where you'd plant your roots. Just give her a bear hug for me. I'll be fine. I'll see you tomorrow, Dave, but you're not staying here."

As Jerry placed the phone in its cradle on the bedside stand, he thought of Jan Young, David's mother. He was sure her love and prayers would embrace him as he tried to put his life back together. She was as dear to him as his own mother had been.

"Mother," Jerry muttered as the sudden memory of his first tragic loss swept over him. His mother had died of leukemia when he was ten.² The tremendous void that remained where she had been was magnified by five years of his father's alcoholism, abuse, and eventual suicide. Now, another tragic twist of fate had struck Jerry with the worst agony he had endured in his twenty-seven years. He had always believed in his heart that life was a divine gift to mankind, ultimately good and infinitely rewarding. However, he wondered if he would ever find that elusive element called joy. Right now all he could feel was one wrenching heartache after another gathering around him like murky clouds of despair. His mind tumbled out of control again.

"Oh, Roxanne, why?" He buried his face in his bed sheet and quietly cried himself to sleep.

Chapter Two

Facing his sorrow and accepting his feelings the previous lonely night had calmed Jerry's emotions. He felt courage beyond himself as he greeted his friends.

His eyes were sad, and he looked haggard and drained, but his cheerful smile relieved the concern on David and Kimberly's faces as they entered his hospital room. Rachel Duncan, Eric's sister who had helped David pull Jerry from the bog, followed and quietly slipped into a corner.

Wearing a forced grin to mask the worry in his eyes, David strolled over to the bed and wrapped Jerry in a hug.

Jerry felt tenderness in David's embrace. He again recalled the terrible fear written on his friend's face as David and Rachel struggled to drag him from the bog; that putrid black pit that nearly claimed his soul as well as his life. Jerry felt a flood of guilt and remorse for the agony he'd put David through.

David cleared the huskiness from his throat as he studied Jerry's predicament. "Man, they don't have any intention of letting you escape for a while, do they?"

"Afraid not. I splintered the bone so badly that this is the only way it can heal. Dumb stunt, huh?" David hadn't fooled Jerry with his cheerfulness, and Jerry knew he wasn't fooling David with his sheepish grin. His face sobered. "Dave, thanks again for being

8

there for me." Jerry blinked hard. "I . . . I love you, Brother." His voice broke as he looked at the tiny scar on the inside of his middle finger. David had one just like it, where they had slit their fingers and mingled their blood, claiming each other as brothers when they were nine years old.

David grasped Jerry's hand. "Me too," he said swallowing a lump in his throat.

Kimberly nodded at Rachel and the two women quietly slipped out of the room.

Finally, Jerry found his voice. "Did Roxy leave for Kodiak with Eric?"

David released Jerry's hand and took a deep breath. He ran his fingers through his short, sandy hair and stared at his boots. Then he straightened his tall slender form. "Yes, Jerry, she did," he answered. The steady gaze in his blue-gray eyes was a mixture of anger and compassion. "I'm sorry, Bud."

Jerry nodded his acceptance and looked away. He already knew the answer, yet he had still held on to a glimmer of hope. His grief was unbearable, so he pushed it away, burying it deep in his heart. He gathered himself together under the gift of courage that he had been granted, and brushed a tear away with the back of his hand as he turned to David. "I'm glad it happened before we were married. That would have been harder." He nodded an assurance to David that wasn't real. "I'm made of tough leather, Dave. I'm all right." He turned away again and cleared his throat, subconsciously laying a row of bricks across the pathway to his heart.

David hoped that Jerry was as confident as he seemed, yet something about his manner made David worry even more.

"I understand my father now. I've forgiven him for everything. My experience in that bog made a different man out of me." Jerry shuddered. "That scared me so bad, David . . . not so much the muck, but the despair. It was so easy to give up, to want to die. He looked David straight in the eyes, his own eyes softening with intense gratitude. "Thank God you came when you did. There's no way Rachel could have pulled me out of my mental state. Within inches of her help, I'd have just let myself slip away." Jerry shook

his head and swallowed hard. "I'm sorry I caused her so much trouble. Is she okay?"

"Sure, in fact, since Sam's crew is returning to rebuild his mining operation, Rachel is applying for a nursing position here so she can take care of you."

Jerry was stunned and embarrassed. He didn't want her pity. Eric's unscrupulous behavior was no reflection on his sister. She owed Jerry nothing. He started to object.

David interrupted. He knew that Rachel had already deemed Jerry as a friend. In her anger at Eric and her concern for Jerry, David was certain that she was developing feelings for his stricken comrade. Everything in Jerry's world had crumbled. David dreaded leaving him in this sorry state, more than a thousand miles from home. With Rachel attending Jerry, however, he wouldn't be alone. Beginning with a bond of friendship, she could become a beautiful cornerstone upon which Jerry might rebuild his shattered life. David targeted his comments with that intent. "Rachel needs a friend, Jerry. She's found one in you. She wants to be here."

It seemed unlikely to Jerry that this young Athabaskan Indian woman might need him, even as a friend. She had a lovely, timid smile that revealed none of her self-assurance and self-confidence. Jerry had seen that first hand. Although she was reserved, she was at ease in her Caucasian father's white world, yet she held such mastery over the wild, harsh elements of her environment. On her Native American side, her unique speech and mannerisms, inherited from her mother, held a certain mystery and intrigue. He had sensed tenderness in her, a great kindness for all life, but this action toward him was surprising. Why would she drop everything and center her focus, and even her career, on him? Rachel didn't really know him that well. He was just an ordinary, nice-looking young man of medium build that any mother would be proud of. If she did consider him to be a friend, why? What had he done to deserve her regard, other than leading her on a treacherous manhunt through the rugged Alaskan wilderness?

Pondering these thoughts, Jerry studied Rachel as she and

Kimberly returned to his room with a round of sodas. He accepted the soda Rachel offered with her shy smile and kind words of encouragement. As she passed his bed and slipped back into the corner of the room he recalled her extraordinary spirit and courage in his behalf. He felt comforted by her gentle ways, and was glad she had come.

Throughout the afternoon Jerry's visit with his friends brightened his spirits and took his mind off his pain as they talked and laughed about happier days.

As time for the evening flight approached, Jerry hugged Kimberly, feeling the softness of her long, auburn hair as it brushed his face. Her sapphire blue eyes brimmed with tears, and her voice quivered as she bid him farewell.

Roxanne was her cousin, invited by Kimberly to bring Jerry with her to Alaska to help search for their grandfather's lost mine. Jerry's pain and grief were a direct result of her invitation. Kimberly knew she was not at fault for Roxanne's betrayal, but she still felt heartsick and responsible.

Jerry smiled and squeezed her hand. "Don't worry about me, Kim. I'm fine. Just keep taking care of David. In less than a month of marriage you've created something wonderful. He has never looked better or been more complete. You are everything, and so much more than the sweet, beautiful, and perfect wife I imagined that David deserved to find." He pulled her closer and whispered. "You're smart too. You know how to push his buttons. He'd do anything for you. Make him!"

Jerry's grin was bright and genuine. Although his arms were empty now and his loneliness was a constant, burning ache, he was filled with joy for David and Kimberly.

Jerry and David's farewell was harder. Then David and Kimberly were gone. Suddenly, home seemed a million miles away. The hospital was a prison, and the heavy traction pulling against Jerry's broken leg was the iron bracket chained to the stone wall of his dungeon. He moaned and closed his deep-blue eyes, resting his curly, black hair against the pillow.

Rachel moved toward Jerry's bed. She sat beside him, taking

his hand in hers. Surprised at her touch, he jumped. She had maintained a silent presence in the background during the farewell with his friends. He had forgotten she was there. Now she leaned forward, her long, black hair falling across his arm. It was sleek and silky, with a mild scent of honeysuckle. She bowed her head, resting her fingers on Jerry's lighter, tanned skin. Her Athabaskan accent was soothing like the sweet strains of a symphony.

"Jerry, I am sorry about Eric. He should not have taken advantage of your kindness and trust to then betray you." She looked up with tears brimming against the dark lashes lining her hazel-green eyes. "I am angry and ashamed that he has caused you such terrible pain and sadness." She shook her head and sighed. "Nedraya, dhech'el, edli like xwyh. Sedraya, dadhk'wn. Si am like sanh to warm nedraya. (Your heart, it is torn. It is cold like winter. My heart, it is burning. I am like summer to warm your heart)."

"What did you say?" Jerry asked.

Rachel smoothed a wrinkle in the hospital gown covering Jerry's chest. "I will tell you sometime," she answered as a tear slipped from the corner of her eye. She lowered her head. "I am sad for you, Jerry. I cannot heal the pain in your heart, but I want to be here for you, to be your friend, to help you anytime you need me. When your heart weeps, I will comfort you."

Jerry took a deep breath and patted her hand. "It's better that it happened now than later, Rachel. Thanks to you and David, I still have my life." He brushed the tear from her cheek and smiled. "I'll be okay."

Rachel stayed by Jerry's side until the nurse prepared him for the night and he fell asleep. Then she left the hospital, walked a block to the furnished apartment she had rented that morning, and dropped onto the couch.

"Nezunh. Drana si have begun. Bedraya edli. It will take oxw to warm him. (It is good. Today I have begun. His heart, it is cold. It will take a long time to warm him)." She sighed, staring blankly at her new surroundings. Then she stood up and unpacked her suitcases and some items from her trunk. After making her bed, she spread a beaded scarf across the trunk, caressing the brightly colored patterns with her fingers—the patterns her mother's skilled hands had created during many long, dark days of winter.

Remembering the soft touch of her mother's hands, Rachel smiled as she returned to the kitchen. She poured herself a glass of milk and sat in the windowsill watching the lights of Fairbanks against the twilight of the Alaskan sky.

CHAPTER THREE

Rachel arose early the next morning and sat at the table in her kitchen nook. She made a list of food and other needs to set up house. Then she pulled Jerry's black-rimmed glasses from her beaded rawhide purse. She had found them beside the log that Jerry had caught his foot on when he fell into the bog. Attempting to straighten the metal frame and replace one lens, she finally shook her head in frustration. "Ohoya, I do not have time to fight these stubborn glasses." She slipped them back into her purse. "I will have them repaired." She showered and dressed, blow-drying her thick hair as she brushed it. Then she went to the lobby and phoned a taxi.

Rachel finished her business and shopping before noon. She put her groceries away and ate a sandwich before walking to the hospital. After presenting her resume, she spoke with the personnel director and was immediately hired to work the day shift as a pediatric nurse. Pending work references from her prior job in Anchorage, she was scheduled to start work in three days. Pleased at how well things were falling into place, Rachel hurried to Jerry's room to share the good news.

Jerry's bed was gone, and an elderly woman lay sleeping where he had been. A twinge of fear sent Rachel hurrying to the nurses' desk to find the reason for his transfer.

✳

As his temperature began to rise again, Jerry continued to chill and began coughing during the night. "Onset of pneumonia," the doctor diagnosed, and he immediately ordered stronger antibiotics and a chest x-ray. Jerry felt miserable. His leg throbbed and his chest ached from coughing. Hypothermia and shock, followed by inactivity as Jerry lay tied to his leg traction, had left him weakened and susceptible to the infection. He was reassured that the medications, along with the humidifier puffing cold mist in his face, would quickly cure him of the pneumonia. Getting some relief from cough suppressants and a pain medication, Jerry welcomed patches of rest between coughing.

Toward morning, following a prolonged coughing spell, the generalized pain in Jerry's chest and thigh was suddenly forgotten, even though it had not diminished. A hot pain sliced through his insides like a knife, ripping his breath from him. Then the pain stopped moving, burning into one central point near his heart. Jerry fumbled for the nurse call button on the bed rail and pushed it.

A nurse entered the room. Hearing Jerry's labored breathing, she took one look at the dusky blue color of his face and pulled the emergency cord on the bathroom wall. Within seconds two more nurses arrived. "I think we've got a blood clot. Let's move!"

Struggling to breathe while someone elevated his head, Jerry fought panic as he watched the medical personnel bustling around him. A portable oxygen tank was rushed to his bedside and an oxygen mask was placed over his nose and mouth. He was quickly wheeled into the elevator, which rapidly descended to the second floor, and a voice echoed over the intercom, "Dr. Bottner to ICU, stat! Dr. Bottner to ICU, stat!" Jerry was rushed through the doors into the Intensive Care Unit. He winced as a nurse inserted an IV needle into his arm, and another nurse applied the wires of a heart monitor to his exposed chest. The doctor entered, snapping orders at the nurses as he listened to Jerry's heart. A portable x-ray identified the cause of Jerry's suffering.

Dazed from the excruciating pain and shortness of breath, Jerry was confused by a barrage of medical terms: Pulmonary embolism, pneumonia rules out surgery, IV therapy, heavy doses of heparin are essential to dissolve the clot, increase dosage of hydrocordone to suppress the cough. If the embolism is dislodged, it may pass through his heart.

"Administer one cc of Demerol per IV to relieve the pain," the doctor ordered, and he continued to bark orders as the nurses hurried to obey. The pain medication gradually took effect and the fire in Jerry's chest began to cool. His breath was less labored and he finally slept.

❊

Rachel slipped into Jerry's section of the Intensive Care Unit and studied his silent features. She was all too familiar with the possibilities of blood clots, especially after surgery or trauma to a leg. The serious implication was that Jerry's blood clot had moved from his leg and was now lodged within inches of his heart. The faint, blue pallor of Jerry's face was typical of his condition; yet, Rachel was shaken. Watching the readings on the monitor she was relieved that at least his vital signs were stable. He had been heavily sedated and was resting quietly.

"Eric, how could you do this? You were like a liga (dog). You have brought shame upon your family. This chila (young man) suffers because of nenh (you)." She sighed, gently passing her hand across Jerry's overly warm forehead. "I am sorry, my friend. I will not leave you tonight." Rachel stayed at his bedside, checking on him whenever he stirred. That night she slept in a chair in his room.

Jerry's condition remained serious for the next two days as pain from the blood clot, labored breathing, and tightness from the pneumonia strained his chest until he thought it would burst.

Except for a quick trip home for a shower or a bite to eat while Jerry rested, Rachel remained by Jerry's side. Her softly spoken words of encouragement—and sometimes words he couldn't understand—calmed and comforted him, easing his fear as he struggled for each breath. Finally the blood clot began to dissolve. Jerry's lungs cleared, and his pain was not as intense.

The first day of her new job, Rachel left the Intensive Care Unit in the early morning hours and walked home. She showered, dressed in her uniform, and twisted her damp hair into a bun. After eating a muffin and gulping down a glass of milk for breakfast, she hurried back to the hospital. She spent a few minutes with Jerry, assuring herself that he was improving and resting. Then she reported to the third floor for duty.

During her two breaks and lunch, Rachel hurried downstairs to Jerry's room to check on him. His color improved throughout the day, his breathing was less labored, and he was resting quietly. After work, she returned to Jerry's room. She released a gentle sigh as she sat down in the chair next to his bed.

Jerry reached out to hold her hand. "You stayed with me last night, didn't you? And every night since I got sick?" Rachel nodded, but her humble smile held Jerry's praise in check. "You angel," he whispered. Drawing her hand to his lips, he kissed her fingers. "I don't know why you chose to be my friend, but heaven was surely watching over me. Thank you." Jerry noticed her uniform and studied her face. "You worked all day; you must be exhausted."

"I am a little tired, but I am fine. You are feeling better?"

Jerry forced a weak grin. "I think so. You're a nurse. Take my pulse and tell me if I'm alive. I'd like your reassurance 'cause I'm still not quite sure."

Rachel withdrew her fingers from his hand and gently placed them on his wrist. "Yes, Jerry. You are most certainly alive. Your pulse is strong and steady."

"Good," he said, nodding his approval. Warm tingles seemed to flow from her fingers as they rested against his skin. Suddenly, Jerry was self-conscious. He nervously cleared his throat. "In that case, I guess I've about whipped this thing."

Rachel quickly withdrew her hand.

Jerry cleared his throat again and reached to push his glasses up on his nose. Realizing for the first time that they were missing, he frowned and scratched his head.

Rachel reached into her purse and handed Jerry his glasses. "They were broken. I had them repaired for you."

Jerry was irritated that he had made Rachel feel uncomfortable. "Oh, thank you. You're wonderful." he said with a remorseful smile. He took the glasses and put them on. "Now I can tell that those specks on the wallpaper are flowers. I thought they were bugs. I could swear they were moving yesterday."

A smidgen of a giggle escaped as Rachel smiled. "You have been quite disoriented at times. Once you scolded a nurse for feeding you a frog. You said it was jumping about in your chest."

"I did? Really? What did she say?"

"She said you had dreamed up your own frog and swallowed him all by yourself, so it was your problem, and you would just have to deal with it."

Jerry chuckled, studying Rachel's serious expression, but he didn't miss the twinkle in her eyes. He took her hand again in both of his. "Thank you, Rachel. You've been amazing. I was so scared. You have no idea how much you helped me. You must get some rest now, my dear little friend. You have dark circles under your eyes. I'm doing much better. You go home and get some sleep."

Rachel smiled and nodded. "The telephone company should have connected my phone today," She said taking a note pad from her purse. She wrote down her new number and handed it to him. "Call me, Jerry, anytime, day or night. I will come." She barely touched his arm as she turned to leave. "Rest well, my friend."

Again, the warmth from Rachel's fingertips flowed and tingled through Jerry's body as she left the room. He sighed and closed his eyes, still seeing her lovely face. Suddenly, the image of Roxanne in Eric's arms, her kiss of betrayal on Eric's lips, flashed through his mind. Jerry's eyes opened quickly. Shuddering, he took a sharp breath and winced in pain. Feeling cold and empty, he forced the cruel memory into a dark corner of his mind and buried it there, feeling a part of himself slip away with it.

CHAPTER FOUR

"David, I am worried. I know you talk to Jerry every day, but something is wrong. Jerry's lungs are clear of pneumonia, and the blood clot is completely dissolved. It has been over a week since he was discharged from the Intensive Care Unit. He will have some discomfort from the fracture for a week or so yet, but the bone has started healing. He should be feeling much better. On the surface it would seem that he is. He appears cheerful when I visit him, but he is eating poorly, which will definitely retard the healing process. He always wants his door shut and his blinds drawn. He won't read anything or even watch television. He sleeps, or pretends to be asleep, most of the day, but he is restless at night. His mind drifts during conversations, and he is too distant and quiet. Has he ever suffered from depression?" Rachel stood at the nurses' desk across the hall from Jerry's third floor room as she waited on the courtesy phone for David's response.

"I've been feeling unsettled about him too, even though he adamantly claims he's fine, and maybe that's why I'm worried."

David recalled every tragedy he and Jerry had endured together since fifth grade—Jerry's parents' tragic deaths, and then the terrible accident involving David's parents. David's anger flared as he remembered the drunk driver who had died in the accident. He took a deep breath and set his personal agony aside. Painful emotions from the past wouldn't help his friend now.

"Jerry had a tough life after his Mom died," he told Rachel. "Then his dad shot himself when Jerry was fifteen. He held together through it all, until my Dad was killed in an accident and my mom was paralyzed. Mom and Dad had always treated him like their own son. The heavy blow just one year after Robert Stone's death nearly destroyed Jerry. He went into a kind of shock. Of course Mom and I needed him as much as he needed us. It was a time of extreme hardship and sorrow. We leaned on each other, helped each other, and just loved each other. He was a great comfort to us, but we couldn't comfort him. He had us very worried. He could hardly eat or sleep for weeks. He got really thin and pale. Then one day, Mom sat him on her lap in her wheelchair. She held him and cried, begging him to take better care of himself, because she just couldn't bear to lose him too. That seemed to snap him out of the shock. They cried together for a long time that day, then he just got better. He said Mom and I were his survival, but in the end, it was his courage and crazy wit that anchored both of us." David paused, checking his emotions. He cleared his throat. "Jerry's more my brother than my friend, to both me and mom. I'll have her call him. Maybe she can help."

"Danny," Rachel whispered as though she had been given a sudden revelation.

"What?"

"I am sorry David, I did not mean to interrupt, but you gave me a thought. I must pursue a possibility here. Please do have your mother call Jerry. I definitely feel that he is in trouble."

Rachel didn't return to Jerry's room. Instead she hurried down the hall to the pediatric wing, feeling a rush of inspiration as goose bumps rose on her arms.

✳

Jerry's mood was dark and cloudy. He didn't care. He was tired of pretending, tired of the facade. He was fed up with the ridiculous mood swings. He never knew which way they would take him. They just jerked him around a lot. There was no reasoning with himself. He would think he had a grip on his brain, then he was crazy again. He felt like a clock spring that was wound too tightly. One more twist from anyone or anything would make it snap, hurdling him off the deep end, whatever that was, into some dark abyss. Then the abyss began to sound inviting—a place without people, or thoughts, or feelings. Somewhere that he could just shut down. He flirted with the idea, too discouraged and frustrated to cope anymore. Yet, a sense of fear held him in check, because nothingness seemed to close around him, making him feel dead. He shook the feeling away, but his emotions went spinning out of control again. Being tied to an infernal bed didn't help. If he could just go for a long, brisk walk or run, he could sweat out the craziness, but he was trapped in his brain, and in his bed. Releasing an exasperated growl, he gripped the bedpan, a symbol of his captivity, and flung it across the room. It bounced off the wall and clattered to the floor. The water pitcher was next in line, because for some reason it reminded him of Eric. Jerry gripped the handle just as the phone rang.

"How's my Jerry Boy?" Jan Young's gentle voice calling him by her pet name squelched his anger.

He was so taken aback that he didn't have time to pretend. Besides, she had caught him at a vulnerable moment. "Oh, Mama Young, I really needed to hear your voice right now!" He choked as his emotions swept over him, and then he quickly regained control, but she had heard enough.

"Talk to me, Jerry. What can I do to help?"

"I'm sorry, Jan. I guess I'm a little down. I'm not very good company today."

"You don't have to be. I didn't call you to be entertained. I called to find out how you are. So, sounds to me like your present reality is wherever your mind is taking you, right?"

"I guess so. But I don't want to be here."

"Healing takes a while. One day is better, another day not so good. In time you will be well."

"I want to be well now. I wish this dumb leg would heal! My

sore behind and I are sick of this stupid bed. The doctors say—"

"Jerry, I'm not talking about your leg. A broken bone would be nothing for you to overcome. I'm talking about your deeper wounds, the wounds inside that you try to hide. The ones that are tearing you apart right now."

Jerry started to cry. "Oh, Jan, how did I fail? What did I do wrong?"

"You tell me, Jerry. You know your own heart. Don't internalize this. You gave her all you could."

Jerry regained control, sitting a little taller in bed. "I know, but it wasn't enough."

"People are free to choose and free to hurt others with that choice. Some people change hearts like clothing, some don't know what they want, and some just get lost. People are the most imperfect part of life, and life happens. For now, work with your present reality. Use it to help you learn and grow."

"What lesson can come from this mess to help me learn and grow? That only two mothers can love me, so forget all this loving wife and family stuff? I wanted that more than anything. I lost it as a kid, and I've lost it now. I'm sorry, Jan. I just don't care anymore."

Her tone softened even more as her love flowed through the words. "I know it's very hard for you right now, Jerry, but you must not bury this bitter pain and disappointment. You have to hold on and work through it. If you try to lose it, you may lose yourself, like you did when Doug was killed. The mind can play tricks on you. Stay in control, and stay on top. Let yourself feel and cry. In fact, you must! Just don't forget who you are."

"How could I forget? You always remind me," he chuckled.

"It's good to hear you laugh," she said. "You're no quitter. You still have a mission in this life, Jerry Stone—an important one. In time you will discover it."

Jan always seemed to say what Jerry needed to hear. He felt comforted by her wisdom and insight, and her love over the phone was as tangible as a warm embrace. They talked a while about her arrival in Indian valley, how nice it was to be near David and

Kimberly, about her lovely mountain cabin, and her beautiful woodland pond. They planned a fishing date for the day Jerry would finally arrive in Slatersville. David would meet him at the small airport and take him straight to Indian Valley to go fishing with Jan. They finally said good bye and Jerry dropped the phone into its cradle.

Jerry's mood was a little brighter when Rachel returned to his room. She saw the bedpan in the corner and picked it up, looking questioningly at Jerry.

He quickly looked away and pushed his glasses up on his nose.

She placed it within his reach, realizing from his guilty reaction that the bedpan hadn't gotten there by accident. Then without a word she began re-arranging the sparse furniture. She had a curious smile on her face and a twinkle in her hazel-green eyes.

Chapter Five

"What's up?" Jerry asked, his interest piqued by Rachel's unusual behavior. She shifted a few more things and opened the blinds. He squinted at the bright light. "Hey, don't open that!" She ignored him, drawing them wide. "Close the blinds, Rachel," he said in a soft, but threatening tone, surprised at his own coldness, especially toward her.

"My people take care of one another, Jerry. It is a good way. I have been worried about you and someone else who is very special. The ancestors have spoken to my heart. You can help him, and he can help you. I will bring him in to meet you."

"Rachel, I don't want to meet anyone. I don't feel that I have anything to offer right now. I appreciate the thought, but I just need to have time to myself to think and work this out."

"No, Jerry, you have far too much time to think, and you are not working through your trial, you are hiding yourself in it. This is not good. I am certain that you should meet him. What you do after that is of your choosing and consequence. I will bring him in."

"No Rachel, I'm not going to see anyone. Now close the blinds."

She looked him straight in the eye with a steady gaze. "I will bring him in." Then she left the room.

Frustration welled up inside Jerry, and for the first time he resented Rachel's commitment to him. "Who does she think she is?" he growled. Taking the IV pole from its slot in the headboard, he tried to reach the blinds, but the pole wasn't long enough. He tossed it into the chair. "Pushy woman, taking a helpless man and forcing her will on him. Well, I won't play her game." He pulled himself upright against the raised head of his bed and folded his arms defiantly across his chest. He didn't like to be rude, but she'd given him no choice. He knew enough about fishing to know when a lure had been set for him, and he was not a stupid carp. He refused to take the bait, no matter how good she had been to him.

A few minutes later, Rachel returned, pushing a wheelchair in front of her. Sitting in only about one third of the chair, silent and meek, was a little Indian boy. His eyes were cast downward, gazing at a piece of driftwood he was carving with a pocketknife. He was very thin and was dwarfed by the large hospital gown he was wearing. Two bare feet stuck out from under the bath blanket on his lap. His brown head was totally bald, perfectly round, and gleamed in the sunlight.

"Jerry, I am pleased to introduce you to Danny Crow. He is my nine-year-old friend from the pediatric wing down the hall. Danny, I would like you to meet my very dear friend, Jerry Stone. Danny cast Jerry a sideward glance but didn't lift his bowed head. He continued to carve on his driftwood.

Jerry was so shocked by this most peculiar, pathetic, heart-wrenching waif that his stubbornness melted like ice in a hot teakettle. An overwhelming feeling of warmth suddenly radiated from Jerry's soul, encircling the little boy with love. His arms dropped to his side, and he blinked hard as he leaned toward the child. "Hello, Danny. I'm glad you came to visit me. That's a fine pocketknife. I had one just like it when I was a boy. My best friend gave it to me. What are you carving?"

"Nothing," Danny mumbled, keeping his eyes on his work. "Just messing around."

"Cool, that's what I do best. Wanna hang out with me, and

we'll mess around together?"

"Why? You're old. You can't do anything fun, anyway, 'cause your leg's all broken and tied up. B'sides, you're a white guy."

"My mind's not tied up, and that's where the fun comes from. Do you think kids have a monopoly on fun? We old men like fun too. And so what if I'm a white guy! You're an Indian! If you don't scalp me, I won't shoot you."

Danny looked up, rather startled, but he didn't respond.

"So our skin's different, but our brains are the same color." Jerry leaned closer to Danny with an unusual twinkle in his eyes. He held his hand to his mouth and whispered so Rachel couldn't hear. "Two brains thinking together always have more fun." He sat back against his pillow and chuckled. "Having a good time starts from the inside. When I was a kid, my friend David and I never stopped laughing. We could think up fun when we were asleep. Once when we were about your age, we went fishing by a canal and caught a small garter snake."

"A snake?" Danny asked, folding his pocketknife and leaning one arm on the armrest. "Did it bite you?"

Rachel smiled and quietly slipped out of the room. Releasing a deep sigh of relief, she bowed her head as she pulled the door shut behind her. "Basi' (thank you)," she whispered. "I nearly caused a war between Jerry and myself, but my little doyona (chief) has brought us peace. Maybe now they will heal each other."

"No, he didn't bite us," Jerry answered. "Couldn't have hurt us if he did. David's father taught us about snakes on a camping trip once, so we knew how to hold him. We decided to keep him as a pet, so we took him home. We sneaked into my house and made a den for him in a shoebox under my bed. Mom called us to have some cookies and milk. When we came back, the snake was gone. We hunted all over my room but decided he must have gone under the door, so we looked everywhere, trying to act normal so Mom wouldn't notice. She was fixing dinner. I didn't know she had seen me sneak under the table. 'Jerry, get out from under there. What in the world are you boys looking for?' she asked. I jumped up and hit my head. David started to laugh. 'Just my red truck,' I answered. 'In front of you right where you left it,' she said, pointing to the top of the table. 'Now go outside and play.' What else could we do? We just hoped Charlie, that's what we named him, was in a safe hiding place.

"The dumb snake curled up on a sack of potatoes in the pantry. Of course, Mom could have made spaghetti, but no, she just had to make mashed potatoes. She opened the pantry door and nearly grabbed Charlie. I don't know who was more scared—him or her—but the whole neighborhood would have voted for her. Mary Jo Lonkey is the only person I ever heard scream louder. Mom ran next door to David's house. On her way over, she asked us how we'd feel if a monster kidnapped us and took us away from our homes. She told us we had better find Charlie and put him right back where we found him, because she wasn't coming home until we did."

Jerry contorted his face into weird, comical expressions as he finished his story. "As usual, David and I spent the next few days pulling faces at each other through our bedroom windows. We even had fun when our moms punished us."

Danny snickered, and then dropped his head and began whittling on the wood again. "My mamma died. She had cancer. She said it's a bad disease that our family gets sometimes."

"Oh, Danny, I'm so sorry. I know how sad you must feel. My mamma died when I was a little boy. She didn't have cancer, but her disease was a bad one too."

"I had cancer," Danny said. "It grew on my kidney, so they had to cut out my kidney and throw it away." He twisted in the wheelchair and raised the side of his gown to reveal a scar. "Rachel said they cut all the cancer away, so I probably won't die, but I have to get medicine in my arm, right here, so I don't get more cancer." He pointed with his knife blade to an intravenous needle taped to the inside of his thin forearm. "The medicine makes me really sick, and I throw up a lot. It made all my hair fall out." Still grasping the driftwood in one hand, he put the knife down and rubbed his shiny brown head.

Jerry was stunned, even though the boy's bald head should

have alerted him to the tiny fellow's plight. His eyes moistened, and he swallowed a big lump in his throat as Danny continued his brave discourse.

"Rachel paints my head sometimes, like my ancestors used to paint their faces. She's my favorite nurse."

"Mine too," Jerry mumbled, feeling very guilty for the anger he had felt toward her. She had been right. Here was a little boy who knew a lot about sorrow and suffering, yet he was surviving with the courage of a warrior. This child had already lifted Jerry from wallowing in his grief. He did need Danny, and maybe he could find something in his heart to offer his small friend. He instinctively reached out to pat Danny's hand, but Danny quickly pulled it away. Jerry smiled. "Hey, Danny, the last white man and Indian war was a long time ago." He extended his hand toward Danny. "Friends?" he asked.

Danny nodded, reaching out to give Jerry's hand a quick squeeze.

"I'm holding you to that. White or Indian, a man's word is his bond of truth, and a bond of truth should last forever. Too bad some of our ancestors didn't figure that out. Do you know what a bond is?" Danny shook his head. "See that scar there? My friend David and I wanted to be like brothers. We cut our fingers and mixed our blood together when we were your age. We promised to be 'blood brothers.' That's an Indian tradition, but I don't know which Indian tribe it came from. Anyway, it's a bond, like being born as brothers. An honorable man will even give up his life, if he's asked, to be true to his bond. Remember that, my friend."

Danny nodded, his black eyes wide and sincere.

"Good, that was your lesson for the day." Jerry pulled a silly face. "Now, let's mess around some more. What do you wanna do?"

Danny chuckled. "You're a funny white man. I liked your story. Tell me another one."

CHAPTER SIX

Kimberly was peeling a carrot in her large country kitchen when the telephone rang. She tucked the receiver against her ear and continued to peel the carrot into the sink. "Hello, this is the Young's," she said cheerfully into the mouthpiece. The peeler suddenly slipped from her fingers and clattered into the sink with the carrot. Kimberly weakly made her way to a chair. "Roxy, where are you?" she asked breathlessly. "Are you okay? How could you do this to us? We've been worried sick for days!" Roxanne's voice was timid and subdued, and Kimberly thought she might be crying.

"I know, Kim, and I'm so sorry. I . . . I'm fine. It's really chilly here in Kodiak. We have an apartment just off the ocean. I'm not used to the ocean air, so I keep pretty bundled up."

"We, as in you and Eric?" Kimberly tried to keep the coldness washing over her out of her voice.

"I . . . uh . . . I know I've really messed up. It was nothing like all our girlhood plans, but we . . . we got married on the way here."

"Roxanne, that was several weeks ago. Why haven't you called us? Whatever happened to that sweet, considerate cousin I used to have? I've been so totally blown away by your choices and actions that I still can't believe it all. Explain it to me. I'll really try to understand, but I'm still deeply hurt and angry, though not nearly as hurt as someone else we both know."

There was a long pause, with some sniffling in the background. Finally Roxanne spoke, her voice quivering with emotion. "How is Jerry, Kimberly? I've been very worried about him."

"I don't really know. He's still in Alaska. He's in the hospital in Fairbanks."

"In the hospital?" Roxanne's voice carried a tone of alarm. "What happened?"

Kimberly spoke through clenched teeth, trying to control her anger. "You and Eric happened. When he saw you two together, he ran away and took a terrible fall into a bog. He suffered a severe fracture in his leg, and he almost died in the bog. David and Rachel were barely able to save his life. The doctors put him in traction in the hospital, and then he became seriously ill with pneumonia. A blood clot almost passed through his heart, and he nearly died again. How did you expect him to be, Roxanne? You were his whole world." Kimberly could hear Roxanne weeping on the other end of the line. "I'm sorry, Roxy. I don't mean to sound so harsh. But it has been a very frightening ordeal for all of us. Then added to all that, I've been in a total panic about you. I'm full of anger and relief, and it's all mixed up together. I am so glad to finally hear your voice."

"I . . . I never meant to cause so much hurt!" Roxanne could hardly speak through her sobs. "It all just happened! When I saw that terrible look of pain on Jerry's face, I knew it was too late to go back. I just wanted to get married and go on with whatever life I'd created for myself." Her muffled sobs overcame her again.

Kimberly was finally regaining control of her anger. "Are you happy with Eric, Roxy?" she asked gently. "Does he treat you well?"

"He . . . he's good to me. His ways are different. I'm getting to know him better. He's a good man, really. It wasn't anymore his fault than mine that we betrayed Jerry. I was the one who was unfaithful to my promise. We just kind of swept each other off our feet. I . . . I think we can be happy, but I've felt so burdened with guilt that I've been miserable. Now, knowing how Jerry has suffered," she burst into tears again. "I . . . I still love Jerry. I'm so sorry I hurt him. Is he going to be okay?"

"Time will tell. He's already had a lot of hurt. Honestly, this was almost the fatal blow. Rachel has voiced some deep concerns for him."

"Rachel's with him?"

"Yes, we found the lost mine, so Sam's got lots of help, now. Tell Eric that Rachel stayed with it until her mission was completed. His father is okay. We also found Grandpa Demeron. He'd been trapped in the mine. We brought him home and buried him beside Grandma Marnie. Rachel went to Fairbanks with us and is working at the hospital, so she's looking out for Jerry."

There was a long silence. Then Roxanne spoke. "I . . . I'm glad he's not alone." She was silent again.

"Roxy, are you okay?"

"Yeah," she answered with a tremor in her voice. "Well, I haven't called anyone else, so I'd better call Mom and Dad. Kim, I hope you can forgive me someday. You've always been more like a sister than a cousin to me, someone I could always look up to. I'm sorry I let you down. I love you, Kim." There was another long pause. Roxanne was weeping again. "Tell David I'm so very sorry."

"All right, Roxy, take care of yourself. Thanks for calling. I'll always love you."

Kimberly replaced the phone and went back to the sink. She peeled several more strips off the carrot and then sat down on the floor and cried.

Having finished his chores, David walked in the door. He immediately noticed Kimberly on the floor, crying. "Honey, what happened; are you okay?" he said rushing to her. She nodded as he reached down and lifted her up off the floor.

Kimberly dried her tears with a paper towel and finished peeling the carrot. "Roxanne called. She and Eric got married on the way to Kodiak."

"Why am I not surprised?" he said, washing his hands and pulling another peeler out of the drawer.

Kimberly ignored David's sarcasm. "She's safe, but she's not doing well. In her words, she said to tell you 'she is so very sorry.' She was already emotional before I told her about Jerry, but when she heard what had happened to him, she completely fell apart. She's carrying a lot of guilt and regret."

"She should be," David said coldly, directing his anger at the carrot he had started to peel. "I'm glad she finally called so you can have some peace. I realize you've been close, like Jerry and me. I can see the worry in your eyes, even though you haven't said much. I try not to judge her, but I'm still awfully angry. I'm sorry, Honey, it'll pass in time."

"I know, David. I understand." They embraced, supporting each other as their love and compassion swept beyond time and distance to their loved ones over a thousand miles away.

⁎

"Brrr, it's an unusually cold rain today, and the wind isn't help-ing," Eric said as he stripped off his raincoat and hat and pulled his feet out of his boots. He ran his brown weathered hand through his black hair. "We've almost got the boat ready to go out. Are you sure you'll be okay without a car while I'm gone? We can still go buy one."

Roxanne was sitting with her back to the door, staring at the rain sleeting down the dinette window. She quickly wiped tears from her eyes, trying to hide them from her husband. She did not want to cry in front of Eric. Then he was as miserable as she was. Once he left for work, she had the rest of the day to cry all the buckets of tears she wanted to. It was easy to do that. The weather inside her matched the weather outside. "No, I don't need a car," she answered, trying to compose herself. "I'd just get lost if I tried to drive, so I don't plan on going outside. If I need groceries, I'll just call a cab. How long will you be gone?"

"It depends, Roxanne. We bring her home when the hold is full of fish. Usually two weeks at the least, a month at the most." He walked over to her, smiled warmly, and kissed her cheek. He paused and turned her face toward him with a concerned frown.

"Have you been crying again?"

She bowed her head, pulling her lips tightly across her teeth and squeezed her eyes shut, but the tears burst free in spite of her resolve not to cry.

Eric cupped her face in his hands and stroked her golden curls. "What is troubling my little fawn this time?"

She pulled away, drying her tears, and went to the kitchen, pretending that she had planned to prepare supper right at that moment. "I finally called Kimberly. She's still angry and upset, more so because I hadn't called. She was worried. So were my parents. It was hard to face them." He waited for her to say more, but she didn't.

"Well, I'm glad you called. Avoidance only magnifies a problem, and you can always imagine that things are worse than they really are."

"That's not true!" Roxanne cried as she crumpled back into the dinette chair. "It's far, far worse!" She laid her arms on the table and buried her face in them. Her shoulders heaved as wrenching sobs burst uncontrollably from deep within her heart.

Eric was startled and confused. He placed his hand on her shoulder, softly patting and rubbing as she wept.

"I almost killed him, Eric! I almost killed him. It was wrong; I knew it was wrong, and I did it anyway. I was so selfish. I didn't even consider the consequences. Worse yet, I broke a faithful trust without an inkling of compassion for the extreme hurt I would cause for someone I dearly loved."

A pained expression entered Eric's dark eyes. He let his hand slide from her shoulder and drop to his side.

More wrenching sobs shook Roxanne's slender frame as she muttered, "I almost killed him. Then I abandoned him, far from home, for your sister to care for."

Eric walked to the coat closet and put on his raincoat and boots, then walked into the drizzling rain. The cold droplets soon drenched his thick, wavy hair and trickled down his neck and back. With his mind deep in thought, he walked for a long time.

Roxanne did not notice that Eric had left. When her sobs

finally subsided, she raised her head and wiped her tear-stained face. "I'm sorry, Eric," she said, turning to look at him, but he was gone. "Eric," she called. She stepped into the bedroom and the bathroom, and then she noticed that his coat and boots were missing. "Oh no," she said sinking into the chair again. "I knew I mustn't lose control. How did I, Roxanne Slater, Demeron, Duncan, Moron, become the happiness wrecker? I hurt everyone I touch." She wanted to cry again, but she had no more tears to cry. "He was wet and cold when he came home, and now he's back out in the rain. What an insensitive and selfish fool I've become. He's my husband by my own free will and choice. I'm even the one who pushed for it before the dirt had time to settle. I owe him far more than what I've been giving. I'll have a hot supper waiting for him. Then, while he eats, I'll draw him a warm bath."

Eric returned, drenched and shivering. Roxanne quickly took a towel to his wet hair as he stripped off his coat and boots. He gently took the towel from her and walked past her outstretched arms, drying his hair and neck as he sat at the table. As she served the steaming supper, he spoke. "We need to talk, Roxanne. Would you like me to fly you home? I'm sure your parents would be relieved to see you. You're cold and miserable here, and you'd be all alone for who knows how long. Besides, I think maybe you're right. Maybe this was all a big mistake." He paused and took a deep breath. "I'll give you a divorce if you want one. Maybe you should go back and see if you can repair things with Jerry." He blinked hard and swallowed, clearing his throat. "I'm sorry I got in the way of your happiness. It was wrong. Maybe it still is. I had hoped we could make it right, but I just can't stand seeing you so unhappy all the time." He got up and left the table. Roxanne followed.

"Eric, your supper, please eat! Then I'll draw—"

"No, thank you, Roxanne. I appreciate it, but I just can't eat tonight. I'm really tired, and I'm going to bed. You think about what I said." He bent down and kissed her lightly on the cheek; then he closed the bedroom door behind him.

CHAPTER SEVEN

Rachel walked home, feeling elated that the past five days had gone so well. Jerry and Danny had spent every free hour together, playing games, telling stories, drawing pictures, and laughing and talking, just like long-time friends. They even shared lunch and supper together in Jerry's room every day. Rachel had been concerned that Danny might be overtaxing himself. However, the interaction was so positive that she and the other nurses decided that they would just take him back to his room right after supper each night. His evening nurse would put him to bed early so he could get more rest.

Tonight he had begged and pleaded to stay longer. He was so upset when Rachel wheeled him to his own room that he refused to give her the hug that he normally gave her. As far as she knew, she was the only person he had ever let get that close. Now, since his friendship with Jerry, his tough act of "I don't need anyone" was quickly disappearing, and he and Jerry were both more open and responsive. Jerry didn't ask to have his blinds drawn anymore. He even asked to be moved closer to the window so he could see the few faint stars that appeared in the deepening twilight of the early September sky.

Rachel entered her apartment and put a TV dinner in the microwave. Then she grabbed a soda from the refrigerator,

dropped onto the couch, and kicked off her white nurse's shoes. "Nezrunh ethtregha drana (It is good. He is not crying today). Neither is Danny," she said, stretching her legs across the coffee table. She took a few swallows and then set her soda on the table by her feet. "Danny is like the sanh xwdhel (the summer heat) for Jerry. Bedraya (his heart) is growing warmer. Danny helped Jerry laugh again. Now Jerry is betlanh (his friend), and he makes Danny laugh again." She laid her head against the back of the couch and sighed contentedly, for the worst of the ordeal had surely passed.

Rachel realized she must have fallen asleep when the ringing of the telephone startled her. For a moment she was disoriented. Then she hurried to the kitchenette and answered it, removing her cold dinner from the microwave as she steadied the receiver on her shoulder.

"Hello, David. I am so happy you called. I have wonderful news. Jerry and a little boy named Danny have become very good friends. They can relate to each other because they have both suffered heartaches and losses. They are healing each other in marvelous ways."

Silence was the only response from the other end of the line. "David, did you hear me? He is much better. Is something wrong?"

David cleared his throat before responding. "Roxanne called Kimberly. She and Eric got married on their way to Kodiak. I'm glad Jerry is better, but I hope your little boy has some kind of miracle up his sleeve. I'm afraid this news might tip Jerry off the edge like when my Dad was killed. I wish I could be there right now, Rachel. It's unfair that this whole mess got dumped in your lap. I am so terribly sorry."

Shaking her head, Rachel sat down in her breakfast nook. "David, you are not blaming yourself for all of this, are you? Asking Jerry and Roxanne to come here was not a wrong thing to do. You asked them for honorable reasons. My Father would have lost everything if you had not come. We can never repay your kindness. Caring for Jerry has been a privilege, not a burden. It is a very small service to three remarkably unselfish people. Please, do not bear this concern for me. Your great worry about your friend is a heavy load. That is enough for you to carry. I will tell Jerry this news when I feel he is stronger and can handle it. I suppose I should be glad to have a sister-in-law, but much healing must come first. Thank you for calling me. Give my love and appreciation to Kimberly. I will stay closely in touch regarding Jerry."

Rachel's cold dinner remained untouched as she arose and placed the receiver in its cradle. "Ohoya! Do'wxt'anh (what are you doing), Eric? Netthi' (your head) has left you." She rehearsed aloud what she wanted to say to her absent brother. "This is irrational behavior for you. What do you know of this woman, taking her to yourself to wife, and betraying a friend in the very act? What happiness can come from a marriage built on disloyalty? Our mother taught you a better way. Her spirit must be very sad. And what now of Jerry? He has found it in his heart to laugh again, to care for a little boy, to turn his sorrow to someone else's good. What will this news do to his grieving heart?"

Rachel slept restlessly that night. The next morning she resolved that she would keep her feelings to herself until she was able to speak to Eric more objectively. However, she called her father with the news, knowing that he would call Eric. In spite of her disappointment in Eric, she had been concerned for her brother. To leave his father in trouble as he had and take such rash action was not like him. She wanted to be certain that he was all right. She got ready for work and walked to the hospital, deeply concerned about the secret that she must keep from Jerry. But for how long? When would he be ready for such news?

"What's wrong, Rachel?" Danny asked as she prepared to wheel him to Jerry's room.

Surprised at his sensitivity to unspoken concerns, she smiled and handed him his pocketknife and wood. "I am fine, Danny. Just a little tired."

"No, I think you have been crying. Are you sick?" A note of alarm was carried in his voice.

Recognizing childish fears rising from his great loss, Rachel quickly buried her anxiety behind a bright, reassuring smile. "No Danny, I am very well." She wrapped his thin body in a warm hug. "Thank you for caring. You are such a special little friend! Now, what mischief do you and Jerry have planned for today?"

"We don't know yet. Two brains are better at thinking up fun, so we'll decide when our brains can think together."

Rachel giggled. "That is a clever plan. Let us go to Jerry right now and put your brains together, then."

Jerry greeted them both with a big grin. Rachel smiled. She dropped Danny off, excused herself, and returned to work.

"Well, Danny, what shall we do today?" Jerry said, pointing to the rubber glove dispenser above the sink. "Think you can sneak over there and get about six of those?"

"Hey, what do you want old gloves for?"

"You get them, and I'll show you."

Danny set his blanket aside and carefully crept to the sink. He stood on his tiptoes and reached as far as his arm would go. He could barely touch them, but making a quick twist with his nimble fingers, he caught the edge of a glove. As he pulled it out of the dispenser, a few more came within his grasp. Five took his best effort.

"Good job," Jerry said, nodding his approval. "Performed like a real warrior. You sneaked into the enemy camp and reclaimed five of your horses they had stolen. That's five feathers in your head band." Jerry slipped the support sock from his right leg and tied it around Danny's bald head. "Ah, yes, feathers," he said pointing to a container of drinking straws on the shelf. Danny crouched down, and in his best stealthy warrior behavior, arrived at the shelf, reached for a handful of straws, and forgot to sneak back as he proudly returned and handed them to Jerry. "Mission accomplished," Jerry said with a grin as he inserted five multi-colored straws into the makeshift headband. "But just think how cold some poor little bird's behind is since you took his biggest feathers."

Danny laughed and gave a war whoop.

"Sit down and cover up before your behind gets too cold,"

Jerry ordered as he blew a glove into a balloon and tied it off for Danny.

Danny tossed it into the air, bumping it with his hand to keep it floating. "Make another one," he said.

"Oh no, we don't want to do that."

"Why not?" Danny argued.

Jerry motioned him closer, inserted the spout of his water pitcher into the top of the glove and filled it with water. Danny watched in fascination as Jerry tied it off and slipped it into his bath basin. Danny held another glove in front of Jerry and grinned as he repeated the same operation. The surgeon and his five-feathered assistant finished their work on the last two rubber gloves and deposited them into the bath basin. Danny didn't ask Jerry what the water filled gloves were for. He just waited in happy anticipation for his next instructions.

"Can you climb from that chair onto the heater beneath the window?"

"Sure," Danny said.

"Pull the window open until you can reach out, and then throw the water balloons at the closest people. You'll have to duck behind the curtain each time, or someone will see you, and we'll both be in trouble. If you're quick, they won't know where it came from. There's lots of room up there, but be careful so you don't fall off the heater, or you might look like me with your leg hanging in the air."

Danny nodded eagerly, reaching for the bath basin. He tiptoed to the heater, set his ammunition in a strategic spot for re-armament, and climbed onto the heater to make his assault on the unwary enemies below.

Jerry sat back, enjoying the little boy's antics and sound effects as he waged war. He missed every target, but he was delighted at the explosion of the gloves on the sidewalk three stories below. When the last glove was gone, Danny turned to Jerry, his bald head shining in the sunlight and his broad grin almost as bright.

"Okay, close the window and get down quick; then sit in your chair, cover up, and act innocent." He tapped the checkerboard on his tray table. "We'll just pretend we've been playing the whole time."

Within moments Rachel appeared in the doorway, her hands on her hips. "What have you two been doing?" she asked. Jerry shrugged and pointed to the checkerboard. Danny studied the black checkers very carefully. "We just got a phone call from the main office. Someone complained about water balloons being thrown from a window. Might it possibly have been that window?" she said, pointing directly at the crime scene.

"What?" Jerry stammered, looking straight at her. "Yeah, just how in the heck am I supposed to be able to reach the window? And Danny's too short." He looked back at the checkers, trying desperately to keep the dogged smile off his face. "Some low flying eagle probably just did a fly-by pooping."

Danny couldn't contain himself any longer. Throwing both hands over his mouth in an attempt to stifle the mirth bubbling up from deep inside, he bumped the checkerboard and burst into peels of laughter as checkers clattered to the floor and onto his lap.

Jerry, still trying to act innocent, could not hold back a chuckle. Then he quickly cleared his throat and pushed his glasses up on his nose. "Danny, just look what you did to our game. I was winning."

Danny's eyes were streaming tears as he clung to his belly and laughed uncontrollably.

Rachel, trying to look very stern, stooped to pick up the checkers. "Yes, Jerry, I noticed that you were most definitely winning, especially since not even one checker had been moved." Laughing quietly to herself, and delighted to hear Danny so gleefully happy, she kept her face downward as she picked up the last checkers. She placed them on the board and tweaked Danny's straw feathers. "I will get you another support stocking, Jerry. You must wear it at all times." Suppressing a giggle, she started for the door. "I do not know how you did it, but no more rubber glove water balloons." She closed the door behind her and collapsed against the wall, holding her sides and laughing. *How can I tell him now?* she wondered. *How can I tell him when his heart is growing so warm and whole?*

Chapter Eight

"She didn't find out that we threw the balloons, did she?" Danny asked.

Jerry pulled the blown-up glove out from under his pillow and flipped it at Danny. "Oh, she knew all right," Jerry said with a chuckle, tapping the balloon back to Danny, who had hit it back to him. "But she didn't have any proof."

"We aren't in trouble, are we?" Danny sent the five-fingered balloon back to Jerry.

"Heck no, I wouldn't let anyone scold you. Besides, Rachel's a teddy bear. She didn't want us to know it, but she was laughing her head off. I could see her shoulders shaking when she was picking up the checkers. She has to act professional because that's her job. She thinks she shouldn't let other nurses know that she treats us special, but they all like us too. They know she's our special nurse. That's why she gets to come over on my wing too. Hey, did you know this hospital can fly?"

Danny let the balloon drop. "Huh uh! That's dumb! A hospital can't fly. It's stuck in the ground."

"Then why does it have two wings? Your room down the hall is on the pediatric wing and mine is on the surgical wing. Why are they called wings if it can't fly?"

Danny started to laugh again. "Eagles have wings. That was

so funny what you said about the eagle. I never laughed that hard before. I was even crying. I didn't know laughing could make you cry."

"That's the best kind of crying, called happy tears. Moms get those sometimes when you give them flowers. I liked to see my mom's happy tears, so I gave her flowers all the time. Did you ever give your mom a gift that made her cry?"

"When she told me she was gonna die, I made a spirit house for her grave out of some sticks. She hugged me so tight that I couldn't breathe, and she was crying a lot, so she must've really liked it, huh?"

Jerry blinked hard. "I'm sure she was the happiest mom in the whole world to think that you loved her so much that you would do something so nice for her."

"I wonder if Rachel was crying happy tears today. Maybe someone gave her flowers?"

"You saw Rachel crying today? When was she crying?"

"Well, she wasn't exactly crying, but her eyes looked like she had been. I was afraid maybe she was sick, but when I asked her, she just smiled and gave me a big hug. So they must have been happy tears, 'cause then she looked happy."

Jerry stuck two more straws in Danny's headband. "That one is for your mamma, because you made her life so happy, and that one is for Rachel. You were worried about her and asked if she was okay. That's one of the nicest gifts you can give someone. Just to let them know you care."

"I care about you. You wanted to be my friend even when I wasn't nice to you."

Jerry felt a sudden rush of guilt as he recalled how ornery he had been toward Rachel, and how stubbornly determined he was not to meet Danny. Her persistence had been a blessed gift to him and Danny, like heavenly powers had really spoken to her. He'd never even apologized to Rachel. "So I am a stupid carp after all," he chuckled to himself. Today would not slip past without a proper apology, he resolved.

"What?" Danny asked, looking confused.

"Oh, nothing. I was just thinking out loud. Hey, you were nice enough. You didn't know I was one of the good guys. Maybe you felt a little scared."

"I'm not scared now, 'cause you and me made a bond. Can we cut our fingers, like you and David did, and be blood brothers?" he asked. "We could use my pocketknife and . . . oh no! Where's my pocketknife and wood?" Danny began searching frantically around his chair for his missing possessions.

"Settle down; it's okay. They're right here, behind my tissue box." Jerry handed them to Danny, realizing the knife and wood were very important to the boy. "I know these things mean a lot to you," Jerry said, looking kindly at his little friend. "I'll help you keep them safe. Where did you get your knife?"

"My mamma gave me the pocketknife for my birthday, and I'm carving the wood for her."

Jerry was deeply moved, yet he was relieved that the blood brother idea had slipped away. He was fearful that any kind of wound, even a poked finger, could cause serious infection to someone in Danny's condition. He hadn't wanted to disappoint a little brother, but Jerry remembered well his dear mother's fragile state. He greatly admired this child's courage, but he wondered what would become of him. He had not anticipated the depth of this little boy's commitment to the bond of friendship he had offered. Jerry was sincere, but now he worried that he might be setting Danny up for greater hurt in the future. He couldn't bear the thought of adding to Danny's pain. Jan had said, "Use your present reality to help you learn and grow." Danny was his present reality, and Jerry felt greatly helped by the child. But was he helping Danny? Separation was inevitable in the future. Maybe getting closer would do Danny more harm than good, only creating more heartbreak and loss for the little fellow.

Danny had become quiet and solemn, carving again on his driftwood. Jerry determined to talk with Rachel about his concerns. For now, Danny's sad face was Jerry's present reality, and he liked to see him smile.

"Okay, my small friend, lunch will be here soon. What

mischief can we get into really fast, besides water balloons?"

Danny chuckled, still carving on his wood. "Tell me some more funny stories about you and David."

"Well, this isn't a funny story, but it's one of my favorite memories of David and my dad. After my mom died, my dad started drinking, so we didn't have much money 'cause he spent most of it on alcohol. He didn't mean to be selfish, but he'd become addicted, and he didn't know how to stop. Alcohol controlled his mind and body and would tell him what to do."

"My mamma told me my Daddy drank lots of beer. She said he was a nice man but that drinking made him mean. One time she took me to my grandma's house when he was being mean, and when we came back home, he was gone. He just de'speared, so I don't have a daddy."

"We have a lot in common, don't we my little friend? My dad was fun until he disappeared into alcohol. Then it was as if he was gone too. That's tough luck, huh?"

"I guess, but I don't remember my daddy. Mamma said we were good without him."

"Hey, this isn't supposed to be a sad story!" Jerry said. "Let's get back to the fun! On my twelfth birthday my Dad did a very unselfish thing. He bought me a really nice used bike. It was a cool green color, and even though I'd wanted a new one like David's, it looked brand new and I really loved it. David got a bright, shiny red one for his birthday a few months earlier. At that time his dad tried to give me David's old gray one, but my Dad told him no. He wanted to buy me one for my birthday.

"It was one of my best birthdays ever. He gave me a big hug and told me he loved me. Then he took me into the garage and showed me the bike. It was terrific! Next to David's, it was the best bike in the whole world, and David and I had a great deal of fun racing down a hill in front of houses. The street lead to some older houses up on the hill, so there weren't many cars that drove on it. It was old and rutty and had a big bump that we called the thrill hill. The faster we went, the more we felt like our stomachs would come up out of our throats as we went over it. It was a weird feeling, but we thought it was the best. Every morning, as soon as we finished our chores, we were on the hill, losing our innards, and loving every minute of it.

"Then one day Dad sent me to the store for some milk. When I came out, my bike was gone. I bawled and blubbered all the way home. Dad was so mad that someone would steal a kid's bike that he called the cops. Then he sat me on his lap, held me in his arms, and bawled with me. Knowing he was as sad as I was made me feel better somehow because I knew he really cared about me.

"That evening he took me next door and offered twenty dollars to David's dad for David's old gray bike. His dad, Doug, smiled and said, 'Robert, you don't have to pay for it. David and I have already told you that the bike is yours.'

"'No,' my dad told him; he put his arm around me. 'I said I was going to buy my son a bike for his birthday, and I meant it. He and I will go buy some green paint tomorrow, and he will have his bike like I promised.'

"Doug was a great man. I loved him almost as much as my own dad. He smiled and nodded, took the twenty dollars, and said, 'Sold!' He shook hands with my dad, tousled my hair, and added, 'Let David and I give it a tune up tonight and we'll bring it over tomorrow.'

"That night I heard banging and hammering and the clanking of tools in David's garage. I was dying to see what they were doing, but Dad said to let them be. The next morning they brought the bike over. Dad and I just stood there in shock. Hanging from the handlebars of David's new shiny red bike was a sign that read, 'Jerry's Bike, Happy Birthday, With Love, From Dad.' David was standing there grinning like a Cheshire cat, holding his old gray bike that was all fixed up and painted. It was as bright and shiny red as the new one.

"Dad started to object, but Doug put his hand on my dad's shoulder and said, 'You wanted to buy David's bike, and you paid for it fair and square. Since both bikes belong to David, he had the right to choose which one he wanted to keep and which one he wanted to sell. He made his choice of his own free will, so that makes it final. He has a fine bike, newly rebuilt, with fresh paint, and as good as new. His bike will last as long as Jerry's, and they will have a great time riding together for years to come.'

"Dad started to cry. He hugged Doug, then he hugged David like he was gonna squeeze the life out of him. When he turned him loose, David was gasping for air and was as bright red as the two bikes. Then Dad held me tight and whispered, 'Happy Birthday, son. Go ride your new bike to your heart's content. Just be home before dark.'

"David never seemed to mind that he had the old bike. In fact, he always beat me in races. We both have the same bikes today, and we still go for bike rides together."

"When can I meet David?" Danny asked as the lunch trays arrived. "He's a good guy like you, isn't he?"

Jerry opened both cartons of milk and set one on Danny's tray. "He's the best, Danny. I hope you can meet him someday. Yumm, fried chicken, mashed potatoes, and green beans." Danny glowered at the green beans. "Hey, none of that! You have to eat everything or I get your chocolate pudding. If you empty your plate first, you get my chocolate pudding. Ready, set, go!"

Rachel stayed busy with her other patients, peeking in on Jerry and Danny as the day progressed. She avoided staying long, though, because their happy interaction just made her more apprehensive about being the bearer of bad news. She decided that maybe she wouldn't even tell Jerry until he could go home and be among his friends and family. However, a strange heaviness hung around her heart, and she felt unusually anxious. Most of her worry focused on Jerry, but there was also a feeling of uncertainty, an uneasiness about Eric that just wouldn't leave her alone. She finally gave in and called her father on her afternoon break.

"Eric seemed glad to hear from me," Sam Duncan said. "He was embarrassed to call because he really felt that he let you and me down. He expressed deep gratitude for you, David, and Kimberly persisting in the search of the mine. He was very pleased to know the mine is being prepared for full production."

"Father, I already know these things because I know Eric. I

was certain he was punishing himself, or he would have called you before. How is he, though? Is he happy? I feel that something is not right."

"Well, Honey, they didn't exactly start this off right. I'm sure they will face plenty of problems. I think he cares deeply for this woman, but I sensed difficulty. He wouldn't really say. How is Jerry?"

"This has been very hard for him, Father. He has finally been doing much better, but now this unhappy news hangs over him, and I am afraid to tell him. He needs to have more time to heal emotionally."

"Sooner or later he will have to know, Rachel. I just hope you're not getting so emotionally involved that you feel the need to suffer with him. You need to stay objective and clear minded if you are to help him through it. Besides, you didn't cause his trouble. You shouldn't take responsibility for it. Help him if you can, but guard yourself and be wise."

"I will, Father. I love you."

When Rachel went to Jerry's room to get Danny, Jerry watched her closely.

"Have you been avoiding us today, or are we still in trouble?" he asked.

"Of course you are still in trouble," she said, smiling. "You are forgiven, though, if it does not happen again."

"We can still do it on her days off," Jerry whispered loudly and winked at Danny."

Danny nodded and smiled, then frowned at Rachel who was giving Jerry a silent lecture with her eyes. "Why do I have to go back to my room every night?" he asked.

"You know bedtime is strictly observed, Danny. You and Jerry have had a very exciting day. You must get some rest to keep up your strength. Sleep helps you heal."

"Why can't I just sleep in Jerry's room? There's room for my bed in here too."

"Danny, if you and Jerry were in the same room all the time, you would stay up half the night. Jerry needs rest and so do you.

Now, no more arguments! Get your pocketknife and wood and tell Jerry goodnight." Danny's objections fizzled. He wrapped his brown spindly arms around Jerry's neck and grunted as he squeezed to make the hug stronger.

Jerry chuckled, feeling a warm spot in his heart as Rachel wheeled Danny from the room. Then he took a deep breath, resting his hands behind his head, and worried about Danny.

Danny pouted and grumbled until he snuggled into his covers and quickly fell asleep. Once he was settled, his evening nurse left the room. Rachel stroked his bald head and then covered it with a stocking cap to keep him warm. "Oh, Danny, how I wish—" she said, kissing his cheek and squeezing his hand. His fingers squeezed back and held on until a deeper sleep overcame him.

Rachel decided she was going to excuse herself early from her evening visit with Jerry. She was too upset and concerned about him and Eric, and she could honestly use tiredness as an excuse. She was exhausted.

"I thought I was in such deep doodoo that you weren't coming in to see me tonight," Jerry teased when Rachel arrived. "I haven't seen much of you today." He grew more serious. "You've stayed pretty scarce. Is there a reason?"

"And when have I not come in before I go home, Jerry? Is that not a given? I just spent a little extra time with Danny tonight. Is that all right with you?" Rachel was startled by the sharpness of her voice and her irritable response. Jerry looked surprised and hurt.

"I am sorry, Jerry," she said, feeling angry that she had let her worries prompt such an abrupt response. "I did not mean to sound short with you. I just had a heavy load today and I am very tired."

"Then by all means, go home and get some rest. I'm pretty tired myself. I'll save what I had to say until tomorrow." He looked out the window at the darkening horizon and folded his arms across his chest.

Rachel sighed and sat in the chair. This was definitely not the atmosphere she had meant to create. Conflict with Jerry was the last thing she wanted. He had spent a perfect day with Danny, and

she didn't want to detract from it. After all, her whole purpose in keeping her distance all day was to protect Jerry from being hurt.

"You were really cute with Danny today. I want you to know how much I appreciate what you are doing for him."

"You really aren't getting what this is all about, are you Rachel? That's what I wanted to tell you, but now I can't find the words. I'm not some noble soul bringing a little boy back from a tragic life, or near death, so that he can laugh and be happy and love again. What he has given me is mine to keep, but what can I give him?"

Rachel sat in silence trying to absorb the deeper meaning of Jerry's words to which her insensitive response had closed the door.

"There's a lot more going on here than I bargained for. There's a lot more to him than I am prepared for. Anyway, why were you crying today?"

Startled, Rachel sat upright. "I wasn't crying."

"Danny said you were."

"When?"

"This morning. He said he thought you were sick. It scared him, but you convinced him they were happy tears. What's wrong, Rachel? We both sensed it. I let him believe that a gift of flowers was the reason for your cheerful smile, but that was a cover up so he wouldn't worry, wasn't it? Your tears were not happy tears, were they?"

Rachel sat quietly, not knowing what to say. Her eyes spoke though, straight from her soul, revealing what her heart could not bring her to tell.

"It's Eric and Roxanne, isn't it? You've heard from them, or about them. You have no right to keep this from me, Rachel. Come clean."

"They got married, Jerry, on their way to Kodiak. I just found out last night. Nobody knew until yesterday. I am so sorry, Jerry, so sorry for everything." She buried her face in her hands.

"That's why I was given peace but no assurance," Jerry mumbled. "It was already a done deal." Jerry's chuckle was cold and bitter. "Well, that's that! Go home, Rachel, and get some rest. You don't have anything to apologize for. I'm tired and want to go to sleep. Please close the blinds on your way out." Jerry rolled as far onto his side as he could with his back toward her, pulled his covers about him, and was silent.

Rachel rose on shaking legs and picked up her beaded purse. She intentionally left the blinds open as she left the room. Departing the hospital she saw a torn remnant of a rubber glove on the sidewalk. Picking it up and pressing it to her heart, she walked home in the crisp September air. She entered her apartment and went straight to bed.

CHAPTER NINE

Jerry slept fitfully. Dreams of Eric and Roxanne had all but ceased. Now every time he closed his eyes, they haunted him. While Doctors were slicing his knee open and grinding steel pins into his bones, Roxanne and Eric were standing in some drab village courtroom, vowing to love each other forever. Forever was the word Roxanne had spoken to Jerry when she promised her love to him. "You and me, forever, forever," she had said. How dare she take precious dreams and stomp them into that sickening black pit! He had survived, but his dreams had died in that putrid bog where she had cast them without so much as a backward glance. How he hated her for that! His little children, with Roxanne's blond curls and dancing brown eyes, had died there. The exquisite dream of his own little family had succumbed to the icy, black muck, just like his family's joy had died with his mother.

Never again would someone have access to his heart. He imagined the walls he would build around it, brick on top of brick and reinforced with iron bars.

Darkness closed around Jerry. It was a thick darkness he could feel, but it wasn't cold like the bog. It was warm, safe, and silent. Here he would stay. Here he could sleep, and sleep, and sleep.

✳

When Rachel arrived at the hospital the following morning, she went straight to Jerry's room. A do not disturb sign was on his closed door. With a sinking heart she inquired at the nurses' desk.

"He hasn't let anyone in the room," the charge nurse said. "He refused breakfast, and he won't tell anyone anything. He asked that Danny not be brought in today. We have no idea what might have happened, do you?"

"Personal problems," she answered. "I fear we may be back where we started. I will see what I can do." Rachel returned to Jerry's room, quietly cracked the door, and peeked in. The blinds were drawn and the room was dark. Jerry's body was twisted awkwardly away from the traction so his back was to the door.

"Jerry," Rachel said softly. There was no response. She approached his bedside. "Jerry," she said again. She placed her hand on his shoulder, but he still did not respond. His breathing was steady and it was early, so she thought he might be sleeping. She quietly slipped back out of the room and closed the door behind her. *Maybe he needs a quiet day to absorb the shock,* she thought. *But this is not going to happen again. I will fight it. Today I will go to Danny, for he will need me. Tomorrow is my day off and I will spend it with Jerry.*

Rachel reported for duty, and Danny was discussed during report. Because census was down, it was decided that Rachel would have a light load so that she could focus mostly on Danny during her shift that day. He was still sleeping, but the nurses knew he would be extremely upset when he couldn't spend time with Jerry. Rachel's associates expressed concern and asked questions about Jerry. They were confused that he would suddenly refuse to see his young friend. They had all delighted in Danny's improvement and were worried. Rachel told them that Jerry had received some painful news and needed time to deal with it. They each gave Jerry their best wishes, knowing that he was Rachel's friend, although some of them supposed he was more than that to her.

As expected, Danny was not only upset, he was irate. "Jerry's my friend. We have a bond. He wants to see me! I know he does! Just take me to him, and he will tell you that."

"Danny, I am very sorry, but Jerry is having a hard time right now. He asked you not to come today—"

"No, he didn't. You're just making that up. He got in trouble because of the balloons, didn't he? We're both in trouble, and that's why you won't let me see him!"

Rachel was startled at his response. "No Danny, of course he's not in trouble because of the balloons. Neither are you. All of us thought it was a funny trick that you and Jerry pulled. We laughed about it all day. Danny, you and Jerry are not in trouble."

"Then he's sick. If he doesn't want to see me, he's really sick! Is he gonna die? I can help him get well. Please let me see him! I know I can help him get well."

"No, Danny, he is not sick. I promise. He is not going to die." Rachel sat in the chair beside Danny's bed and reached for him to gather him into her arms, but he pulled away and moved to the far side of the bed.

"I don't like you anymore," he said as several big tears slipped over his lashes and rolled down his cheeks.

Jerry's words the night before struck Rachel like a thunderbolt. This was what he had realized. She had been so relieved for both of them that she had not anticipated how strong the bond could grow between Danny and Jerry. Now, she had to find solace and comfort for both of them in their anguish, because neither of them had anyone else to lean on. Her shoulders felt very inadequate for the situation she had put herself in. Yet, she had felt powerfully inspired to do what she had done. So, somewhere, somehow, there must be an answer. Her heart prayed for that answer as she stood and lifted a resisting stiff child in her arms. He twisted and squirmed, but she held him fast.

"There, there, Danny. Shhhh, shhhh," she said, gently rocking him. She swayed back and forth and whispered soothing sounds to him as if he were a baby. He suddenly went limp in her arms and burst into a full barrage of tears. She felt his little arms reach around her neck and hold on tight, his small body melting against hers as the grief from all his fears and sorrows poured from his broken heart. Rachel thought her own heart would break as she held him close and tried to comfort him. She sat in the chair, rocking and soothing, patting and caressing. "It is okay to cry Danny, it is okay. Cry as long as you want. I am here. I will hold you." She was crying with him. She cried for Danny, for Jerry, and for Eric.

Danny's tears were finally all gone. He settled in her lap and snuggled against her. "Why doesn't Jerry want to see me? Did I do something wrong? Is he mad at me?"

"No, Danny, he is not mad at you. He has some sadness right now because of personal problems. He was sad before you met him, and you helped him laugh and have fun again. You have been his little hero. He heard some more sad news yesterday, and he just needs to work through it. I am sure he did not want to be sad in front of you. He was probably afraid it would make you sad too."

"No, I could make him feel better again. I'm his friend. I should be with him when he's sad. I should tell him that I care so he will feel better."

"Just give him a few days, Danny, maybe—"

"I know, I can pray for him like I prayed for my mamma. She said my prayers helped her a lot. She said she knew God would take care of both of us even if we couldn't be together, and he gave me you and Jerry. I know he can help Jerry. Can I pray for him right now?"

"Yes, Danny, I think that would be fine." He squirmed from her lap and placed his bony little knees on the floor at her feet. He leaned across her lap and offered the sweetest prayer that Rachel thought the angels had probably ever heard. It was a simple prayer, uttered with a child's unequaled love for a stricken friend and placed with enormous faith at the throne of Deity. Rachel took hope in the child's unwavering faith, for in that faith she felt power.

Rachel tried to visit Jerry the next day, but he insisted on his chosen isolation. For the next few days he talked to no one, ate poorly, and kept his blinds closed, and the Do Not Disturb sign remained on his door. Each day Rachel tried to draw him out, to at least regain his acceptance of her as a friend, but he seemed to have locked the doors to his heart. Calling David hadn't helped, because Jerry refused to accept any phone calls.

Rachel devoted her time to Danny who was probably hurting as badly as Jerry.

Danny waited patiently, hoping each day to go to Jerry, accepting the disappointment, and trusting that maybe tomorrow his friend would feel better. He remained faithful and fervent in his little prayers for Jerry, never once doubting that Jerry would one day ask for him.

Danny fell asleep one night after a desperate prayer pleading that Jerry would want to see him the next day. Rachel tucked him in and kissed his tear-stained face.

Emotion and anger welled up inside her. She had vowed that she would fight if Jerry closed himself in again. He had done that, and more. It was time to take action. She went directly to Jerry's room, tore down the Do Not Disturb sign, and pushed the door open. She walked to the blinds and opened them. Jerry rolled over in bed and glared at her. Before he could complain, she walked to his bedside, flipped on the overhead light, and said, "We need to talk." He opened his mouth, but she didn't want to hear any excuses, so she continued, "All right, it has been five days since you found out that your unfaithful fiancée married my despicable brother. What can you do about it? Hibernate in here like some growling old bear? You told me once that you were glad you still have your life. What life? To lay in here, day after day, feeling sorry for yourself while a little boy down the hall suffers with a broken heart?"

Jerry sat upright and started to speak, but she cut him off.

"Ohoya! I know it is my fault that he suffers. It was I who introduced you. I understand what you were trying to tell me about his strong attachment to you. I am sorry. I was so relieved for both of you. I should have noticed what was happening, but I did not notice. That is my mistake." She paced beside his bed, nervously rubbing the beads on her purse handle.

Jerry sat back, folding his arms across his chest, and watched her in silence.

She suddenly stopped pacing and whirled toward him. "But it was you who made this bond he speaks of. It was you who told him to always be true to a friend. Every day he says the sweetest little prayers, begging for you to feel better, and every day he vows that you will be true to your bond. Every night he cries himself to sleep, faithfully hoping that tomorrow you will ask for him to come. If you do not wish to see him again, then you must tell him. He will not believe anyone but you." She turned away, brushing hot tears from her face, and started for the door.

Jerry remained silent, staring at the blue squares on his hospital gown.

"I know you did not want to meet him in the first place, Jerry, and I know I have no place to tell you what to do." She turned again and met his gaze as he looked up. "I only know that a little boy loves you." She turned and walked from the room, closing the door behind her.

Jerry grabbed the pull string and turned off the light. He lay in the dim room, gazing at the fading horizon. He had been so numb the past few days that he decided he must have journeyed into the abyss he had previously feared and fought against. He had not realized he could actually go there. Part of him resented Rachel, because her emotional little speech had forced him out of his comfortable black hole. Part of him was grateful, because he really didn't want to be there. But here was sadness. Here he could feel all that he had lost. His own beautiful little children, their laughter and squeals of delight as he gave them piggyback rides, or just tickled them. His sweet wife, looking on and smiling, with her hands covered in flour as she prepared biscuits for supper. Suddenly, he realized that this dream, this memory, was his own. It was his mother and father. It was his three older sisters and himself playing with his father. The laughter echoing in his heart was his own. This was his dream. This was what he had wanted for himself. This was what he had lost again.

Jerry's body shook as he wept. He buried his face in his blankets to muffle the sobs that he could not control. The pain in his aching heart was worse than any blood clot because it was an emptiness that could not be filled.

Jerry didn't see the door open slightly and then close. He didn't hear the patter of bare feet across the hospital floor. He didn't notice the thin shadow quietly moving the chair against his bed and then climbing up on it, but he did feel a little hand stroking his curly hair, and another one softly patting the back of his hand as it held the blankets over his face. Jerry froze. Choking back a sob, he quickly dried his eyes and lowered the blankets. A face, about ten inches from his own, was visible in the dim twilight. The small features portrayed deep compassion as tears streamed down two little cheeks.

"Danny," Jerry gasped. "How did you get here?"

"I've been prayin' and prayin' for you, 'cause Rachel said you're sad. She said I couldn't come unless you asked for me, but I heard you cryin' in my dream. So I got out of bed and sneaked like a real warrior so nobody saw me. I was afraid they'd make me go back to bed, and I knew you needed me."

Jerry stifled a sob as he lifted the boy and pulled him into the bed beside him. He planted a big kiss on Danny's bald head. "Thank you, Danny," he choked. "You are right. I really needed you." Tears fell unheeded now as Jerry wrapped his blanket and strong arms around the little orphan boy, holding him close. *What a miracle of faith, loyalty, love, and healing lie in the enormous capacity of this small child's heart,* Jerry thought as Danny gently patted his arm.

"It's okay to cry, Jerry. I'm here." Danny cooed in soothing tones. "You can cry as long as you want to."

CHAPTER TEN

Danny was sitting in his wheel chair, eating breakfast in Jerry's room. "Was your leg hurting last night, or was your heart hurting 'cause someone was mean to you?" he asked.

Jerry smiled as he spread a thick layer of jam on his toast. "My leg doesn't hurt anymore, Danny. It's getting better. I guess I was just missing my family."

"You must've been missing them a whole bunch, 'cause you were really crying. I didn't know a big man could cry. I had to cry too 'cause you sounded so sad."

"We did cry together, didn't we?" Jerry reached down and hugged Danny. "That was a tough night. You helped me a lot, Danny. I don't know how you dreamed about my problem, but I really did need you. Thank you for coming to me. I'm sorry I left you to worry all those days. I was kind of lost, I guess. That's not a good excuse, but it's the only one I have."

"That's okay. I felt lost when my mamma died. I just couldn't figure out what to do. I tried to be brave. I tried so hard to be like a warrior so I wouldn't cry, but the tears just kept coming and coming, and I couldn't stop. Then, when I cried for you 'cause I was missing you, Rachel said it's okay to cry. Now I know it is 'cause you're brave like a warrior too, but you cried a lot."

Jerry chuckled. "So I did. Danny, you are the bravest warrior

I've ever known. But you can cry anytime you feel like it, and I owe you one, so if you ever need a crying partner, just ask me. Deal?" he said, giving Danny a high five.

"Deal!" Danny grinned.

✳

Rachel had gone to bed emotionally and physically exhausted. She had slept through her alarm and suddenly awakened with a start. "Oh, no, I am late for work!" She rushed to the kitchen and called the hospital. Danny would be worried if she was not there when he awakened. "Connie, I am so sorry; I overslept. Tell Danny I am on my way. I will be there shortly." She hung up the phone and rushed to get ready. Stuffing a muffin in her mouth as she half ran down the sidewalk, she reached the hospital and ran up three flights of stairs. She arrived at the nurses' desk and clocked in. Then she picked up her list of patients. "Is Danny all right, Connie?" she breathlessly asked the head nurse.

Connie's green eyes twinkled. "Danny is just fine. I told him you would be late. He didn't mind." She chuckled, but said no more as Rachel hurried to his room.

Seconds later she was back with a puzzled expression on her face. "Where is he?"

"Where would he want to be more than anything?" Connie said, her smile sending a thrill through Rachel.

"How? Connie, I am sorry, I know I am already late, but—"

"Yes, of course, I'll keep an eye on your other patients. Just go." She motioned down the hall, but Rachel was already running toward Jerry's room. Connie threw back her head of gray hair and laughed out loud.

Danny's giggles echoed through the open doorway as Rachel reached the room. She stopped for a second, gathering her composure as she heard Jerry's cheerful voice. She entered the room just as a spit wad flew in front of her face.

"Danny, shame on you. You almost shot Rachel."

"You mean you almost shot her! Mine wasn't ready yet."

Danny put his drinking straw to his mouth and blew a soggy scrap of napkin at Jerry, who was aiming a guilty grin at Rachel. The spit wad bounced off Jerry's nose, and Danny immediately doubled up with laughter.

Rachel leaned against the wall and smiled, too overcome to speak. What miracle had brought this about? Then she noticed Danny's knobby little knees poking out from under his gown, and she had her answer. She didn't need to wonder anymore.

Several happy days passed with spit wads, pudding painting on dinner trays, and yes, a few more water balloons, not to mention the goofy-looking faces drawn with markers on sheets of paper and taped all around the lower part of the walls. (Rachel thought Danny to be the better of the two artists).

One day Danny arrived in Jerry's room wearing a gloomy face. Jerry was puzzled, but he didn't ask any questions, and Danny wasn't volunteering any information, either. As Danny listened to Jerry's stories with a waning smile, the mischievous sparkle was missing from his eyes. Jerry tried to cheer him up by pulling silly faces, but Danny just smiled sadly, without his natural, happy glow.

By the time Rachel checked in, Jerry was becoming concerned. "What's wrong?" he whispered to her when Danny wasn't looking.

She took the breakfast menu and wrote on the back of it, "He starts chemotherapy again tomorrow. It is hard on him. He is brave, but he does not like to talk about it. He will be glad to have your company today. It will take his mind off his fears. Thank you, you're wonderful! With all my love, Rachel."

Jerry read the note with worry on his face, and then he took a double take at Rachel's signature and cast her a questioning glance. She smiled and lightly ran her fingers through Jerry's curly hair. Then she excused herself to go back to work. Jerry stared at the note as a warm tingling passed through him.

"Why do you have that funny look on your face?" Danny asked. "What did Rachel write to you?"

Jerry quickly stuffed the menu under his pillow. "Oh, nothing important." He batted a glove balloon to Danny.

Danny caught and held it. "Your face didn't look like it wasn't important. I think you'd better tell me."

Jerry chuckled. "Well, a guy's gotta have some secrets. I'm sorry my small friend, but this one's none of your business."

"Danny got an all-knowing look on his face. "I'll bet she likes you—I mean, like a girlfriend." Danny snickered.

Jerry threw a pillow at Danny to hide the flush on his face, then pushed his glasses up on his nose. "You think you're pretty smart, don't you?" He heaved another pillow at Danny.

Danny threw both pillows back at Jerry and then grabbed another one off the chair and threw it as well. Pillows and a five-fingered balloon were soon flying about the room, and a full-scale war was declared and vigorously acted out. The yelling and laughing from Jerry's room caused the nurses to close the door, and for a time, Danny's fears were forgotten.

As Rachel came to take Danny to bed, he said, "Wait, I gotta tell Jerry something." He climbed out of the wheelchair, pushed the other chair up to Jerry's bed and climbed onto it. "I didn't want you to worry about me and spoil our fun, so I didn't tell you that I probably can't come to see you tomorrow. I hope you'll be okay without me, but I've gotta get my cancer medicine tomorrow. If I come to see you I might throw up and that wouldn't be cool. So when I get done with all that yucky stuff, I'll come back." He gave Jerry a big hug, which Jerry returned, holding the youngster closely for some time.

He swallowed hard. "I'll be waiting for you. Don't forget to come back. We've got a bond, you know."

"I know. You let me come back when your sadness got better. I'll come back when my throwin' up gets better." He waved bravely as Rachel wheeled him to the door. Jerry smiled and heartily waved back; then his eyes met Rachel's, and no words were needed to tell of their love and concern for a courageous little boy.

Jerry didn't see much of Rachel or Danny the next day. Several times Rachel wheeled him to Jerry's room, all bundled up and looking very pale and tired as he peeked out from his blankets. But his smile was bright as soon as he entered Jerry's door.

They only stayed a few minutes, but the visits were most welcome. Jerry sent Danny notes, jokes, or fun origami animals and objects folded out of note pads from the nurses' desk. He made a paper airplane covered with notes of encouragement and praise, with silly quips mixed in to make Danny chuckle. Jerry lay awake that night thinking of his little friend. This time Jerry was the one doing the praying.

Sometime in the middle of the night, Jerry was awakened by the sound of someone whimpering, and a weak, shivering little boy climbed into bed with him. As he wrapped his big arms around the thin child, he felt wetness on his skin. "Danny are you okay? How did you get here?" Jerry asked with deep concern.

"I had a dream about my mamma when she died," he answered. Jerry wrapped him tightly in a blanket hanging on the bed rail. Danny started to weep, and Jerry was true to his promise as he wiped tears from his own eyes. Finally, Danny spoke. "I wish she didn't have to go away, but it's okay 'cause she hurt really bad and threw up a lot. She doesn't hurt now, and she can smile and sing and make pretty flowers with beads every day. I'll be with her again someday. Is she with your mamma now?"

"Probably so," Jerry answered. "Maybe they're best friends, and maybe they are smiling down on us from heaven this very minute."

Danny snuggled closer. "I think you're right." He snuggled still closer, gave a gentle sigh, and his steady breathing told Jerry he had finally found peace in sleep.

Fearful that the nurses would be alarmed to find Danny missing, Jerry pushed the nurse call button. "Shhhh," he whispered, when the nurse entered. "Come over here. I think someone may be looking for a barefoot runaway. Why don't you see if they will just let him stay here until he wakes up?"

"Are you sure? He may get sick and throw up on you!" she answered.

"So, what's a little puke? If he can take what he's going through, I'm sure I can endure a wipe down and a bed change."

"Very well, I'll call peds and alert them."

As she left the room, he heard a worried nurse greet her. "Did

Danny come down here? He was sound asleep when I did rounds. I went to check on him when I finished, and he was gone."

"He's settled in with Jerry. I was just coming to call you. They are both resting, let's leave them be." Jerry smiled, checked Danny's covers again and relaxed with a deep, contented sigh.

The same pattern continued for the next two nights. "Why don't you just move his bed in here?" Jerry asked Rachel. "That's what he wants anyway. At least he won't be wandering the halls in the middle of the night. I can call a nurse if he needs one."

"That is really sweet, Jerry, but it can get bad and you may not get much rest. They are hitting him pretty hard with the chemo this time, because they are hoping it is his last. Kind of like a booster shot." She was shaking her head doubtfully.

"Rachel, first of all, I owe you an apology. Forcing me to meet Danny was the best thing you could have done for me. I was a jerk about it, and I am deeply sorry. You were so right, and I was so wrong." Jerry folded his arms behind his head. "I hope I've made his life happier. I was afraid when we were getting close because separation is so hard. Now, I have huge anxieties about that little boy because I don't know where he'll go when he leaves this place. I just hope something I've done or said can always stay with him." Jerry smiled. "I know he will be with me every day for the rest of my life. Do you know what he did for me?" Jerry lowered his arms and leaned toward Rachel.

"One night I was a total wreck. In fact, it was the night you threw that Do Not Disturb sign on my bed and told me off. Well, I really needed to be told off. When I was alone, all the rotten stuff I'd dealt with caved in on me, stuff I'd pushed away for years. I lost it. I was wasted. Then while I was bawling and blubbering like a big baby, I felt two little hands touching me and patting me. I didn't see or hear him come in. He said he knew I needed him." Jerry paused to swallow his emotion. "He just crawled up in my bed, wrapped his arms around me, and bawled right along with me. Now, do you think it's going to bother me if he needs help in the middle of the night? He wants to be in here. Get it cleared and bring him in. It's my turn to say to him, "I knew you needed me.""

CHAPTER ELEVEN

The head nurse cleared Danny's transfer with the doctor, and she and Rachel wheeled Danny and his bed into Jerry's room. The effects of the treatment had taken their toll on the child. Jerry was frightened by Danny's appearance. His little brown Indian looked rather washed out. Jerry motioned for them to bring Danny's bed alongside his own.

"Are you sure?" the head nurse whispered. "Sometimes the vomiting can be projectile." Jerry's answer was to grip Danny's bed rail and draw it tightly against his own. She smiled at Rachel and shrugged as she left the room. Rachel got them settled and then returned to her other duties.

Danny had slept through the transfer, and he continued to sleep for a long time. On occasion it seemed to Jerry that his slow, unsteady breathing disappeared altogether. Several times he panicked and called the nurse. She smiled and reassured him that Danny was really doing quite well. Finally, he reached his hand through Danny's bed rail and laid it against Danny's chest until he was convinced that there was no pause in his breathing. He could feel Danny's heart beat through his skinny ribs. It was beating too rapidly, but it was steady. In time, Jerry's eyes became more accustomed to the slight rise and fall of the covers, and he relaxed.

Rachel balanced her duties among her other patients, and

the long walk to Jerry's room to frequently attend to Danny. She smiled to herself at the clucking mother hen Jerry had become. More and more she felt herself caring for this remarkable man. He had his darker, sullen side, the tendency to hide his own pain and suffering, and maybe even himself, but his compassion and tenderness toward others was a trait that impressed her the first day she met him. Every touch, every word, and every expression revealed the rightness of his heart.

Rachel laid a reassuring hand on Jerry's shoulder. "I know he looks bad, Jerry, but he is holding his own. When we disconnect his IV, you can cuddle him if you want to." She hugged Jerry's shoulders and ran her fingers through the short, curly hair at the back of his neck. He grasped her hand and pulled it to his lips, kissing her fingers. Her closeness was comforting, so he didn't let go until she had to adjust the IV.

She and Jerry were quietly visiting when Danny awakened. He looked confused as his black eyes darted around at his different surroundings, and then he spotted the artwork on the walls and quickly turned to find Jerry. "I get to be in your room all the time? I don't have to go to bed in my old room anymore?"

"That's right," Jerry said with a grin. Danny's bright smile brought with it the sunshine, and Jerry felt its warmth.

Rachel had hoped she would be there when Danny awoke. She had anticipated his delight and hoped she wouldn't miss it. She wasn't disappointed by his reaction, and she winked at Jerry and kissed Danny's bald head before she returned to her other duties.

Danny stayed awake long enough to assure himself that he was not dreaming, that his bed was in Jerry's room to stay, and that he wouldn't have to leave. Then he drifted off to sleep again. However, his rest was short lived. He started to fuss and whimper in his sleep; then he suddenly cried out and sat up.

Jerry could see that Danny was retching. He quickly grabbed his bath basin, twisted around in his bed, and held the basin under Danny's chin. "Nurse!" he called out, forgetting about the call button as Danny's angry tummy released its contents. Kelly,

Jerry's nurse, hurried to Danny's side. Jerry wiped Danny's mouth with a tissue, and then with a moist wash cloth that Kelly had handed to him. He stroked Danny's head as the nurse emptied and rinsed the basin.

Danny cried quietly, shivering and whimpering until he finally snuggled back under his blankets and closed his eyes. An enormous ache tugged at Jerry's heart as he tucked the covers under Danny's chin and took the small brown hand in his large one.

Closing his fingers tightly around Jerry's hand, Danny was calmed by the touch of his special friend. He slept again, his hand still clutching Jerry's fingers.

Rachel entered the room. "Was it pretty hard?" she asked, removing the empty chemotherapy bag and opening a rapid fluid drip into Danny's IV.

"Yeah, I thought his insides were going to come out with it. Is it always this bad?"

"Not always, some people don't even get sick," Rachel said. "It depends a lot on dosage, different types of drugs, and different types of cancer. This was a heavy dose. It could get worse. Jerry, you don't have to—"

A stubborn shake of Jerry's head closed the subject. Rachel gently wiped a tear away that had slipped from the corner of Danny's closed eye. Then she walked to the other side of Jerry's bed and surprised him with a kiss on his cheek. "I have never seen an angel in a hospital gown before today," she said as she returned to the side of Danny's bed and listened to his heart with a stethoscope. She took his blood pressure and then sat down. She watched him for a while, holding his other hand in her own brown fingers.

Jerry smiled, thinking how right Danny and Rachel looked together. He pushed his glasses up on his nose, still feeling her gentle kiss hot on his cheek.

After Rachel left, Jerry dozed while Danny was sleeping. He frequently roused to check on Danny. Then he slipped into a deeper sleep. He was awakened suddenly by a cry from Danny as he bolted upright in bed and spewed the yellow green contents of his stomach onto his bed and gown.

"Nurse," Jerry yelled, too groggy and disoriented to remember the nurse's call button again.

Rachel had slipped in and out of the room to find Jerry and Danny both asleep, with Danny's hand still holding fast to Jerry's fingers. She was talking with Kelly in the hall when Jerry called. Both nurses immediately rushed into the room. Rachel stripped Danny's soiled gown from his bony chest and began bathing him as Kelly pulled the covers from the bed. Danny was crying and shivering as Rachel dressed him in a clean gown.

"Let me hold him while you change the bed." Jerry's voice sounded abrupt.

Rachel glanced at him, surprised to see anger in his eyes. "He might throw up again," she cautioned.

"So if he pukes, he pukes. I can take better care of him if he's here with me." His arms were reaching out, ready to place Danny beside him. Rachel pushed the smaller bed away from Jerry's and slipped between them to lift Danny into Jerry's waiting arms. Her eyes were questioning. Jerry expressed his anger with whispered hostility as he tucked his covers around the shivering child. "He was fine and happy. Why was all this harsh treatment stuff necessary? I respect medicine, but right now I'm deeply questioning its logic."

Rachel nodded her understanding and moved the IV onto the post in Jerry's bed. She smiled and placed a kiss on Danny's head and another one on Jerry's other cheek. Then she turned to help Kelly make the bed.

After Rachel and Kelly left the room, Jerry blinked hard, still frowning as he pulled Danny against him, petting his little bald head like he would a puppy and soothing him by humming tunes. Danny snuggled up to him. His shivering finally ceased and gave way to peaceful sleep.

An intense feeling of awe suddenly poured through Jerry as he recalled his anguish the night he and Danny had wept together. This was the longing he had felt so bitterly that night; the emptiness for his own little son, now filled at least for the moment by the small, living, breathing, reality of someone else's child. He kissed the boy's head with all the yearning in his heart, and a few tears trickled down his cheeks. He carefully settled himself against his pillow and relaxed as he brushed them from his face with the back of his hand.

Chapter Twelve

"Did you find this young man in your father's gold mine?" Connie asked as Rachel returned to the pediatric nurses' desk. "You'd better hang on to him. He's a keeper."

Rachel laughed as she caught the merry twinkle in her charge nurse's eyes. "Jerry is one of a kind. I had hoped that he and Danny could support one another in their confinement. However, I did not anticipate this wonderful friendship between them. Now, through Danny's illness, Jerry has become very much like a doting daddy."

"And you?"

"What?"

"Doting! We all do it with Danny, especially you. But Danny's not the only one being doted over. This Jerry of yours is more than you have said." Connie's prying eyes studied Rachel as she leaned forward, looking directly into Rachel's face. Rachel just smiled self-consciously. "I thought so," Connie said, her smile broadening.

Her all-knowing expression and insight surprised Rachel. She had thought the warm feelings swelling in her heart were less obvious. "He is a nice man," Rachel said simply. "We shall see."

"There's no 'we shall see' to it. Rachel, you might as well admit what you are trying to hide, even from yourself. You are madly in love. It's written all over your face." Connie laughed again, tucking a loose strand of gray hair behind her ear. "If you three stay around here it'll be too warm for Fairbanks to freeze this winter."

Rachel felt a flush of color on her brown skin. Avoiding Connie's gaze, she pulled Danny's chart from its slot. Unable to think up a quick response, she cast a smile at Connie, and buried her nose in the chart.

Connie nodded her approval of Rachel's unspoken love. "You're an excellent and sensitive nurse, Rachel, and a hard worker. We're lucky to have you. While you're caring for Danny on the other wing, don't hesitate to take time to care for your Jerry as well." She gave Rachel a hug. Then chuckling to herself, she turned to take orders off a chart a doctor had just left at the desk.

Rachel finished writing on Danny's chart. "Thank you, Connie," she said placing her hand on Connie's shoulder. "I shall take my break with Danny and Jerry. Apparently you know why better than I do. I will think about what you said."

Rachel took her purse from the break room and bought an orange juice from the vending machine. She entered Jerry's room and sat quietly in the chair, resting her tired feet on the bottom of Danny's empty bed. Jerry was sleeping with a contented smile on his face. His arm was wrapped around Danny who was snuggled peacefully against Jerry with his covers carefully tucked under his chin.

An overwhelming rush of tenderness surged through Rachel, warm goose bumps rising on her arms. *What am I feeling?* She thought as it swept from the prickling hair on the back of her neck through her entire body and tingled in her toes. The feeling was profound, something greater than she knew, but she had no explanation. Rachel loved the beauty of nature, the gifts of God—the magnificent mountains of her native homeland, the brilliant fireweed, and the fields of lupine growing on the frozen tundra—but she had never looked upon anything more beautiful than the scene in front of her. With humble awe, she felt the love between a broken man and a little orphan boy. Surely, this too, was a gift from God. How had this oddly matched pair of humanity made such a welcome and comfortable space for themselves in her life?

And what lay in store for each of them? She gazed upon them, resting side by side, and she could not separate them from her heart.

"Oh, Mother dearest, what have I done to myself?" she whispered, fingering the brightly colored flowers that had been carefully beaded into the fabric of her purse. Her mother had put them there with painstaking love during her own long illness when Rachel was seventeen. The purse was to be a high school graduation gift, but her mother gave it to her early, sensing that she would attend the graduation only in spirit. *No matter,* Rachel thought. *She was there. The love of a mother for a daughter transcends time, and space, and life, and death.* "I will watch over you," her mother had said. "Listen for my call of love in the cry of the wolf on the frozen air. Look for me in the golden wings of the eagle as it soars in the pale blue vastness of the sky. Feel my presence in your heart when you are in sorrow or in joy. I will always be there." Rachel could see her mother's beloved smile and the light of love in her eyes. She could feel the soft touch of her hand upon her face. Rachel knew she was here with her now. She thought of Eric and found comfort in knowing that their mother would be with him as well.

And then, somehow, she felt the presence of some other mothers nearby. One was alive with love, very young, brown-skinned and beautiful, dressed in a white buckskin tunic, and wearing silken braids of long, black hair. The other, gentle, with fair skin and a white gown, smiling with love and compassion, reaching beyond days and weeks and years, trying to touch the wounded heart of her cherished son. Rachel closed her eyes and let the vision from deep within her soul bathe her with a spiritual warmth of understanding. She, Eric, Danny, and Jerry had all been loved and nurtured by their own precious mothers. They were not alone . . . ever.

Rachel sipped on her juice, glancing at her watch from time to time. Then she arose, kissed the fingers of both of her hands and ever so lightly touched Jerry's lips and Danny's cheek. Then she returned to work.

❊

In Kodiak, with its rain-drenched fall climate, Roxanne finished packing Eric's bag for the dreaded fishing trip early the following morning. She set the heavy bag by the front door, stepped into the bathroom to brush her short, blond curls, and applied a touch of lipstick. Then she hurried to the kitchen and pulled a casserole from the oven. Eric would be home soon, and she wanted everything to be perfect for him on his last night at home. She was setting the table when he walked in the door and removed his rain gear.

He glanced at the bag she had prepared for his departure, and then at Roxanne who was reaching across the table with a plate and a glass. His feelings caught him off guard as her slender form brought back memories of the few times he had felt that she could truly love him as much as he loved her. There had been times of closeness that they had shared when he was filled and content, believing, or at least wanting to believe, that this could last forever.

Now a pang of fear and mistrust made him question her true intent in packing his bag for the perilous journey out to sea. He had never before dreaded the hard profession he had previously embraced. The danger and excitement of the job and the acrid smell of fish seething from the ship's hold now seemed loathsome, and he didn't want to go. He wondered what he would come home to. He expected it would be an empty house. But he longed to come home to a lovely and exciting wife who had found it in her heart to build a future with him rather than live in the sorrow of past mistakes? He had tried desperately to console, comfort, and encourage her, to win her affection with his tender care and passion. But if he were absent, she might leave, for he was powerless to keep her here.

Suddenly, he resented everyone who sat in gluttonous indulgence at dinner tables in warm, comfortable homes devouring feasts of fish. How dare they blindly and selfishly dismiss any hardship, risk, and suffering of the fishermen who struggled to stand on heaving decks with fish water running down their necks and freezing their hands and feet?

Roxanne folded the last napkin. Then she turned to face him. Smiling brightly, she hurried to his side with a dry towel.

"Hi, Eric. Welcome home. Did you have a hard day?" she asked, gently wiping moisture from his face and neck.

"Not too bad, Roxanne. The rain let up some, so final preparations were easier."

"I'm glad. I just put dinner on the table." She ran her hand across his cheek. "After we eat I'll draw you a nice, warm bath and scrub your back, then I'll give you a massage. You must be sore from all your hard work." She hugged him, kissing him full on the mouth, something she hadn't done for some time.

She seemed genuinely happy to see him. Her sweet face showed no telltale sign of tears. She smiled, showing the dimples he seldom saw. Her brown eyes were dancing, and her lips were soft and inviting. Overpowered by his love and longing for her, he embraced her, his fears lost in the passion of his kiss. Then he held her tightly, pressing her small body close to his. Her reaction to his affection seemed to hold no reservations, and her response was open and enticing. They shared a pleasant evening and retired in each other's full embrace.

The morning dawned wet and stormy, with rain sleeting down the windowpane. Eric lay quietly, warm with contentment, still cradling Roxanne in his arms as he had all night. She was awake but did not attempt to get up. If only he could believe this was where she always wanted to be, or was her cheerful countenance, her special care and affection so freely given, her way of saying goodbye? Eric pushed away the thought. As for now, his wife had given herself to him, and she was still warm and willing. He would cherish these moments even if they were his last. His arms drew her closer, his kiss revealed his heart, and her lips were soft and responsive.

The time had slipped away far too fast, and the departure of Eric's fishing boat was drawing near. His fears were now in full effect, choking his throat with emotion as he tried to control his voice. "Here is the ticket if you decide you want to visit your parents while I'm gone." He placed it on the table, reluctant to remove his fingers, as though with releasing it he would allow it to fly from his hand, like he feared she may fly from his arms and be lost to him forever.

"Thank you, Eric. You are far more kind and caring than I deserve. Be safe, husband, be safe." Again her kiss was full and warm.

He held her and his arms just wouldn't let go. "Thank you for last night and this morning, Roxanne. I will not hold you here, my little bird, if you must fly away. Just know that somewhere out there on the ocean swells is a fisherman who is very much in love with you." His voice cracked as he blinked and swallowed hard. He bent and kissed her, and she felt the truth of his words in his kiss. Then he grabbed his bag and was gone.

Roxanne stood staring at the closed door for some time. Then she walked to the table and picked up the ticket. "I should have told him I love him," she whispered to herself, "but I just couldn't say it. I just couldn't." She picked up the phone and called the number on the itinerary in the folder with the ticket.

"I'm flying from Kodiak to Anchorage to Seattle," she said into the receiver. "How much extra would it cost if I change my ticket to fly from Anchorage to Fairbanks for a layover, and then back to Anchorage and on to Seattle?" she asked.

When she hung up the phone, she sighed and walked to the window overlooking the gray swells of the ocean. Her heart throbbed in agony as if it were being torn in half. One half cried out for her husband—a loving, handsome, young Indian, fighting the harsh elements aboard a storm tossed vessel; and the other for a beloved young man, suffering untold pain and anguish while bound mercilessly to a hospital bed by her own cold betrayal and broken promise.

The tears she had managed to hide so well from Eric burst forth uncontrollably now. She wept bitterly, like the rain sleeting down her windowpane. *Even God can't stop crying in this bitter, rain drenched land of the North,* she thought.

Chapter Thirteen

"I'm really sorry I threw up on you and your bed, Jerry," Danny said as Rachel stripped off his gown, moved him onto the bath blanket on his bed, and cleaned him up. His eyes were sad and his lower lip puckered like he was about to cry.

"Hey, I invited you to share my bed knowing full well that might happen," Jerry said as Kelly took his soiled gown and handed him a bath basin of warm water. "Remember our bond? You'd do the same for me if I were sick, wouldn't you?" Danny hung his head, but nodded his willingness to do anything for the bond. "Then why the gloomy face? Look, I'm not ruined. I wash." Jerry scrubbed his shoulder, arm, and stomach while Kelly placed a bath blanket over him and stripped his bed.

Rachel settled Danny in his bed and covered him up, and then she took his blood pressure and listened to his heart. He was still on the verge of tears. She hugged him. "Are you all right?" she asked. "Does your tummy still hurt?"

"No," he mumbled.

"Rachel leaned over him, soothing him by gently stroking her fingers across his head. "Then what's wrong, Danny?" she asked.

"I won't be able to stay with Jerry now in his bed. I sleep good when he holds me, and I'm not scared anymore."

"Who says you can't stay with me? Just let me get cleaned up, and you can crawl right back over here. Deal?" He reached his hand over to Danny.

Danny raised a shaky little hand and gave Jerry's big one a feeble slap "Deal," he said weakly as a slight smile flickered across his face.

Rachel was deeply moved. How many men would purposely expose themselves to a second dousing of throw up? Jerry would make a wonderful father. She wished she had the power to give this little boy to him, but that was out of the question, of course. Danny was Native American, Jerry lived in another state and was single, and Danny already had foster care planned for him as soon as he recovered from this last treatment. Rachel pushed the longing away because it hurt. She could not change the course of action taken by the State Department of Children's Services.

For now, Jerry and Danny were free to enjoy each other, and she could see no good reason in spoiling their remaining time together by sharing the sad news. Jerry had been concerned about separation. Now, as it was drawing near, Rachel was terrified for both of them. They had become so extremely close. Maybe her decision to introduce them had been a mistake after all. She had hoped that the separation would not happen until Jerry was ready to go home. Beyond these concerns was her own unspoken attachment, an awareness of how terribly lonely and empty she would be without them.

Rachel turned to help Kelly. Watching Jerry as she worked, she perceived the grave concern in his eyes as they focused on the child. He suddenly leaned forward with a grin on his face.

Jerry had learned through plenty of hard times that a light attitude always eases a heavy burden of sorrow or suffering. Danny needed that now. "You know something, Danny? You're the most colorful person I know," Jerry said.

"I'm only brown," Danny responded looking confused.

"Just on the outside. Take jelly beans, for instance. What colors are they?"

"Lots of colors—green, red, yellow, orange, and purple."

"See? That's what I mean! You're full of colors too. In fact, you can throw up in Technicolor. You proved that today."

Rachel was startled and just stared at Jerry. Kelly grabbed her mouth as a snicker escaped. She turned her back, trying to maintain self-control, and stepped into the bathroom to dispose of the soiled linen.

Jerry continued. "The first time was red Jell-O, and the second was yellow and green stuff all mixed together. This time it was orange Jell-O. Now we need to find you something purple to eat. Oh, yeah, and a blue raspberry Popsicle. Then when you throw up the next two times, you will have gone through all the colors of the rainbow." Danny chuckled and Kelly laughed out loud. Before Rachel and Kelly could finish making Jerry's bed, Jerry had Danny laughing out loud too.

"Hey Rachel, you got any purple Jell-O for Danny?" Jerry asked as she arranged the bedspread around his suspended leg. "He's only got two colors left."

Rachel rolled her eyes, amused, but refusing to show it. "Ohoya, Jerry! Only you could think up such a silly game! Yes, I can get Danny some purple Jell-O."

"Cool," Danny said.

Later, Danny was sleeping beside Jerry while Jerry watched muted television. Danny suddenly woke up nauseated and started retching again. With Jerry's help, the bath basin saved the bed and their hospital gowns. Danny's tummy was still contracting as Jerry wiped his face. "Hey, Jerry, I did it! It's purple this time!" the sick little boy proudly announced.

Jerry's heart ached for Danny. Rachel was right. This color thing was the most ridiculous idea he'd ever had, but he was desperate to relieve the little guy's suffering. As he'd hoped, making light of the most dreadful side effect had eased the trauma. Jerry pushed the call button. "Tell Kelly we have purple and now we need blue," He told the voice on the intercom.

"What?" the intercom asked back.

"Just tell Kelly, she'll understand."

Danny had taken in very little food, all of it clear liquids. Jerry was amazed at the volume his tummy had sent back out. Jerry ordered a clear liquid supper for himself so that he would not be eating a meal in front of a child who couldn't even hold down Jell-O. The blue Popsicle Danny ate returned shortly after dinner.

"I did it, Rachel! I did it!" Danny said when Rachel came back to visit after supper.

"You did what, Danny?"

"I threw up a whole rainbow. Jerry said he's gonna make me a special award tomorrow."

Rachel laughed. Silly as it was, Jerry's weird color game had turned the tide of a child's suffering from misery and tears to excitement and smiles. She felt she could learn much from this unique and sensitive man. She bent over him and quickly kissed him on the lips. He looked up at her in surprise. She smiled and threaded her fingers gently through his hair, wrapping her other hand around his. "You are amazing, Jerry. You have been better for Danny than the best medicine. If awards are being given out, you deserve a double one. She bent to quickly kiss him again.

But this time Jerry responded by reaching up to cradle her head in his free hand as he kissed her back. Wonderful sensations flowed with his blood as it pulsated through his body. Feelings he had buried deep inside swelled in his heart, trying to burst through the brick walls he had built around it.

Danny's giggle broke the spell.

Rachel gently pulled away, a red glow on her brown cheeks. Her hazel-green eyes twinkled as she tried to reclaim her reserve. "I . . . uh . . . that was the only award I had on me. It was the best I could do."

Jerry slipped his arm around her. Cradling her silky bun of hair with his other hand again, he guided her lips back to his, reveling in the sweet warmth of another kiss.

Danny squirmed beside him and sat up. "I didn't know you and Rachel did that kind of mushy stuff. I was right. She is your girlfriend!"

Jerry and Rachel laughed. "Didn't you hear her, Danny? That was her award to me for letting you puke on me today. See, you didn't have to feel bad about it at all. You earned me the best award

ever from the prettiest girl we both know." He wrapped Danny in both arms and squeezed him tightly.

CHAPTER FOURTEEN

With the days of nausea finally passed, Danny began eating heartily, regaining his health day by day. The washed-out color of his skin gave way to the rich, natural bronze of his people. He remained fairly weak at first, but slept less and less during the day. By the end of the week, Jerry was seeing some of the spark and vitality growing strong again in the child. He was amazed at his stamina and his ability to bounce back from such a deadly illness.

At first, Jerry entertained Danny with stories, which he eagerly devoured while faithfully carving on his driftwood. "I like to hear stories," Danny said one day. "My mamma used to tell me lots of stories when the sun hides most of the time, and it's too dark and cold to go outside and play. I wonder who will tell me stories and take care of me when I go away from here? I miss my mamma's stories and her hugs." He grew quiet and thoughtful. Jerry swallowed hard. He waited until Danny spoke again, not wanting to disturb Danny's sacred memories. "Sometimes an elder from our tribe comes to visit our school and tells us stories," he continued, without looking up. "She's really old, but she gets happy when she talks about the ways the Indians used to live. She tells us legends, and sometimes she makes us laugh like you do. I like your stories too, 'specially about you and David. They're the best ones."

As Danny's strength grew, so did the mischief. Small chunks of soggy napkins always littered the floor from their spit wad wars. Laughter from Jerry's room was a given, so the door was kept shut to reduce the volume of noise for the other patients. Checkers were often strewn on the floor and on the top of the heater beneath the window, along with chess pawns, kings, queens, knights, bishops, and castles. The chess pieces being the targets, and the checkers being the cannon balls.

One day Rachel entered the room and stopped abruptly. "Jerry, what have you done to this boy?" she asked, trying very hard to look stern. Danny grinned at her through chocolate pudding and mashed strawberry war paint from his lunch tray.

"He wanted me too," Jerry answered with a guilty chuckle. "What was I supposed to do, disappoint a warrior?" Jerry opened the tray on the bedside table so Danny could grin at himself in the mirror. "Don't get all excited, Rachel! He's a kid, and he'll wash. Now, be a good nurse and hand me one of my support socks and some straws for feathers so we can make him look like the real thing, okay?"

"Here we go again," she said as she handed Jerry the items for the Indian headdress and left the room. Within a few moments, Danny began receiving visits from most of the nursing staff of both hospital wings.

"See how important you are?" Jerry said with a grin. "I'll bet you are brave enough and good enough to be a Chief."

Danny's face suddenly grew solemn. "You need some war paint too, Jerry, so we can both be Indians. Then you can cut my finger and your finger and we can be blood brother's before I have to go away." He picked up his pocketknife and climbed from his bed onto Jerry's. Then he dipped his finger into the pudding and very carefully and ceremoniously painted a stripe across Jerry's nose and cheeks.

Jerry was surprised. "What's all this going away stuff you're talking about?" he asked as Danny painted another chocolate stripe. "Has someone told you you're going away?"

Danny wiped the remaining pudding on Jerry's napkin and

then dipped his finger into the strawberries. He carefully painted a red stripe between the two brown ones as he gave his simple answer: "I dreamed it last night, and another night too. I want to be your blood brother so we will always have our bond, like you and David, even if I can't see you anymore." Jerry put his arm around Danny as the little Chief settled himself beside him, sticking Jerry's neck with a straw feather. As Jerry rearranged the feather, Danny handed him the open knife and held up his forefinger. "Okay, I'm ready. You can poke me now."

This is seriously for real for this little guy, he thought. *I can't get out of it this time. What am I going to do?* Suddenly, he remembered the IV needle taped to the inside of Danny's arm. Rachel had said it would be removed tomorrow after his last bag of morning fluid was empty. "Wait, I've got an idea. We don't have to poke you to get your blood. Give me your arm." Very carefully Jerry withdrew the tubing plug from the needle, avoiding contamination. He'd seen the nurses do it and knew how to keep it sterile. "Okay, now raise your arm up just a little bit."

"Cool," Danny said, when several drops of dark red blood dripped onto his arm. "That won't even hurt. Will the bond still work?"

"Sure, it's your blood, isn't it? Now, hold still and I'll plug the tube back into the needle." Jerry secured the plug with a gentle twist. "Aha. I should have been a nurse."

"What?" Danny asked.

"Nothing, we're doing important stuff here, just focus. He opened the pocketknife and touched the tip of his finger. Danny shuddered and squeezed his eyes shut as Jerry gave a quick jab. "Okay you can open your eyes now."

"Are you bleeding?" Danny asked, with his eyes still closed and concern in his voice. "Did it hurt really bad?"

"Hey, why were you so brave when you were waiting for me to poke you?"

"I'm used to getting poked, but I didn't want to hurt you, ever."

Jerry chuckled at the deep compassion of his little friend. "I'm fine, Danny. Hold your arm up here."

Danny's eyes were wide as he saw the drop of blood on Jerry's finger. Then he watched breathlessly and reverently as Jerry placed his bleeding finger on the drops of blood on his small brown arm and mixed them together. Jerry looked at him and smiled, surprised to see tears brimming in the little boy's eyes. He wiped Danny's arm with a washcloth.

"Now I'm not alone. I have a real brother, and our bond can't ever be broken. Even if I can't see you anymore, I know you will be with me, just like my mamma." He threw his arms around Jerry as tightly as his small muscles could squeeze and started to cry. Jerry blinked back his own tears, but a few escaped, dropping onto Danny's bald head as he wrapped the child in his arms with all the love he could give to his new little brother.

"Where did the blood on this wash cloth come from?" Rachel asked, as she went to Jerry's bed to take Danny's blood pressure. She never knew which bed he would be in. He migrated, depending on moods and activities.

"Ah, it's nothing, I just poked my finger with Danny's knife when I was helping him." He winked at Danny, who smiled back, his precious secret tucked safely away in his little boy heart.

"What are you two up to?" Rachel asked, sensing that she had missed something significant between them. Then she saw Jerry's face and laughed. "Oh, I see. Some special Indian Powwow you have been holding? Very well, I will leave you to your important council meeting. I will see you after work." She kissed Danny's head, avoiding his feathers, and kissed Jerry's cheek, avoiding his pudding paint.

Except for an occasional trip to the bathroom, Danny hadn't moved from Jerry's side all day long. He had fallen asleep still wearing his pudding when Rachel arrived after supper. Jerry was still wearing his as well. She giggled. "Would you like a wash cloth?" She asked.

"Yes, please. It's itching like crazy, but I didn't want to scrub it off while he was awake. This has been a very important day for both of us."

"I see," Rachel said, but the question in her eyes required a commitment from Jerry that Danny's secret must be as sacred to him as it was to Danny. Now, Jerry had two brothers, and this small one warmed his heart in marvelous ways he had never imagined. He was so grateful for Rachel's insight that had brought Danny into his life. How he would miss him when he left this place!

Jerry didn't reach for the warm cloth when Rachel brought it to him. He laid his head on his pillow and closed his eyes. She smiled, and her gentle touch was relaxing as she wiped away the dried pudding and strawberry juice from his handsome face.

She smiled more as the memory of her two painted warriors engraved itself in her heart. Yet, a part of her was crying out in agony. Every day that Danny improved was a day closer to his discharge. How she had grown to love this man and this boy. She set the washcloth on the bedside table beside Danny's Rainbow Award, specially made by Jerry and displayed for all to see.

Remembering the tender kiss Jerry had initiated the night of the award drew her to him now. She bent and kissed his forehead, then his brow.

✳

Jerry was sad and tired as he lay basking in the comforting touch of the washcloth against his face. It was soothing and pleasant, so he let himself drift. He felt Rachel near. He felt her soft lips press against his forehead and brow. Suddenly, his buried heart began beating rapidly in his chest as her closeness stirred him. His free arm encircled her back and pulled her to him as his lips met hers in a warm caress. Somehow, this was so right.

As Danny whimpered and squirmed, Rachel gently pulled away. They smiled at each other, then looked at him. A frown furrowed his brow, and a tear slipped out of the corner of one of his closed eyes.

"Do you want to take a break, Jerry? I can put him in his bed to sleep."

Jerry shook his head, wiping away the tear. "He needs me tonight. I'm fine. He's going to be discharged soon, isn't he?"

"How did you know?" Rachel asked, startled at the question and dreading the answer.

"He knows, he told me today. It's true then?"

Rachel nodded. "He will be placed in a foster home as soon as he is well enough. I did not have the heart to tell either of you. I wanted you to be able to enjoy your time together. I suppose this is best so you can both be prepared, but how did he know?"

"How did he know that I was falling apart that terrible night? He's been having dreams." Jerry ran his fingers through his hair and shook his head. "I think they're more than dreams."

Rachel looked at two little bumps under the covers where Danny's knees would be, and she understood. "He has a direct line to heaven." She gently rubbed his knees through the blanket.

Jerry nodded. "That must be where he draws his reservoir of courage from. He is so much more grown up and knowing than his few years. How soon will it be?" he asked.

"His last IV is tomorrow. As well as he is doing, it might even be the next day. I am sorry, Jerry. Maybe I should have told you. I was going to tell you tomorrow night, just in case. I wanted you to have one more happy day together first."

Jerry reached for Rachel's hand. She gave it to him and sat on Danny's empty bed. "Then I guess it better be the best day yet, right? Maybe you should alert the staff to look the other way tomorrow." He winked at her, and his eyes twinkled with mischief, but there was also a great sadness in them. The sadness was greater than she had ever seen, as though he was bravely preparing to forfeit his most priceless possession, or maybe even his own life. It troubled her, because she could sense the depth of his sadness, but did not understand it. Losing Danny was tearing her apart too, but it was something far more significant to Jerry. Jerry continued speaking, unaware that she had glimpsed into the darkest and saddest corners of his heart.

"Since he already knows, let's give him a huge going away party tomorrow night and invite everyone, the off-duty staff as well. Maybe we could even invite his foster family so he can meet them. That might make it easier for him when he has to go. We should buy him a huge cake with candles, ice cream, and presents—" Jerry suddenly couldn't speak. He placed his hands across his face, trying to bury the emptiness swelling inside him that he couldn't hold back. But it was useless. Rachel slid her feet to the floor and reached across the child to comfort Jerry. Danny was sleeping peacefully now, unaware of the embrace of two people, each filled with deep compassion and concern for a beloved little boy.

Chapter Fifteen

Roxanne packed her bags and tidied the house, putting everything in place. She would leave tomorrow evening for Anchorage. She hung the last of Eric's clothes neatly in his closet, running her fingers across his shirtsleeve before closing the closet door. Sighing, she sat on the bed, staring at Eric's pillow, which was vacant of its owner. She pulled back the covers and crawled between the sheets, remembering how satisfied and comfortable she had been lying in his arms.

She looked at a picture of him on the dresser. He was very handsome, posing with his crewmates aboard their fishing boat. She wrapped her arms around his pillow and breathed in the lingering scent of his musk aftershave, still fresh on the fabric. Then she set the pillow back in its place, rolled over, and nestled against her own pillow. She pulled open the top drawer of her nightstand and took out the handkerchief Jerry had given her to wipe off his glasses on the plane ride to Alaska. She could still smell the mild pine and Sweet William scent she remembered so well. She turned off the lamp and closed her hand around the handkerchief. It was a long time before she slept.

❊

The late September morning was brisk in Fairbanks as Rachel took the list Jerry had written for Danny's big farewell party and climbed into the taxi. It was her day off, perfect to go shopping for the special gift Jerry had requested. Children's Services had agreed to contact the foster family and notify them of the party. Hospital personnel responded immediately to the idea, and the maintenance department blocked off a portion of the sidewalk below Jerry's window with wet floor signs and a yellow "caution" ribbon. Several off-duty nurses volunteered to decorate for the event.

With all the errands delegated out, Jerry was free to show Danny the time of his life. Well, as much as was possible in a hospital room with his leg tied to a bed, of course, but Jerry wasn't the least bit hindered. He grinned as he reviewed his plans. The fun began right after breakfast. First on the agenda was more water balloons, a whole bath basin full of them. Such enjoyment they both took from the bombardment three stories below. Danny's magnificent sound effects and excitement were as delightful to Jerry as if he could rise from his bed and walk to the window himself.

Then Danny and Jerry made a special poster on a poster board that Rachel had delivered to them on her way to fulfill her assigned duties. Drawing stick figures with markers, they sketched a collage of their adventures together. Danny's depiction of the water balloons doubled Jerry over in laughter. Danny liked the drawing of him and his Indian headdress best. Of course, the poster was to go home with Danny. To change pace, they had several skirmishes between the chess pieces and the checkers. Then on Jerry's instructions, Danny filled Jerry's water pitcher again and again until the bath basin was full of water. Jerry taught Danny how to fold note pad paper into tiny boats to float in the basin. Soon the project turned into boat races. Each person blew on his boat to push it to the finish line on the other side of the bath basin. Jerry slyly directed most of his wind toward Danny's boat so it always won. Then he ranted and complained because his boats just weren't fast enough. Danny took pity on Jerry one time and blew on his boat. The result was a cross wind crash, and Jerry's boat sank to the bottom of the basin.

After lunch, Danny seemed rather tired, so Jerry told him stories until he fell asleep, nestled beside his new big brother and friend. Jerry held him, desperate to treasure every last moment with this precious little boy who had made him smile, laugh, and love again. He finally fell asleep too, dreaming that he and Danny were sitting beside Jan Young's lovely woodland pond fishing together, and that Danny was his own little son.

Jerry woke up with his heart aching, wondering where Danny's life might take him and hoping that kind Providence would someday allow their paths to cross again. Jerry looked at the fresh puncture wound on his finger. It was near the scar that David's pocketknife had left many years ago when they vowed to be brothers forever. At nine years old that vow had been the cement of a life-long friendship which had blessed both David and Jerry thousands of times over.

Jerry recalled the tears welling up in Danny's eyes, the serious and reverent attitude, and the earnest commitment to the "bond" this boy had demonstrated. The childlike ceremony he and Danny had performed yesterday was every bit as heartfelt to Danny as it had been to him and David when they were nine years old. Jerry knew Danny would not forget. Someday, sometime, somewhere, Danny would find him again. In the meantime, Jerry's spoken wish to Rachel, that he wished he could give something of lasting worth to Danny, had been granted. Danny would always stand tall and true to his word, and he would never forget his big brother. Jerry was certain that he would see Danny again.

Danny began to stir, so Jerry turned his thoughts to his goal to make Danny happy, and he tucked his ache safely away inside his heart. A few moments later, a sleepy-eyed boy stepped into the bathroom. He slid the roll of toilet paper from the dispenser and collected two more rolls from the bathroom. More awake now and under Jerry's instruction, he laid a pillow on a bath blanket in his wheelchair and pushed it into the hall.

"I'm takin' my puppy for a walk," he proudly announced to some unseen nurse in the hall.

Jerry listened, grinning with anticipation, and tried to picture in his mind the little bald-headed boy pushing his strange looking puppy down the hall in a wheelchair with his oversized hospital gown hanging almost to his ankles.

"Okay," the unseen nurse responded. "Just don't wander too far."

Jerry chuckled. Danny knew exactly where he was going. He had learned the floor quite well during his nightly wanderings. The clean supply room was just down the hall.

"What have you got there?" another unseen nurse asked.

Jerry strained to hear.

"See that pillow. He's my puppy, an' I'm takin' him for a walk. I won't go far."

The unseen nurse laughed.

Everything was quiet for a time, and then Jerry could hear the slight squeak of the wheelchair and the patter of little feet drawing near. The door was pushed open and the wheelchair bumped into the door and bed as Danny entered the room wearing a most mischievous smile.

"How did you do?" Jerry asked, straining to see into the wheelchair.

"I got a whole bunch of ammunition," Danny said as he removed the pillow puppy and uncovered a large stash of toilet paper hidden in the seat of the chair.

"Good job! Let's count 'em! Then you take yours in the wheelchair to the other side of your bed so you can use your bed as a shield." Jerry soon had a dozen rolls of toilet paper tucked beside him in bed, and Danny had another dozen in the seat of his wheelchair. He ducked behind his bed with a roll poised for attack.

"You say go, Jerry," he called.

"Okay, are you ready?"

"Uh huh,"

"Set, go!"

Danny jumped up and pelted a toilet paper roll at Jerry. It bounced off the traction and sailed into the wall. Jerry retaliated, gently tossing a roll that glanced off Danny's chest. Danny grabbed another roll and threw it as hard as he could at Jerry. Jerry returned fire and a roll caught Danny in the side of the head. He laughed and heaved another roll, hitting Jerry on his suspended foot. Jerry winced and bit his lip.

"I'm sorry, did I hurt your leg?" Danny asked with concern. Jerry answered him with a roll to the stomach. Danny bent over laughing, then leaped up and knocked Jerry's glasses off with another direct hit. Jerry sent two rolls flying toward Danny and then quickly put on his glasses when Danny ducked behind the bed. Rolls of toilet paper flew faster, and, from Danny's arms, harder as the battle escalated into full warfare. When Jerry's ammo supply was depleted, they took a time out while Danny restocked his bed, and then the battle ensued again, more ferocious than before. Frequently Jerry caught the rolls Danny threw, returning fire as he snatched them from the air, helping him save his stock of ammunition.

After a few contacts with a target or object, the toilet paper rolls began to get loose. Soon the flying rolls trailed long strands of paper behind them, and without planning it, Jerry's bed, Danny's bed, the bed curtains, the chair, and the bed tables were soon fully toilet papered. Jerry was wearing strands of paper in his curly hair and on his gown, and some was wrapped around Danny and draped around his shoulders from him whirling and ducking.

The war continued with full assault and vengeful fervor until Rachel walked in just as Danny ducked and a toilet paper roll sailed across the room and bounced off the wall. Jerry and Danny stopped as though frozen in action, staring at her with trepidation on their guilty faces. She was too stunned at the sight to react for a moment. Then she collapsed into the chair with peals of laughter as a strand of toilet paper from the curtain floated down and landed across her face. The frozen stance of Jerry and Danny melted with her laughter. Danny climbed onto Jerry's bed, overcome with delighted giggles, and Jerry laughed with rapture as though laughing had the power to transcend him beyond the pain of separation that was soon to follow.

"Well, I guess I should call the girls and tell them not to bother." Rachel said when she could finally speak. "It appears to me the decorating has already been done." She unwound another strip of toilet paper from her long, black hair. "Where did you get all the toilet paper? I know you did not ask for it. No one would have been foolish enough to give it to you."

"I took my puppy for a ride in the wheelchair to the room with lots of toilet paper," Danny chortled. "He helped me hide it under a blanket he was sitting on."

"Puppy! What puppy?" she asked. Jerry held up a pillow and pointed to it. "That was the puppy?"

"The nurses just thought he was being really cute," Jerry said with a chuckle. "He walked right past them with their full approval, loaded up, and—" Jerry held his hands out, showing off the results, as Danny nodded with a proud grin.

"Ohoya! What will you think up next?"

"See, Jerry was right. Two brains working together can have lots more fun, just like him and David. Suddenly, Danny looked worried. "We aren't in trouble, are we?"

"No, Danny, you are not in trouble. I will have to think about Jerry, though. He should be." She hugged Danny and smiled, shaking her head at Jerry. "I am quite surprised that you did not tie the ends of the toilet paper rolls to your beds and send some of them out the window." She left the room to get several garbage bags, and Jerry and Danny grinned at each other. Quickly tying several rolls to Jerry's bed rails, Jerry rolled them across the floor to Danny, who put Rachel's suggestion into action. Rachel alerted the surgical wing staff that pilfering and a full-fledged war had taken place under their noses. As the nursing staff peeked in a few at a time to see the aftermath, Rachel walked to the pediatric wing and informed them as well. Of course, the war was soon the top news story buzzing through the hospital, and Jerry and Danny's war zone was visited often over the next hour. Jerry sat in bed with a sheepish grin as Danny proudly explained the strategic details of

the victory he was sure he had won.

The strewn toilet paper was eventually collected and stuffed in garbage bags beside the toilet and behind Jerry's bedpan in the bedside stand. The only disciplinary action taken against them was that no more toilet paper would be allowed in the room until the bags were empty. Some toilet paper still hanging from the curtains accented the streamers of colored crepe paper and balloons for the party, which was to commence shortly after supper. Danny's curiosity was aroused as the decorations went up, and he was becoming suspicious.

Jerry and Rachel asked if they could be the ones to break the news of the forthcoming discharge and foster home to Danny. Rachel held him in her lap and cradled him in her arms. "Danny, you and I and Jerry have become very close during your illness, and we are so happy that you are getting well. The doctors are waiting for one more blood test to come back from the lab. They expect it will tell them that you are well and ready to leave the hospital. A nice family has asked for you to come and live with them. They will put you back in school where you can make lots of friends and be a healthy, happy boy again."

Danny sat quietly listening as his little black eyes, all too knowing, gazed longingly at Jerry. He blinked back tears, trying very hard to be brave. Then he looked up at Rachel. "How soon will I have to go away?" he asked.

"You will probably be able to go to your new home tomorrow, so now we can tell you why we decorated your room. Jerry wanted to have a big farewell party for you tonight. We invited everyone who has taken care of you. We invited your new family too, so you can meet them. Jerry and I have been planning all day long to surprise you. He wanted to have a really fun day with you first, though, before we told you about the party."

"Okay, I've never had a big party before." Danny suddenly threw his small arms around Rachel and started to cry. "Do I really have to go? Can't I stay a little bit longer? I'll let them put the needle back in my arm and give me some more throw up medicine if they'll let me stay."

Rachel hugged Danny tightly as her reserve crumbled. She wept quietly, hiding her face and trying to control the convulsive sobs building up inside her.

Jerry, who had been fighting to keep a reassuring smile on his face, tried to stop some tears forcing their way past his eyelashes. It was hard to calm his voice, but he could see that Rachel needed help. "Bring Danny here, Rachel," he said. "I made him a promise I have to keep."

She arose and gratefully placed the skinny little boy clinging to her into Jerry's arms. The instant he felt Jerry's hands reaching for him, he released Rachel, and she fled from the room as Jerry wrapped his strong arms around the child.

"Okay, Danny, I promised if you ever needed a crying partner I'd cry with you. This seems like a good time." Danny threw his arms around Jerry's neck and buried his little face in his chest. Jerry held the child and let his own tears roll down his cheeks and drip onto Danny's gown. Rocking his upper body back and forth, he cooed and consoled as he puppy-petted the little bald head that was snuggled against him.

Danny's crying finally ceased, but he still held fast to Jerry's neck and didn't move. Jerry continued to rock the child as he spoke, forcing a lighthearted tone into his voice.

"Now, why would you want to do a crazy thing like getting that needle jabbed back into you and doing all that throwing up stuff again? No one's fun enough to do that for, not even me! Why, you threw up every color in the rainbow to get rid of that stupid needle in your arm. You were a brave warrior, the very best! You don't want to suffer through that again. You're a kid! Kids are supposed to run, and play, and throw water balloons at girls. Kids are supposed to be free and have fun. Do you know how lucky you are? You got set free from your needles and tubes. Look at me? I'm still tied to this dumb bed, and I can't even take my puppy for a walk in the hall and sneak past all the nurses to steal toilet paper. I can't even see the ground from here. All I can see is some buildings and the sky. But you can play on the ground, and you can pick up all the balloon pieces we exploded down there and bring them

to me so I can remember you and all our fun. We can't keep the toilet paper, though, as a keepsake. I'm gonna need that for other purposes. We'll just have to remember our toilet paper war in our heads, right?"

"Right," came a muffled reply. Danny still clung to Jerry, not moving.

"Danny, you and me worked hard to get you well. I want you to be well. Don't you want me to get better and get out of this traction mess so I can go to my home someday?"

"Yes, but I wish I could go with you," the muffled voice replied.

"Yeah, I know. That's the hard part, but remember our bond. We're brothers now. You just go out there and have the best time of your life for me too. Part of me is stuck here, but remember part of me gets to go with you. We need to dump this place and discover the world and all the fun it has to offer. Will you go to your new home and see how much fun you can think up in your little brain for us to do together? Remember, you said you know you're not alone."

"Okay," Danny said, still not moving, but his grip around Jerry's neck was less desperate.

Pulling his sheet up with one hand, Jerry dried off his face and then patted Danny's back. "What's the most fun thing we did today?"

"The toilet paper fight," Danny answered, releasing Jerry's neck but still snuggling close.

"I can't believe you knocked my glasses off!"

Danny giggled and propped his head up on his hands, his little elbows digging into Jerry's chest. Jerry ignored the discomfort and dried a little tear-stained face with the same wet spot on his sheet. "You look funny without your glasses."

"Yeah, well that was a low blow, you little punk. The only thing I could try to knock off you was your shiny round head, but you kept ducking."

Danny sat up beside Jerry and grinned.

"Didn't Rachel look funny when that toilet paper fell across her face? She was really laughing hard."

"That was the best part. Hey, are there any rolls of paper left, or did they take them all away from us?"

"There's a small roll in my bag by the toilet."

Jerry lifted Danny down from the bed. "Hurry and get it. We'll attack Rachel when she comes back."

"Cool!" Danny laughed, scurrying off to the bathroom.

Rachel was sitting at the nurses' desk, still fighting the flow of tears. Kelly stood beside her, patting her shoulder. "They are so close. I cannot bear to see them separated. I never dreamed it would be so hard for me, either. I was only trying to be a caring nurse, but Danny wrapped his little heart around me and tied a knot that I cannot sever. Actually, both of them did. How did I allow myself to get so emotionally involved?"

"Because you're a good woman, Rachel. Nursing is a profession, but compassion is a gift, and you're loaded." Kelly smiled. "Maybe the party will make it a little—"

"Did you hear Danny laughing?" Rachel said, springing to her feet and drying her eyes.

Danny was standing on his bed with the bag of toilet paper, and Jerry was poised with the small toilet paper roll in his hand when Rachel entered the room followed by Kelly. Danny emptied the bag of toilet paper on both of their heads as Jerry struck Rachel's bun, knocking the clip out. Her long strands of silken hair fell past her shoulders while the clump of Danny's toilet paper rolled off her head and fell at her feet.

Kelly laughed with delight, pulling the wad of paper from her head and throwing it at Danny, but Rachel was too surprised to move. She just stared at Danny, who was rolling on his bed, laughing and holding his tummy. Then she looked at Jerry in amazement. He rubbed the small wound on his finger and smiled reassuringly. She didn't know Danny's secret, but Jerry did. Danny would be okay.

Danny and Kelly were involved in their own toilet paper war as Rachel moved to Jerry's bedside. She clasped his hand, drawing it to her face. "Jerry, you are wonderful. Thank you!" She kissed

the palm of his hand. "I don't know what you did, or how you did it, but thank you!" She cupped his face in her hand, bent down, and placed a quick kiss on his lips. Then she left the room.

CHAPTER SIXTEEN

The foster family, a kindly Indian couple in their late forties who had already raised their own children, had been selected to care for Danny. They had readily accepted the invitation to the party, eager to meet their foster son. Danny accepted them with respect and openly shared his and Jerry's artwork.

"I will leave most of this stuff on Jerry's walls, 'cause he'll be missing me a lot, and my pictures will help him feel better," Danny told them. "Will I have my own bed?"

"Yes, Danny," Mrs. Birchwood answered. "You have your own bed in your own room, and some nice toys in a toy box too."

Danny wasn't interested in the toys waiting for him. "You'll have to let me keep my poster right by my bed so I can see it, 'cause it's really important. Me and Jerry made it. I have to keep it forever to remember a bond. And you have to let me keep my Rainbow Award 'cause Jerry said I throw up in Technicolor. He gave it to me 'cause I really earned it." He proudly held it up for them to see.

"Of course you can keep them both by your bed, because they're important to you," Mr. Birchwood answered with a broad grin.

"Okay, then I guess I can live with you."

"That will be fine, Danny. We are glad to have you come."

Mrs. Birchwood patted his bald head as she and her husband exchanged amused glances.

Jerry looked on in silence, his eyes carefully scrutinizing Danny's foster parents. People in such situations were always on their best behavior. He didn't want to miss any tell tale signs that they might not be as kind and caring as they seemed—as though he could do anything about it if he didn't like them—but his reasons were justified. He knew the pain and suffering of a child. He had lived it. He remembered how often he cried himself to sleep at night, his weeping heart drawing his only comfort from a picture his mother had hung on his wall before she died. It was a picture of the good shepherd lovingly cradling a little lamb in his arms. *The gift of a little child is supreme. No child should ever be hurt, or . . . lost,* he thought. He looked at Danny and choked on a huge knot in his throat. His own ravaged dreams cried out their empty longings from the depths of his soul. They could only be silenced tonight if he knew that Danny would be in the loving care of someone who cherished that gift.

Jerry felt his eyes boring through these people. It wasn't fair to doubt them. He didn't even know them, but he watched them just the same. As the party progressed, he began to think they might be acceptable, but his judgment remained guarded.

The Birchwoods were not oblivious that they were under harsh surveillance, but they cheerfully interacted with Danny and the group of hospital personnel, aware that Danny and Jerry's relationship was very important to the child. Through the games and fun, Danny became more and more at ease with his foster parents. He even let Mrs. Birchwood hold him on her lap as she presented him with a toy snowmobile that raced across the floor on tiny wheels hidden in the skids.

Jerry finally relaxed and joined in the merriment and games. After all, this was his party for Danny, and it had to be the best!

The outpouring of love for Danny touched the Birchwoods, but they were even more touched by the people expressing what Danny had done for them. One patient, a little old grandma suffering from gallbladder surgery and heart problems, peeked in the door with a gift her daughter had brought for Danny. She had been walking the halls in misery the day Danny took his puppy for a ride in the wheelchair.

"If you close your eyes and pet him you can pretend he's a real puppy, and he'll lick you better. That's what puppies do," Danny had told her. He had lifted her spirits so much that she wanted Danny to have a real puppy. Her gift was a little stuffed mechanical dog that responded to love by barking, panting, wagging his tail, walking, and sitting and cocking his head. The celebration moved into the hall while Danny proudly took his new puppy for a ride in the wheelchair. Jerry was listening from his bed, but watching with his heart.

As the evening grew late, refreshments were served. Then it was time for the last gift. Danny stood beside Mrs. Birchwood with her arm around him as Rachel, smiling the most beautiful smile Jerry had ever seen, wheeled a shiny new red bike into the room. A sign hanging from the handlebars read, "Danny's Bike, Happy Memories with Love, from Jerry and Rachel." Danny's eyes grew wide, and his mouth dropped open. He ran, not to the bike, but to Jerry. He climbed onto the bed and threw his arms around Jerry. "I never had a real bike before. It's just like David's, isn't it?" He leaned back to see Jerry's nod, and then hugged him as tightly as his little arms could squeeze. "Thank you, Jerry." He slid to the floor and ran to Rachel. She got down on her knees to receive his hug as he wrapped his small arms around her neck and long strands of hair, adding a vocal grunt to his tight squeeze so she would know that he meant it. Then he petted the bike like it was a puppy and said, "Thank you, Rachel."

As the guests said goodbye to Danny, the Birchwoods approached Jerry, and each of them shook his hand.

"We have seen the great love you have for Danny this night," Mr. Birchwood said. "You have helped us see into this child's heart. I promise you on my word of honor that we will be good to the boy and give him the most tender care."

"Thank you," Jerry said, but he could say no more. He smiled and nodded.

Later, Rachel held Danny in her lap for a while, gently talking to him as they shared memories and expressions of love. Then she tucked Danny into his bed and kissed him good night. She kissed Jerry on the cheek. "That was the most wonderful party, Jerry. I shall never forget your great kindness. Thank you for letting me share in the planning with you. I wonder if you even know what a remarkable man you are." She ran her fingers gently across his cheek and then left the room.

The night was cool, but her heart was warm as she walked home, yet an empty melancholy only added to the emptiness of the apartment. The order had been given. Danny would be released early the next morning. Jerry's leg was healing, and he might be casted by the first of the week. Then he would be ready to go home. Beyond the emotional ups and downs that are a part of nursing, Rachel felt that Jerry, Danny, and she had been given a unique journey, even a marvelous journey into one another's hearts. The journey had felt so right for the final destination to feel so incomplete. She went to bed, but she felt a need to remove her heart and just put it away for the night so she could rest.

✳

Danny sat up after Rachel left and pulled his carving from the tray of his bedside table. Jerry had seen the crude carving gradually taking on some distinct shapes, and he had watched with curiosity. However, his respect for Danny and the great love of the child for his mother had held back any questions about the carving.

Danny climbed down from his bed. Using the chair as a stepping stool, he climbed onto Jerry's bed, sitting Indian-style and facing him. "You know what I've been making for my mamma?" he asked.

"No, I figured it was kind of sacred to you, so I didn't ask. It's very nice though."

"Well, it's a robin—right here." He pointed out a shape carved against the backdrop of the driftwood, like a raised carving on a plaque. "My mamma loved to see the robins and the chickadees come in the spring. She always opened the windows in the mornings, even if it was cold, so she could hear them sing. The robin chirps kinda loud, but it's a pretty sound, and the chickadee sings its own name. This Robin is flying, 'cause it's free like my mamma's spirit, but it's taking something with it from the earth that it loves—a wild rose. See the flower in its beak?"

Jerry nodded, feeling a reverent stillness as the little boy shared his treasure that he had worked so long and hard to complete.

Danny continued. "My mamma loved wild roses, so I gave her lots of them. She couldn't take me to heaven with her, 'cause I have to stay here and find out what God wants me to do. So my mamma is taking one of the roses I gave her to heaven. That way part of me can be with her, because the rose is my love."

Jerry looked in awe and amazement at the beauty of the little boy's simple masterpiece. Now, he could see the bird, its wings wide spread and each feather visible. The beak was pointed to the top of the carving, and what Jerry had thought was a series of small bumps was very clearly the wide petals of a flower. Day after day, as Danny carved, all Jerry had seen, and what most men would see, was a crude piece of child's play, even though Jerry had an insight into the love involved in its creation. And now, catching a glimpse into heaven through the beautiful eyes and faith of a child, he was spellbound.

Danny thrust the carving toward Jerry. "I want you to have it 'cause it could be your mamma too. Her spirit is free like my mamma, and you said you gave her lots of flowers, so she can take part of you to heaven with her. Your love was in your flowers."

"Oh, no, Danny! I can't take this! It's beautiful, and you worked so hard to make it for your mamma. I'm extremely honored that you would want to give it to me, but it's too special."

"But that's why I want you to have it, because you are special too, and you said we have a lot in common. I think that means part of you belongs to me and part of me belongs to you, 'specially now that we're brothers. You gave me a shiny red bike, so I'll think of you when I ride it. And I'm giving something to you to remember that we're in common."

Jerry took the precious gift and wrapped his arms tightly around the little boy. "Thank you, Danny! This is the most wonderful and sacred gift anyone has ever given me. I will treasure it always."

"Okay, now I can go away, 'cause I have your love in my bike and you have my love in that," Danny said, pointing to the carving. "And don't worry about my mamma. She doesn't mind. I can make her another one, 'cause I have her love in my pocketknife.

"I feel tired now, so I better go to sleep." His small arms circled Jerry's neck and he squeezed tight. Jerry wrapped his big arms around Danny and hugged him back.

"Thank you for my fun party. I love you, Jerry. I know you will really miss me, but we have a bond. We're brothers."

Danny pulled the covers up and tucked them under Jerry's chin. "I think I'm gonna sleep here tonight, 'cause then I won't have to miss you until tomorrow, okay?" he said as he snuggled beneath the covers.

"Okay," Jerry fought to keep his voice lighthearted and steady. "Goodnight, little brother. I love you too." He kissed Danny's bald head, and while Danny slept, Jerry prayed. "Please, God, will I ever have a son?"

CHAPTER SEVENTEEN

Danny woke up excited and eager to get dressed. "I get to wear my caribou hides my mamma made me," he proudly announced. "Rachel said I could when I went home."

"Caribou hides?" Jerry asked.

"They are right here, Danny, just like I promised." Rachel removed a beautifully beaded tunic from the plastic bag she had hung it in when she admitted Danny to the hospital weeks ago for his final stage of chemotherapy. It had been no easy task for her to convince him that the handmade clothes should be exchanged for a hospital gown. They had remained safely packed with his other sparse belongings that had come with him to the hospital.

Danny slipped into the soft breeches and beaded moccasins and tied the rawhide strings. Then he proudly donned the tunic, caressing the beaded flowers and designs with his fingers. "Mamma learned how to make these from her grandma. She had to scrape the skin until all the hard stuff was gone, then she cut the pieces and sewed them. She made it too big for me, 'cause she said I would be growing bigger while she made it. She sewed all the beads on, and it took her a whole year, and she let me help her cut this stuff. He ran his hand through the fringe hanging at the bottom of the tunic. She made it because she said I'm a real Indian, and I should look like one. Do I?"

Rachel smiled and hugged him. "Yes, Danny, you look like a very real, very handsome Indian"

Jerry gazed at the little boy in front of him, suddenly looking so grown up and strong. Except for the shiny brown head, Danny looked like any other healthy child. Yet, he was so Danny . . . and yet . . . so different, somehow.

"Wow!" he said. Now you look like a real warrior . . . well, almost. Rachel get me a support sock and some drinking straws. Our little chief needs a headdress to make him authentic. We'd better skip the war paint, though. The Birchwoods wouldn't want chocolate pudding smeared in their car, would they?"

Danny shook his head as Jerry followed the twisting head with the sock. Soon headband and straw feathers were in place. Rachel had brought a camera, and many pictures were taken, of Jerry and Danny with the poster and award, Jerry and Danny and his carving, Danny and Rachel, all three of them together posing with Danny's bike with Kelly behind the camera, and then a picture of Kelly and Danny. Pictures were also taken of Danny with Connie and the pediatric nurses and pictures of Danny with Kelly and the surgical nurses who had adopted him to their wing. Rachel took a picture of the grinning grandma and Danny and the little stuffed mechanical puppy she had given him. Then there were lots of pictures of Danny modeling his full Indian attire.

How handsome he is, Jerry thought. *I couldn't be prouder of Danny if he were my own son.* No matter—Danny was his little brother, and nothing could change that or remove the pictures Jerry was taking in his heart, where Danny would stay for the rest of Jerry's life.

The Birchwoods arrived, and Danny greeted them. "I'm sorry, but you'll have to wait, 'cause we've been really busy, and I've gotta do something for Jerry before we go." He whispered in Rachel's ear. She nodded, and she and Danny left the room. They were gone for some time as Jerry answered questions for the Birchwoods. His answers were short and to the point since he didn't really feel much like talking, and he wished Danny and Rachel would hurry. The Birchwoods seemed to understand.

Then Danny bounded into the room with Rachel behind him, crawled onto Jerry's bed, and handed Jerry a rubber gloves box filled with rubber scraps and twigs from the sidewalk below the window.

"You remembered to pick them up for me!" Jerry grinned. "How did we do?"

"We did good! These were all over the sidewalk and hanging in the bushes too, where they exploded! I had to walk into the bushes to get some of the biggest ones."

"Felt great to touch the ground, didn't it? Look, you even brought me some." Jerry peeled a small glob of damp earth and wood chips from Danny's moccasins and kissed it. "Aw, good old dirt," he said.

"What did ya' do that for?" Danny asked with a puzzled twist of his mouth that made Jerry laugh.

"Because I miss it, that's why." Then Jerry motioned for everyone to leave the room. He held Danny's face in his hands and looked deeply into his black eyes. "We've had a great time, Danny, and we'll always have our memories. Now, you go play in the dirt, and get muddy, and roll down hillsides, and run, and jump, and ride your bike, and be a kid! And remember, you're doing it all for me too." He pulled Danny into his arms and held him tightly as Danny hugged him back. Jerry blinked and bit his lip hard. He kissed Danny's bald head and then cradled it against his chest. "Now, go, and I'll go with you. He pressed the wound on his finger to the Band-Aid inside Danny's elbow and winked, and then he set Danny on the floor and gave him a gentle push toward the door.

Danny nodded, squeezing the Band-Aid to his arm as he hung his little head and slowly walked away. At the door, he stopped and looked at Jerry as tears trickled down his cheeks, but he had a big smile on his face. "We'll always be together 'cause we have a bond. We're brothers!" he said, waving. Then he disappeared as the door slowly closed behind him.

"I love you, Danny," Jerry whispered as he lay down and pulled the covers over his head.

Danny pulled the door shut and stood facing it for a moment; then he bravely dried his eyes on his tunic and turned to face his new life. Rachel squeezed his shoulder and left her hand there as she, Connie, and the Birchwoods wheeled the hospital's own little celebrity past waving nurses and doctors to the waiting car. Outside the open car door, Rachel knelt on the pavement and held Danny in her arms.

"Where's my bike?" he asked anxiously looking around.

"I put it in the trunk, Danny," said Mr. Birchwood. We left your poster and your award on the seat so you'll have them with you on the drive home." The Birchwoods settled in the car, leaving Rachel and Danny to say goodbye in private. Connie stood back a ways, dabbing at her eyes and waiting for Rachel.

"With his mind settled about the safety of his treasures, Danny wrapped his little arms around Rachel. He held on tightly as his brave performance began to crumble, and tears streamed down his little face. "I don't wanna go. Can't I stay with you?"

Rachel tried to be brave for both of them. "Danny, what would Jerry tell you?"

"He said for me to go be a kid."

"Don't you want to do that?"

"I guess Jerry wants me to, and I know he loves me, so maybe that's what God wants me to do too. I've been tryin' to figure that out."

"Then you won't be alone, will you?" she said, tickling his knobby little knees. "When you get sad, remember to use these, like you taught me when Jerry was sad."

Danny nodded his understanding. "Okay, Rachel." He stood taller and squared his shoulders under the tunic as he dried his eyes with his arm. "Tell Jerry I was brave like a warrior. He'll be proud of me."

"I'm proud of you too, Danny, I love you."

"He gave her one last ferocious hug, then climbed into the back seat. As she fastened his seat belt, he said, "I love you too, and tell Jerry I love him. I forgot to." He twisted around in his seatbelt and raised up onto his knees, waving at Rachel until she was out of sight, and then he turned around and sat down, placing his poster on his lap and hugging his rainbow award to his heart.

Rachel thanked Connie, giving her a hug, and then sent her back to the floor alone with Danny's empty wheel chair. Feeling the need to walk, she did so aimlessly. This was her second day off, and at that moment, the last place she wanted to be was in the hospital. Removing a large clip from her bun she gently shook her head, letting her hair fall free. She walked for a long time. She worried about Jerry, but she felt he would want to face his grief in private as she did, and she worried about Danny. How lonely was his journey in the back seat? Under the circumstances, twenty minutes could seem forever to a child in pain. How far away was his new home? Was he smiling and playing with his new toys, or was he just sitting on a bed in a strange room, clinging to his precious keepsakes. She couldn't think about it anymore, so she switched her thoughts to Jerry.

With Danny gone now, Jerry's confinement would be long and lonely. It was good that his leg was nearly healed. His emotional state had been so much better, but Rachel didn't want him to have a chance to close himself in again.

Suddenly, she wanted to be with him. She should have gone back up with Connie and at least checked on him. She should have been there to comfort his sorrow. If she had felt this blue and empty, how must he have felt? She turned quickly and walked toward the hospital. She was far away and quickened her pace. Somewhere in the back of her mind she could imagine the Do Not Disturb sign back on his door, the blinds drawn, and the room dark. When she finally reached the hospital, she ran up the three flights of stairs and hurried to Jerry's room.

His door was open and she could hear him visiting with Kelly. Rachel caught her breath from her brisk walk and calmed herself. Feeling greatly relieved, she entered the room and quietly sat in the chair. Kelly filled his water pitcher and then smiled at Rachel as she left the room.

"Are you okay, Rachel?" Jerry asked. "You just disappeared. You've been gone quite a while."

Rachel nodded. "I am sorry, Jerry. I went for a long walk. I should have come back and told you first. I am fine though. How—?"

"Well, I'm glad you are," interrupted Jerry, "because I'm not! This room is about as empty and quiet as a tomb. They moved his bed out, and I almost blubbered in front of the housekeeping personnel. Every time I feel like I'm going to bust out bawling, I look at his funny little drawings, or think of some cute thing he did, and I just have to laugh instead. Man, if I'd known it was going to hurt this bad I'd probably have gotten out of bed and run the other way, broken leg and all that first day you brought him in. I guess that's why the pain is at the end, not the beginning." Jerry chuckled and picked up Danny's wood carving. "He sure knew how to brighten up a lousy world."

Rachel smiled, filling her mind with memories of the little boy. "Yes, Sanh (summer) was in his smile. I could not, but he warmed nedraya' (your heart)." She spoke more to herself than Jerry.

He didn't understand her, but he loved to hear her speak her native tongue. It was like gently falling waters as it came from her lips. The interpretation would detract from its beauty. She had spoken of Danny's smile, and it comforted him to think of it.

"He gave me his precious carving," Jerry said. "I never dreamed such a magnificent piece of work was being created under my very nose. I'm supposed to be an art dealer, to see into the passion of an artist's work, but I totally missed it this time. I felt his love and commitment to his carving, but his transcendent journey into his little masterpiece totally escaped me. It was my loss, but through his love I inherited the finished treasure. Come, let me show you."

Rachel arose and stood at Jerry's bedside. She put her arm around his shoulder.

Jerry slipped his arm around her small waist and drew her closer.

As he shared Danny's story, heavenly rays seemed to emanate from the drab and weathered piece of driftwood. The child's pure love filled her being, and so did the sweet remembrance of this man who had so nobly cared for him day and night. Emotion swelled in Rachel as she turned in Jerry's arm to face him, but there were no words she could find. Her eyes were tender, seeking, longing. Could he ever find it in his heart to love her as dearly as she had grown to love him, or was his heart still buried in the depths of the sadness that she had glimpsed in his eyes? He would soon go away as Danny had, and she might never know.

"What?" Jerry asked, his questioning eyes searching hers.

Suddenly, she bent and threw her arms around his neck. The fragrance of honeysuckle drifted from her cascade of black hair as it fell against his cheek. Surprised, Jerry wrapped his arms around her, softly running his fingers through her hair. Her closeness stirred emotions and feelings he had buried deeply in his heart. "Rachel, are you all right? What is it, Honey? I know you miss him terribly. What can I do to—?"

"It is only partly Danny," she whispered, holding onto Jerry as though he might vanish if she let go. She had felt such an empty sadness. Now, it was wonderful and warm in his strong arms as he held her. How gentle his hands felt stroking her hair. If only he could hold her like this forever.

"Tell me, Rachel, how can I help you?" He pulled her closer, smoothing the silky strands on her head as he kissed through her hair. "Come, my little friend," he said pressing his face against her cheek.

She didn't want to speak. She just wanted to feel him near, and she wanted him to feel her near. Oh, how she longed to melt his sorrows and grief, to heal his wounds with the radiant heat she felt flowing through her veins, to mend his broken heart with all the love and tender care she felt for him. "Just hold me," she whispered. "Just hold me."

He responded by tightening his arms around her. He kissed her head more fervently and continued to stroke her hair with a gentle caress.

She finally loosened her arms around his neck enough to turn her face toward him. He kissed her forehead and smoothed strands of ebony hair away from her face.

"Are you okay, Honey? What's troubling you?"

She shook her head, struggling with her feelings. There were still no words.

"Please, tell me," he whispered. His deep blue eyes were filled with compassion and concern, and his handsome face was so kind. Rachel ran her fingers across his shaven chin and up his cheek, feeling ever so slightly the shadow of his beard. Her hazel-green eyes were soft with sadness and yearning. Then they fluttered and closed behind thick lashes, holding back the tears that wanted to break free. As her closeness overcame him, Jerry yielded, reaching for her kiss, this time with fervor.

Jerry's heart beat rapidly, straining against the walls he had so carefully built up around it. He didn't want to hurt again-not ever. The darkness of his mind raged in defiance against vulnerability. The previous kisses shared with her were simple, sweet, and warm, filled with care and comfort, but this kiss, all consuming and disarming, was reaching into his deepest reserve and drawing him to commitment. An air of foreboding surrounded the kiss, yet he could not draw away. He embraced the beautiful woman, so warm and soft in his arms, drawing her to him with all the empty longings of a broken heart and gave himself to her, at least for this precious moment in time.

CHAPTER EIGHTEEN

As their lips parted, Jerry was breathless. What had just happened between them? He felt a weak fluttering in his heart as a tremor passed through him. He was not prepared for what had just transpired, nor was he inclined to soon forget. He released Rachel, but held her hand. "Rachel, you are a beautiful and amazing woman with remarkable compassion. Thank you for so many sweet gifts of kindness. Heaven blesses me with your presence. Go, pull the chair over here, and tell me what's in your heart."

Rachel withdrew her fingers and brushed the back of them across his cheek. She sighed, and went to get the chair, leaving her soft touch tingling on Jerry's face. Pulling the chair against his bed, Rachel sat down, and Jerry reached again for her hand, waiting expectantly. Finally, she was able to speak.

"It…it is all very good, really. Danny is well and can be a happy, healthy child again. You will soon be free from your traction and able to return to your family and friends." Rachel was uncomfortable with being put on the spot as she searched for words. "It is just that for a brief time we had our own little hospital family here, and—" she paused and swallowed hard. "It…it was all very special. I am happy for Danny, but I miss him so much already, and—"

Jerry grinned and wrapped his other hand around her hand that he was holding. "You don't want me to go home, do you?"

"I want you to be well and whole, but . . . I will miss you." She quickly glanced downward. The fire of Jerry's kiss was still burning on her lips, a promise that maybe he could love her as she loved him, but there was so little time. Then he would be gone, with a thousand miles between them, and she would be alone again.

Suddenly, Jerry remembered David's words. "Rachel needs a friend, Jerry. She's found one in you. She wants to be here." She had changed her whole life to be there for him, and she had been ever true to her commitment, expecting and asking nothing from him in return. How could he think to leave this precious friend behind?

"Rachel, now that Danny has gone home, do you have any ties to hold you here in Fairbanks?" he asked, looking deeply into her eyes as though really seeing into her heart for the first time.

"No, just the wonderful people I work with."

"Come home with me. David and Kimberly have been trying to find a full-time nurse for David's mother, Jan. She's confined to a wheelchair. They had one, but she quit because her father had a stroke. They'll be thrilled to hire you. They already love you, and you'll fall in love with Jan. She is the most dear and beloved woman. She practically raised me after my mother died when I was ten. I adore her. There is no one I would rather see caring for her than you. No other nurse I've ever known has angel wings and wears a halo for a nurse's cap." Jerry squeezed Rachel's hand so tightly it hurt. "Come home with me to Indian Valley."

Rachel was too stunned to speak. Jerry's eyes were pleading, and there was a tenseness in his grip that hinted of more than he was saying. Although he wasn't asking her to come for himself, he had given her reason to hope. There was no real chance that Jerry could grow to love her if she stayed here. Her father was busy with the mine and had Jack and Molly to watch over him, now, and Eric was married. She had no one to stay for. She lowered her head and closed her eyes, letting the profound reality sink in.

To go would leave her beloved Alaska behind, though, and all that she had ever known. She cherished her native homeland and its people, its wonders and beauties, its towering mountains and rugged valleys, and its crystal springs. She loved the harsh terrain, the rich green moss, the rivers and thick forests of black spruce, and the permafrost on the tundra, covered with millions of brilliant wild flowers. She loved the moose and caribou, the bears and Dall Sheep, the willow ptarmigans, or grouse, and she especially loved the lonely cry of the wolf in the frozen night air while the yoyekoyh (northern lights) danced its colors across the Alaskan sky. Alaska had made her who she was. Tears welled up in her eyes as she thought of all she would leave behind. But she had given her heart to this kind and humble man, one who would give her little brown-skinned babies a home filled with love, laughter, and joy. This was still only a dream, but it was a dream she had to believe in. She would go, but she would forever leave a part of her heart behind, for she would always be an Athabaskan and an Alaskan. Rachel raised her head and looked into Jerry's deep, blue eyes, her own now brimming over with tears that were beginning to slip over her lashes and trickle down her cheeks.

"Basi', Jerry. Sedraya' dadhk'wn'. Ehe' nezrunh. Si . . . tr'etodel. We will go.(Thank you, Jerry. My heart, it is burning. Yes, it is good. I . . . we will go, we will go.)"

Jerry threw his arms around her, nearly pulling her onto his bed with his hug, and then he gave her a quick kiss on her lips and released her as he cleared his throat and pushed his glasses up on his nose. "That's wonderful!" he said, squeezing her hand a little too tightly. "I'll call David right now and share the good news."

Rachel laughed and dried her eyes, as hope grew brighter in her heart. "I will go and turn in my notice and tell Connie and my friends on pediatrics."

The rest of the day was busy with phone calls and arrangements. On Jerry's insistence, the doctor gave him a date when he felt Jerry could safely be put in a cast. It would be another week, and then he could be discharged almost immediately, especially since he would be in the company of a nurse for his journey home.

Night came too quickly, and it was time for Rachel to leave. She stood beside Jerry's bed, running her fingers through his hair as she said goodnight. However, she intentionally avoided

bending to give him the quick goodnight kiss he had become accustomed to. As she stepped away from the bed, he caught her hand and pulled her again to his bedside. Cradling the back of her head in his hand, he drew her face near as her silken hair bathed his face and chest with its soft touch and fragrance. Then he placed his other arm around her waist and pulled her to him as he gently caressed her mouth with his lips in a sweet kiss that felt very much like a promise.

After Rachel went home, a lonely feeling of melancholy hovered in the room as Jerry looked through the dim light to the vacant place where Danny's bed had been. How he missed that little guy! Jerry picked up the carving, tracing with his finger the carefully placed grooves of the pocketknife blade. He recalled Danny's intense expression, his tongue, barely visible, following the line of his lips as though it were directing the movement of his knife blade. Jerry tucked the carving beside him in the bed, and Danny was with him in spirit.

With the warm memory of his little brother in his heart, Jerry turned his thoughts to Rachel, to her enchanting smile and the luster of her long, black hair as she wheeled Danny's red bike into the room. Until that moment, he had never noticed how beautiful she was. Then today, Jerry remembered how she had thrown her arms around him, pressing herself so close, and held him almost desperately, as though he might vanish from her grasp. Jerry closed his eyes, remembering her face so close to his as he smoothed her hair, her hazel-green eyes beseeching, her long black eyelashes closing, and her lips against his. Jerry felt it again, burning through him and out the ends of his toes. And again tonight his kiss was given openly and freely of his own desire.

What of Rachel? Her touch, her care, could stir things in him that he had tried so hard to lock away. Why did she move him so deeply? Jerry couldn't go there now, his heart wouldn't let him, not yet. But he was so glad she was coming with him—coming home with him. The emptiness without her and Danny would have been unbearable.

"We will go," she had said, as tears representing her own

sacrifice—the things and people she loved and again willingly left behind at his request—welled up in her eyes. Why had she made of him such a special friend?

Suddenly, Jerry sensed he was not alone. He started and opened his eyes. Staring into the dim light, he beheld a ghost—but it wasn't a ghost. The warmth and comfort that had embraced him only seconds before shrank into the shadows of the twilight, and coldness filled Jerry's heart.

Standing at the foot of his bed, with tears streaming down her face, was the last person in the world Jerry wanted to see. Her hand was reaching for him, and a look of anguish scarred the sweet, pixie face of Roxanne.

Jerry was too shocked to speak, nor could he find words in the darkest corner of his heart where he had recoiled. He viewed her through glassy eyes, feeling nothing but coldness. But his gaze was strong and steady as she left the foot of his bed and moved to his side. She reached for his hand, but he jerked it away.

"Oh, Jerry, I did this to you. What a horrible, horrible thing I have done!" she said, looking at the traction as if it were a monster.

The traction was no monster, but there was a monster present. It was the worst kind of monster—the one who preys on trusting souls willing to give their deepest love. It binds them in ropes disguised as garlands of wild flowers, and then casts them, and all that is precious to them, into the murky and icy depths of a black, slimy bog.

"Forgive me, Jerry. Please forgive me for hurting you so!" Roxanne was kneeling beside his bed with her face against his mattress, and her sobs were jostling his bed.

He wanted to shove her away, but he didn't want to touch her either, so he just held himself rigid, clenching his fists and gritting his teeth. There was no forgiveness in the blackness of Jerry's heart where he had withdrawn even more when he pulled his hand away. He had never hated and had never dreamed that he could hate anyone, not even his own father the night he killed himself. But, now, Jerry knew hate, and he drew still deeper into the darkness.

"I still love you, Jerry! I have no excuses for what I did. I ruined my life and Eric's—" She rose and clenched her hands into fists against her breast. "And see what I've done to you! I can't bear the guilt anymore, I just can't bear it!" She desperately threw herself at Jerry, her arms around his neck as her tears seeped through the gown onto his chest. "Say something, Jerry. Please! Say anything!"

He had lunged backward against the mattress and tried to twist away when she cast herself upon him, jerking the sandbag as a sudden pain shot through his thigh. He bit his lip against the pain and hit the nurse call button with force. Then, gripping her wrists, he pried them from his neck and pushed her away.

She crumpled in a heap on the floor and buried her face across her arms, weeping uncontrollably.

A new nurse, unfamiliar with the patients, entered the room and stood aghast trying to access the situation. "Get her out of here!" Jerry ordered.

"Yes, Sir." The nurse rushed to Roxanne and pulled her to her shaky feet, quickly ushering her toward the door. Roxanne looked back at Jerry, and the agony of remorse written on her face jolted him like a gunshot in his mind. "I'm sorry, Jerry. I didn't mean to hurt you. I'm sorry. I'm so sorry!" She buried her face in her hands and wept. Jerry was in a state of shock as he saw his father in her face and actions, and the same exact words echoing from the deepest, most haunting memories of his life. He had never seen his father alive again.

In Roxanne's state of mind, Jerry would not be responsible for helping her to choose the same escape from shame and defeat that his father had. Jerry was only a beaten and heart-broken fifteen-year-old kid then, and although he had feared that his father might choose suicide, he really hadn't thought he would ever do it. Somewhere in his mind, Jerry had always blamed himself, thinking that if he hadn't screamed "I hate you" at his Father, his dad wouldn't have belted him and then shot himself in anguish and remorse after David and Doug Young took a scared and bleeding boy home with them.

"Wait," Jerry called out, burying his face in his bed sheets as he tried to recover from the shock. With his face still covered he motioned toward the chair. "Sit her down and leave the room," he ordered, "and turn on the light."

From behind the sheet, Jerry could see her slender legs and the feet that she always used to curl under her when she sat down. Memories came flooding back, sweet memories, and in each memory he saw her dancing brown eyes and the warmth of her smile. How he had loved her! He heard her muffled sobs coming from the chair, and he didn't want to see her like this. Jerry lay back against the raised head of his bed, took a deep breath, and shuddered. The darkness in his heart was slowly giving way to the light in the room. Jerry wiped cold sweat from his face and neck, still holding the bedclothes between him and Roxanne. She remained still. Only her sobbing broke the heavy silence in the room.

Finally, Jerry closed his eyes and lowered the sheet. He took another deep breath, reaching for courage and control, pulled his glasses off, and ran his hands across his face and through his hair. He folded his hands behind his head, intentionally leaving his glasses off so he couldn't see her clearly. He opened his eyes.

Roxanne was curled in a pathetic ball in the chair, and her sobs had turned to gentle whimpering sounds like her cocker spaniel, Spooks. Jerry used to have staring contests with the dog to see who would break eye contact first. He always knew when he was about to win, because Spooks would start to whimper and whine, which would increase in volume as his endurance crumbled. Then he would finally let out one yelp, like Jerry had pinched him or something, and run from the room.

Suddenly, Jerry chuckled as the memory broke the ice in the room. "Hush, Roxanne, you sound like Spooks."

Her whimpering stopped immediately, and she sat up, staring at Jerry as she wiped her eyes on her jacket.

Jerry tossed her his box of tissues. "Here, you need these more than I do." He waited while she blew her nose and wiped her face. When he saw her reach to smooth her crumpled dress and sit up straight, he put his glasses on and looked directly into her alluring

brown eyes that he had loved so much. The ache was intense—
the longing to gather her in his arms and kiss away her pain, but
that responsibility belonged to her husband, now. Neither could
Jerry's grief and hurt be removed by her tears and apologies. His
heart could not be healed by her. He took the memories and longings and put them away. The past was in the past. What had Jan
said? "Work with your present reality. Use it to help you learn and
grow." This seemed like a good time to follow her wise counsel.

"Jerry, I'm so very—"

He cut her off. "You already said that. It doesn't matter now.
What in the Sam hill Pete are you doing here? Where's Eric?"

"He's out on a fishing boat. He bought me a ticket so I could
visit my parents while he's gone."

"Roxanne, this isn't Slatersville, in case you somehow haven't
noticed. Like I said, what are you doing here?"

"I just had to come, Jerry." She started to tear up again.

"Stop, we can't make sense in a conversation if you're sniveling.
The time for tears is past. Bring that chair here and sit down."

Roxanne pulled the chair close to Jerry's bed. "Kimberly told
me what happened, and I was just so worried—"

"That was more than a month ago, Roxanne. It's a little late to
be concerned. It's over now."

She started to cry again. The tissue box was still over by the
window, so Jerry fished a string of loose toilet paper from the bag
behind his bedpan and handed it to her.

"Does your husband know you're here?"

"Not exactly, but he told me I should probably come back and
talk with you."

"What for?"

With tears welling up in her eyes, she rose from the chair and
approached his bed. "Things aren't working out very well for us.
I've been terribly unhappy. He said to—" She clasped Jerry's hand.
"Jerry, is there anyway we could go back and start all over again?"

Jerry withdrew his hand. "Why would I want to do that?
You're a married woman, now, and I'm no marriage wrecker."

She dropped her head and dried a couple tears that had

escaped. "He's offered me a divorce if I want one. I know in a million years I could never make it up to you, but . . ."

"Not on your life, Missy. You chose him over me. You married him instead of me. He's your husband, and it certainly didn't take you long to marry him, did it? You dumped me, and we weren't even married yet, but you and Eric are. We're talking marriage vows, covenants, promises, a bond. How dare you go back on a bond as important and eternal as marriage? You promised me forever in words, without a bond, with only a promise ring."

Jerry grabbed Roxanne's left hand and shoved her wedding band in her face. "Whatever was going on in that little head of yours at the time doesn't matter. Roxanne, you, of your own free will and choice, told him forever with a binding promise and a binding ring, didn't you?"

She bit her lip as it began to quiver, and a few tears slipped from her eyes, but she stood quietly and listened.

Jerry ran his finger around her ring. "Tell me, Roxanne, where does the ring start and stop as it goes around? Show me the beginning or the end. Uh huh, that's right. There is no beginning or end. What should that tell you?" Jerry released her hand with a warm, firm squeeze and then he was silent.

Roxanne stood quietly turning the ring on her finger, obviously deep in thought. Finally she looked up at Jerry and nodded as several more tears trickled down her face.

His expression softened. "Sit down and let's talk. You said you aren't getting along? Do you argue a lot?"

"No, never."

"Is he controlling or forceful? Is he cruel or abusive in any way?"

"No, he's really very kind and patient. He's considerate, and he worries a lot about me because I'm so unhappy."

"Why are you so unhappy?"

She started to cry again. "Because I hurt you terribly. Because it was wrong, so very, very wrong." She leaned forward, resting her forehead against Jerry's bed. "And because I still love you," she told him, with tears choking her voice.

Jerry sat quietly and let her cry, controlling the urge to reach out and smooth her blond curls—the curls he had wanted his little girls to have. He fought the urge to embrace her and kiss away her tears, to heal the pining for him that was now so misplaced. He almost reached out to touch her hand, to comfort her, but Eric's ring stopped him. He swallowed the emotion welling up within him as he reminded himself of his place, and he withdrew his hand. Instead, he reached into his bedside stand and pulled a long strip of toilet paper out of the bag. He stuffed it into her clenched fist, took a deep breath, and tried to clear the lump from his throat. He stared to speak, but couldn't. He cleared his throat and tried again. "Roxanne, does Eric love you?"

She nodded.

"Does he tell you, or does he show you?"

"Both, he's really very good to me, and I know I've hurt him terribly."

"A very wise woman once told me, 'Some people change hearts like clothing. Some don't know what they want, and some just get lost.' I know you well enough to know that you aren't one of the heart and clothing changing kind, and you may be confused, but I don't think you're lost. I think you just need to figure out what you really want, so I'm going to help you.

"When you left me for Eric, I thought it was the end of my world." He cleared his throat again, trying to keep his voice calm and steady. "But it wasn't; my world has gone on without you. I am healing, and I will find my own happiness without you. So you need to let go, Roxanne. If you are truly sorry, I will accept that, and forgiveness is a given. But the only way to be truly sorry is to not make the same mistake twice. Learn from the current reality and from the pain we have all suffered. Go back to your husband and let him be what you want. If you give him all the love you once promised me, you will find happiness, and you will have a wonderful marriage.

Jerry reached out and took Roxanne's hand, gently pulling her to her feet. He cupped her blond curls in his hands and kissed her on the forehead. "Go home, Roxanne." His voice was soft. She embraced Jerry, and this time he embraced her back, letting go of all the heartache and tears he had cried. He took a deep breath and forced his voice to remain gentle but firm, kissed her forehead again, and said, "Go home to your husband."

She bowed her head and nodded, and then turned and left the room, unaware that she was trailing a long piece of toilet paper behind her.

Jerry held his composure until the door was tightly closed, and then he started to chuckle, but the tears he had held back tumbled from his eyes. Then his body began to shake with sobs as he finally laid Roxanne to rest beside her little blond-headed babies in the bog.

Chapter Nineteen

Rachel stopped by Jerry's room on her way to work the next morning. His door was closed. She peeked in, but he was sleeping. *I'll check on him during break,* she thought quietly, closing the door behind her. She was passing the nurses' desk on her way to pediatrics when a disturbing conversation between the charge nurse and Jerry's doctor caught her attention. She paused at the fountain and got a drink, pretending not to listen.

"Jerry asked for pain medication last night and again this morning, and he didn't sleep well."

"Okay, we'd better order a portable x-ray of his leg and see if there was any damage." He shook his head. "Does anyone know anything about this woman?"

"The evening staff had never seen her before. It was late, and Jerry was settled for the night. She never checked at the desk, and no one saw her slip into his room. He was very angry when he called for the nurse, and he demanded that she be taken out. Then he suddenly changed his mind and told them to let her stay. He ordered the nurse to leave and close the door."

"What happened then?"

"She was in his room for some time, but she had calmed down a lot before she left, and so had he."

"Has he said anything about the incident?"

"No, he hasn't said a word. The evening and night shift said he's been very quiet even though he hasn't slept much."

Rachel glanced at her watch as the charge nurse and doctor started down the hall to visit the rest of his patients. It was fifteen minutes before she had to report to duty. She would not report early today. She wished this wasn't Kelly's day off. Kelly wasn't afraid to share information with her concerning Jerry because she understood their relationship. She treated Rachel as she would his family. Since Rachel was not related to Jerry, and she worked on a different wing, she was not ethically entitled to any information about him. His chart, resting on the nurses' desk, contained information Rachel desperately wished she had access to. Feeling deeply troubled about the bits and pieces she had overheard, Rachel knew she would have to wait.

What could have possibly happened to re-injure his leg? she thought, dreading the possibility of extended time for him in traction. *And who was this woman they spoke of?* Rachel returned to Jerry's room and sat quietly in the chair that had been moved close to his bed by this mysterious visitor. Rachel had put it back in its usual place when she had left last night.

An air of foreboding hung over Rachel as Roxanne's image kept flashing across her mind. Who else might visit Jerry that would trigger his anger? If it was Roxanne, where was Eric? He had been on Rachel's mind. An unsettled feeling about him had plagued her for some time, but her father advised her to let him follow Eric's situation. Now, with this turn of events she worried even more. She would call her father today.

Rachel studied Jerry's face as he slept. His glasses were on his bedside table beside a wadded bunch of toilet paper. A frown furrowed his brow, and he fidgeted in his sleep. He stirred and moaned as though he was in pain, then was quiet again. Rachel watched with concern as his hands and arms moved in small jerking twitches. Too soon, her wristwatch progressed to clocking in time. She arose, placed a gentle hand over Jerry's, and laid a soft kiss on his troubled brow; then she reported for work.

Jerry was still asleep when she checked on him during her

break. His breakfast tray lay untouched on his bedside table. When Rachel hurried to Jerry's room during her lunch break, the breakfast tray had been replaced by his lunch tray, which was also untouched. However, he was resting more quietly. By her afternoon break, Rachel was quite anxious. She found Jerry sitting upright in bed, staring blankly out the window.

He turned to greet her. "Hi, Rachel," he said, and then he was quiet again.

"Jerry, I happened to overhear the doctor say they were concerned that your leg may have been re-injured. What happened?"

He smiled, but only slightly. "Ah, nothing, I was just being stupid. I jerked it really hard last night. They x-rayed it and found out that I broke some calcium loose, but they don't think I re-fractured it. The doctor said it'll just be pretty sore for a few days. I hope they can still cast it as planned. I'm sick of this place."

Rachel noted disheartened frustration in his voice, and a hint of anger. "Are you in a lot of pain?" she asked.

"They gave me a pain pill this afternoon, so it's not too bad. It's just that my butt is petrified to this bed, and I want out. Yesterday would have been five weeks too long."

Rachel stroked her hand through his hair, but he gently caught her hand and gave it a quick squeeze and then let it go. "Not today, Rachel. I'm in a grumpy mood, and I'm not very good company. I'm sorry."

"Is it just your leg, or is something else troubling you?" She opened the door of communication, hoping he would reveal the details of the previous night, but she saw his jaw stiffen as he shook his head.

"Nah, I'm just tired and discouraged. I'll get over it. I think I'll try to rest for a while if you'll excuse me, Rachel. I didn't sleep much last night." He laid his head against his pillow and closed his eyes. The subject was closed, and so was the visit.

Rachel bent and kissed his cheek, but he didn't respond. She went straight to a phone booth and called her father.

"Eric is out to sea for several weeks," her father told her. "He said he was sending Roxanne to stay with her parents while he's gone. That's all he would say, but he sounded like he was unhappy."

Rachel didn't tell her father she believed Roxanne had visited Jerry. There was no reason to cause him consternation when she had no facts. "Thank you, Father. Call me if you hear anything. I love you, and if you hear from Eric, please give him my love."

Anger boiled inside her as she hung up the phone. She was certain now that her feelings were valid. Roxanne had probably waited until Eric was gone, and then, behind his back, when she was supposed to be with her parents, she had come here to Fairbanks. Rachel's concerns about Eric had probably been justified all along.

Now, when Jerry was finally recovering and moving forward with his life, when he was finally starting to open up his heart again, Roxanne had dared to come here and inflict herself upon Jerry. Something she had done had startled Jerry enough to re-injure his leg, and who knew the toll her visit might take on his emotional state. If the mood Rachel had just left Jerry in was any indication, he might still be in for a rough ride. Why now, after all these weeks? Why hadn't she ever tried to call or come sooner? No, she waited until Eric was out to sea, struggling with his sadness alone, and then she had taken this brash action. Rachel questioned Roxanne's intent with great suspicion. Was she planning to leave Eric so that she could try to rekindle a relationship with Jerry? Why had he let her stay after he had demanded that she leave? Was he still so deeply in love with her that she could make him vulnerable again to her deceit?

Rachel remembered the warm and stirring moments she and Jerry had shared the previous day. He had touched her, held her, and kissed her. How special he had made her feel, and how much his kisses had hinted of promise. *What now?* Rachel thought with a deep sigh as she returned to her duties. *What now?*

Jerry was pleasant, but quiet all the next week. He was too quiet. Rachel gave him many opportunities to open up, but he remained subdued and reserved, even toward her. She was relieved when the doctor announced that the calcium should adhere back to the bone, and the fracture had not separated. He would cast Jerry tomorrow as planned. Kelly hadn't been able to shed much more light on Jerry's visitor than Rachel had already guessed. She was described as petite, with blond, curly hair. There was no information on how he re-injured his leg, and he wasn't talking.

Rachel was relieved that he would be discharged tomorrow or the next day. She had spent less time with Jerry as she made preparations and secured tickets for their departure. He talked about her coming home with him, and was glad, but the spark of enthusiasm he had shown the day she consented had disappeared, and so had the close interaction between them. Rachel found a box, and Jerry carefully packed Danny's pictures and his carving away for the trip. *Well, at least he shows some emotion*, she thought as she watched him from the corner of her eye. She had expected he would regarding Danny. She was certain some of his melancholy was loneliness for his little friend, but there was also something deeper inside, something guarded.

❋

Kimberly ran to meet Roxanne as she walked down the stairs from the commuter plane that had just landed at the Slatersville airport. She gave her a firm hug, wanting to assure Roxanne that whatever mistakes she had made, she still had a cousin who loved her. "Let's get your bags and take you home. Your parents are anxious to see you."

"I don't want to see them yet, Kimberly. They think I'm arriving later. I was hoping just you and I could talk first."

"Sure, whatever you say. Where do you want to go?"

"Let's hike up the trail on Buckskin Peak to our favorite old climbing tree. I feel the need to be young and innocent again, like before all this happened."

Dressed in blue jeans and sneakers, Kimberly was prepared for the hike. "Why not?" she said, remembering all the pleasant walks and talks she and Roxanne had shared through the years. Roxanne was mostly quiet and thoughtful as they walked. Once they had reached the old cottonwood and settled on their favorite branches, almost side by side, with their backs resting against the huge trunk, Roxanne opened the subject Kimberly had been expecting.

"I need to talk to you about Jerry."

"Okay," Kimberly answered.

"You need to promise that what we say here will be buried at the base of this tree when we leave. You'll never speak of it to anyone."

"I promise, but what are you trying to tell me, Roxanne?"

"I can never forgive myself for what I did to him."

"No, I suppose not, especially since you still care for him so much."

"He's a wonderful man. I gave up far more than I realized when I ran off with Eric, but it's too late now to go back."

"That's true."

"I saw him."

"Who?"

Roxanne dropped her head. "Jerry, I went to the hospital."

"You what?" Kimberly cried, whirling around to face her cousin and nearly losing her balance on the limb. "Roxanne, how could you? What good could that possibly have done? Rubbing salt in the wound, prolonging the agony, bringing all the pain back to the forefront? How could you do that to him?"

Roxanne's head dropped lower. "I know it was a dirty trick, but I had to know."

"Had to know what? How miserable and alone he was? Hadn't he suffered enough torment? I don't understand you anymore, Roxanne. What were you thinking?"

Tears were beginning to trickle down Roxanne's face, and she wiped them on her shirtsleeve. "Maybe I shouldn't have come," she said, shifting her position to stand up.

Kimberly reined in her anger and regained her self-control. If Roxanne had visited Jerry, she'd better find out the whole story so she could help Jerry in some way. Right now she was too upset to want to help Roxanne much.

"Sit down, Roxanne," she said. "I don't mean to scold. I just worry a lot about a situation that's out of my hands. I feel so bad for him!"

"I know," Roxanne said, resettling on her branch. "I asked him if there was any chance for us, for me to make amends."

"I hope he said no. You're married now, and you have a husband."

"He did."

"Good."

Roxanne was silent. Kimberly looked at her and saw the grief in her face and her voice softened. "How was he, Roxanne? I worry about him every day."

"He's good. He was really upset at first. I didn't blame him, but it hurt to feel him so hard and cold, and know I did that to him. He's such a kind man, really."

"What did you expect, a joyous reunion?"

Roxanne ignored the snide remark. "I needed to feel his anger, to understand the full impact of what I had done to him. I needed to feel his hate and bitterness. It was devastating! I'd never seen him like that, but it was necessary."

Kimberly's expression was incredulous as she stared at Roxanne. She felt it better not to voice her feelings at that point.

Roxanne continued. "Somewhere in the back of my screwed up little mind I had to know that I could never go back. And I'm fine with that now. But although Jerry seemed changed, although he looked sad, and maybe a little haggard and older, he hasn't changed—not really. He's still kind and good—" The tears began to flow again. "He forgave me, Kimberly. Can you believe that? He forgave me, after all I did to him. He taught me a valuable lesson. His forgiveness is conditional, that I mustn't make the same mistake twice. He made me see the importance of the promises I have made to Eric. He made me see the hurt I've already caused him." She started to weep. "He made me see what a dear and caring man Eric really is. He gave me new eyes to see what I do have. He gave me a new chance for true happiness. Jerry held my head in his hands and kissed me, hugged me, and then sent me back home to my husband." She folded her arms across her knees, laid her head on her arms, and wept.

Kimberly remained quiet, trying to take in everything Roxanne had said. Jerry, even in his own suffering, had opened a bright, new door for Roxanne's happiness. He had set her free from the bitter anguish and guilt that had haunted her for weeks, the anguish and guilt Kimberly had feared in Roxanne's voice on the phone. As Kimberly listened now to Roxanne's sobbing, a humble recognition of commitment to move forward, she could feel the healing power of Jerry's gift to her cousin. Her heart was filled with love for this precious friend, still tied to a hospital bed more than a thousand miles away.

✳

Jerry exited the taxi with help from Rachel and the cab driver. He was awkward on his crutches, and the cast felt like it was made of steel. He struggled through Rachel's door and into her small apartment. She took him to her bedroom, laid him on her bed, and propped pillows under his full leg cast. "I'll sleep you in here because the sofa is too low. I can sleep on it."

Jerry caught her hand as she started to leave to get him some lunch. He pulled her to the bedside and encircled her in his arms with a warm hug. "Thank you, Rachel, for everything from the bog to here. You owed me nothing, but you gave me everything. Thank you, my beloved friend." He planted a moist kiss on her cheek, and released her before she could turn her face toward him. The moment had passed, and her lips hungered for the kiss her cheek was wearing.

She only had until morning to be alone with him, and then they would be on their way to Indian Valley and his home, friends, and family. How she wanted to be held in his arms again, as she had been on that day when, in a moment of time, she had belonged to him in his heart. Two kisses and two embraces had been filled with sweetness, hope, and promise. She would hold onto those few moments forever, and she would give him time. Jerry was the dream and desire of her heart. He was worth waiting for.

After lunch, Jerry slept for a while, so Rachel finished her last minute packing. Following supper, she would wash dishes and pack them away in her trunk, the bedding and towels the next morning, and her little apartment she had made her home would be vacant. She had given Kelly a key and told her to take all the food and then turn in the key. She would miss Kelly and Connie the most. They had been good friends.

As she prepared a supper tray for Jerry, she heard the creaking and clicking of his crutches. He appeared in the kitchen doorway.

"Jerry, you did not have to get up; I was bringing dinner to you."

"No thanks, I've had breakfast, lunch, and dinner in bed enough for a life time. I'm finally free. I'm sitting at a table like a normal human being for a change."

Rachel giggled. "Jerry, I only have a little breakfast nook, you cannot fit in it."

"Who says so?" Jerry said as he clumsily hobbled to the booth and sat sideways on the bench with his leg cast stretching across the floor.

"Fine, I will get a stool for your leg. You are a stubborn man, but I love you." Rachel surprised herself. The words just came out as naturally as breathing.

Jerry took a second glance at Rachel, startled by her simple, honest statement as she pulled a stool to the table and gently lifted his leg onto it. Jerry watched her brown hands lifting his heavy cast and her shiny, black hair sweeping across her arms and tickling his bare toes peeking out from the bottom of the cast. He watched her face—so soft and lovely, and her hazel eyes filled with tenderness. She placed his dinner plate before him and smiled.

He caught her hand, pulling her down toward him. Reaching through her silky strands of hair, he cupped the back of her head in his other hand and drew her lips to his. The kiss was simple, sweet, and only for a moment, but again that moment belonged to her in his heart, and she felt hope in its promise.

CHAPTER TWENTY

The flight to Seattle was long and uncomfortable for Jerry. Rachel was worried, because after a layover here, there were two more connecting flights before reaching the remote town of Slatersville. The airline personnel met Jerry with a wheelchair. He was looking a little ragged around the edges, his face grimacing with each move, and his wrinkled brow revealing the extreme discomfort that he kept to himself.

Watching his misery, Rachel was frustrated. Jerry's leg had healed so nicely, and his pain was completely gone until Roxanne had come. She was married to Rachel's brother after choosing him over Jerry, and was, in a large part, the cause of all this suffering in the first place. Why couldn't she have just stayed away, been true to Eric, and left Jerry alone? Rachel gave Jerry another strong pain pill, hoping he could sleep a little during their layover. As she stood beside him, she gently ran her fingers through his hair. He had not let her do this since Roxanne's visit that night.

Jerry leaned his head against Rachel, relieved by her comforting and gentle touch. He suddenly sat upright. His body stiffened and his hands clutched the arms of his wheelchair. Roxanne was standing in line, waiting to board a flight that the loud speaker had just announced was scheduled to fly to Anchorage. She was dabbing at her eyes with a tissue, but her small frame stood erect, her head held high like someone who knew what she wanted. She had completed her visit with her family and was returning to her husband as Jerry had told her she must. While he had waited for her to gain control in his hospital room that painful night, he had struggled between his immense anger and his desire to help her in her grief. He had prayed with all his heart to feel forgiveness, and for the strength to turn his bitterness into good. Peace filled his soul now, as he watched his little pixie love walk out of his life once more and into the arms of another man—a man who loved her and would take care of her. As Jerry wiped a tear from the corner of his eye, he felt gratitude toward Eric. He sat back in the chair and dropped his head. Closing his eyes tightly, he took a long, deep breath and relaxed.

✳

As Rachel ran her fingers through Jerry's hair, she felt another ray of hope. He was not only allowing her to finally touch him again, but he was responsive, relaxing under the gentle caress of her fingers. Then he leaned his head against her. The noises of the loud speaker and the busy travelers were lost to her as her heart grew warmer.

Jerry raised his head and stiffened suddenly, gripping the armrests of his wheelchair. Staring toward the passengers waiting in line to board a plane, he bit his lip and took a quick breath. Rachel's eyes followed his gaze, and her heart felt a quick jolt of anger. Roxanne was standing in the line. Rachel watched Jerry as he watched Roxanne. Deep pain filled his eyes, and then turned soft with tenderness as a faint smile ever so slightly creased his face. He sat erect, gazing for a moment, and then leaned back in the wheelchair, wiping the corner of his eye. He dropped his head, squeezed his eyes closed, and took a deep breath.

Rachel's heart sank to the bottom of her shoes, and her hopes and dreams lay open and defenseless against the truth she had just witnessed. For almost six weeks of compassion for a dear friend, which had turned to heartfelt care and fondness and then deepest love and passion, she had given Jerry all the strength and soul she had in her. Everything in her life had centered on him. She recalled her father's words, "I just hope you're not getting so emotionally involved that you feel the need to suffer with him. Help him if you can, but guard yourself and be wise." There were other words too, forgotten until now, offered by a loving father with a benevolent heart. "He's been deeply hurt, Rachel. That can make a man bitter. I don't want you to get hurt." She remembered her response to her father, "Time can heal the deepest wounds, Father, and so can love."

Alaska suddenly seemed a lifetime away. The throaty bugle of the caribou and the cry of the wolf called to her spirit to go home, right here and now, to just turn around and go home. Rachel sighed and leaned against the pillar behind her as she looked at Jerry's bowed head and broken body. Defeated as she felt at that moment, Jerry still needed her, and she still loved him. Only about seven weeks ago, this good and humble man had traveled this same journey in the company of the love of his life to help Rachel's father in his time of need. Yes, she would go with Jerry, to the end of the earth right now if he needed her. She had told her father, "Time can heal the deepest wounds, and so can love." She had both of them. Roxanne could not make her dream die so easily.

She stepped against the side of the wheelchair, and reaching down, ran her fingers through his hair again. He caught her hand with his and pulled it to his lips, gently kissing the palm as he placed his other arm around her waist and laid his head against her breast. Neither of them could speak for a moment. Jerry was not aware that Rachel had seen Roxanne. He only knew this lovely woman standing beside him had been his true and faithful friend, and he wanted to feel her near.

Jerry's leg was awkwardly wedged in front of him as he sat slightly twisted to the side in his seat during their final flight. Rachel sat across the isle, sensing Jerry's great discomfort, yet she was helpless to do anything to relieve it. The difficult journey came to an end as the commuter plane touched down on the Slatersville runway.

As Jerry arose and hobbled through the door of the plane with Rachel behind him, a pretty young woman began waving and doing a little jumping dance. She was slightly older than Jerry, with blue eyes, short, brunette hair, and a huge smile. Standing beside her were David and Kimberly. Jerry smiled and waved back. Then, straining to hold his cast away from the steep stairs, he gripped the railings and struggled down the steps of the plane. Finally Jerry touched the ground, and the attendant who had carried his crutches while backing down the stairs ahead of him handed them to him. Jerry had only cleared the steps a few feet, when the young woman burst through the gate and ran toward him.

"Jerry," she screeched, throwing her arms around him and nearly knocking him off balance.

He grinned and hugged her against one crutch and then buried a kiss in her hair. "Sally, I missed you so much. No one to boss me around or nag at me. How did I ever survive without you? Do I still have an art gallery, or has my talented sister and her classy fashion designs converted it into a dress shop?"

"Your sister took very good care of it for you, but you owe me big time, now, brother. You recruited me for two weeks, not two months."

Leaning his armpits on his crutches, he held his arms out in a futile gesture. "You want I should kneel and beg your forgiveness?"

"No, I hate it when you grovel!" she answered, hugging him again and burying her face against his chest. She held her embrace for some time. Then, still hugging him, she looked up and smiled. "Welcome home, Jerry, welcome home."

"Hey, Sally. I want you to meet someone special. This is—"

"Rachel," Sally said, releasing Jerry as she wrapped her slender arms around the young Indian woman standing quietly to the side.

Rachel, a little surprised by the warmth of this stranger, responded by patting Sally's back lightly with her hand. She smiled at Sally.

"Thank you for taking such wonderful care of Jerry for us,"

Sally continued. "How terrific you are. We all love you. Oh, I'm sorry, you don't even know who I am! I'm Sally, Jerry's big sister." She grinned at Jerry, who was wrapped in a firm embrace in David's arms.

Jerry and David, each fighting a show of emotion, just held their embrace until Jerry was able to speak. "Good to see you, brother. I've missed you."

"Me too," David responded, swallowing the knot in his throat. He couldn't find his voice, so he just wrapped his long arm around Jerry's shoulder and smiled. No words were needed. Jerry read the greeting in David's eyes, delivered from his heart.

Kimberly hugged Rachel. "Welcome, Rachel, we're so thrilled you could come. Thank you is a very small word to say to someone with a huge heart. We love you." Rachel nodded and smiled.

David took Rachel's hand and led her a few feet away as Jerry reached for Kimberly. "How can we ever thank you, Rachel? He's only here because of you. I could never have found him in time, and then your constant care for weeks through all his anguish and suffering. How can we ever thank you?" He wrapped his arms around her. "Surely heaven sent you to us. Bless you, bless you!"

Sally stood beside David, her head bowed, nodding approval to his words.

As Jerry embraced Kimberly, she couldn't hold back the tears. She was not responsible for her cousin's actions, but she had introduced Roxanne to Jerry. Her sadness for his suffering had been very personal to her. She clung to him and wept. "I am so sorry, Jerry. If I hadn't asked—"

"Hey, Kim, you don't owe me any apologies." He held her tightly, leaning on his crutches, and gently rocked her in his arms. Then he smoothed a strand of long, auburn hair from her face, pulled a handkerchief from his pocket, and dried her eyes. "No more tears now. It's all over, okay?" He embraced her again, stroking her head. "No more regrets. I'm fine, Kim, I'm fine."

Remembering the air of confidence, the look of hope, and the spirit of commitment that Roxanne had carried with her as she boarded her flight earlier that day, Kimberly hugged Jerry again more tightly. "Jerry, you are a truly wonderful man." She stepped back, and her blue-sapphire eyes carried an unspoken message of enormous gratitude. Jerry nodded. Kimberly smiled and kissed his cheek. "I'm so glad you're finally home!"

"Jerry has had an extremely long and uncomfortable journey, David," Rachel said. "He re-injured his leg several days before we left. It's not serious, but he has suffered pain all the way here. We must get him where he can rest for a while. Is his apartment very far?"

"Not far," David answered. He and Kimberly loaded the luggage into their Jeep, while Rachel and Sally helped Jerry slide across the back seat of Sally's car. They drove to Jerry's art shop where David jumped out of the Jeep to help Jerry into his apartment at the rear of the gallery.

"That's not the plan," Jerry said. "All I need from home is my fishing gear. I have a beautiful woman waiting for me in Indian Valley."

"Jerry, you must rest now," Rachel said. "There will be much time to fish later."

"I agree with Rachel, Jerry," Sally said. "She's the nurse. Jan wouldn't want you to overdo, and it sounds like the trip was very long and tiring. I think you should rest. We can go to Indian Valley later."

"Great, now I have two bosses," Jerry quipped. "Tell them, David, how do I get the most rest?"

"Hey, bud, who am I to argue with a professional and a sister? The nurse knows best, and you have to live with the sister after the argument. I'm sorry, but I'm not touching this one. Besides, you know Mom. Whose side do you think she'll take if you don't mind them? Then she'll be after you as well."

"But I have a date! I promised; I can't stand Jan up. She's waiting for me, and so are the fish."

Kimberly joined them and said, "What's going on? Aren't we unloading Jerry's things and going in?"

"He wants to go fishing," David said, grinning at his wife.

"Right now?"

"Yup," Jerry answered, defiantly folding his arms across his chest.

Sally switched off the engine. "My car, my keys, my decision—end of argument." She opened the car door. "Let's go inside and put my stubborn brother to bed."

"Whoa, there, Miss Bossy; just 'cause I'm on crutches doesn't give you the upper hand!"

"Wanna, bet? It's payback time, baby brother. Rachel, how long did you say he'd be in the cast, a month?" Rachel nodded. Sally giggled, "One whole month of paybacks. This is gonna be fun." She closed her car door and walked away to unlock the shop.

David shook his head and chuckled as he opened Jerry's car door. "When did you ever win an argument with Sally? Let's go in so you can rest."

Jerry grumbled all the way to his bedroom. David helped him lay down, and held his cast while Rachel supported it on pillows. Jerry's grumbling turned to mumbling the second his head touched the pillow. Rachel gently ran her fingers up and down on his shoulder while David unlaced his boot. Jerry was sound asleep before David could pull the boot off Jerry's foot.

CHAPTER TWENTY-ONE

When Jerry woke up several hours later, Kimberly called ahead to tell Jan they were on their way. Jerry stretched his leg across the pillow in the back seat of Sally's car, hugging his fishing gear as if it were a long lost friend. Sally drove the twenty miles across Slater Valley to the base of the mountain pass. David and Kimberly followed in their Jeep Wrangler. Driving the winding forty miles to the summit, Sally and Rachel chatted, getting to know each other as Jerry snoozed comfortably against the other pillow propped behind his back and head. He had not felt this peaceful for six long weeks. When they reached the summit, Jerry awakened like an alarm went off in his head, and as the car descended the seven miles into Indian Valley, he whistled in the back seat while getting his gear in order.

Rachel enjoyed this lighthearted side of Jerry, frequently glancing at him over the seat. She had not seen him this happy since he and Danny were caught throwing rolls of toilet paper out the hospital window.

Jan had already driven her wheelchair to the pond when they arrived. Jerry was like a child on Halloween night, frustrated at the cumbersome cast as he tried to bull his way out of the car to go get his treat. He hobbled down the seventy-five yard pathway toward the pond at a pace that made Kimberly nervous as she followed him with his pillow and a reclining lawn chair. Sally carried his fishing gear.

David unloaded Rachel's bags and trunk from his Jeep and carried them into her room in his mother's cabin. Neighbors and part time professionals had been helping with Jan's care after her nurse had resigned. David and Kimberly had often stayed at night so she would not be alone, although she insisted that she would be fine. He felt a huge concern lifted from his shoulders, knowing that not only did Jan have full time care now, but her nurse was a very dear and trusted friend.

Rachel followed David through the tidy cabin to her own new home, which was a most pleasant, comfortable, and even spacious room, decorated with creamy lace curtains. A beautiful handmade quilt covered the bed, and those same skilled hands had made matching rocker cushions. Rachel felt a touch of home, because the quilt was the magenta color of the brilliant Fireweed growing on the tundra.

As she began to arrange her belongings, she answered David's many questions about Jerry and informed him of the recent troubling events.

David felt anger burning inside him as Rachel told him of Roxanne's visit.

"I do not know what transpired, except that he was extremely upset, and he somehow re-injured his leg, but he would not tell anyone what had happened, or who had visited him that night. It had to be her, though," Rachel said. "I only caught bits and pieces, but there was an instant and dramatic change in him."

"Uggh," David growled. "I wish he'd never met that wench. She was a sweet little disaster waiting to happen; one sugar coated nightmare after another for Jerry. And it still goes on." David placed Rachel's trunk in the location she pointed out under the window. "I wish she could just drop off the planet or something," he said, angrily kicking a piece of lint off the floral print rug and onto the hardwood floor. "I have tried to be sensitive and keep my anger to myself, though, because she is Kimberly's cousin, and they're very close. Sometimes my tongue gets pretty sore from me

biting it." He stooped and picked up the same piece of lint, dropping it into the cream-colored wastebasket.

"I have learned to know Jerry well these past weeks," Rachel said, hanging a clothes carrier in the closet. She turned to face David. "He is bright, clever, and inventive. Much of his value is humility, and not clearly visible unless one is watching for it, but he has a ready, giving, and gentle heart." She brightened as she spoke of Jerry, and David felt he was getting a glimpse into her heart.

"I wish you could have seen him with Danny. He was truly amazing! He healed a very sick child with a power of love and compassion that I cannot put into words." She paused again, and her eyes were joyful as she spoke of David's best friend, the Jerry that David knew so well.

David sat in the oak rocking chair, carefully watching Rachel's expressions, seeing more than she meant to show, and listening beyond her words.

"Danny is a beautiful child, full of faith and courage. When Jerry had no will, Danny gave him a reason to believe. Danny is a little nine-year-old boy who had the power to open Jerry's heart and make him hope, feel, and love again." She sighed and her eyes saddened as she stooped and opened the trunk. Removing her mother's beaded scarf, she laid it across the top of the trunk. As she lovingly ran her fingers across the beaded flowers, she continued, "When Jerry is deeply troubled or is in pain, he hides himself from others, even when he knows they care, and he becomes more distant. I cannot reach him when he goes there, because I do not know where to find him. Danny knew, though. He could always bring him back."

"You loved that little boy, didn't you?" David asked.

Rachel sat on the bed and crossed her feet as her ancestors had done for centuries. "Yes, he was very special," she answered. "I miss him terribly, and so does Jerry. That was my greatest frustration with this whole situation with Roxanne. Danny had just left that very morning. I know Jerry was grieving for him. That was hard enough without—"

"You love Jerry too, don't you, Rachel?" Rachel dropped her head and ran her fingers along the quilted lines of the bedspread. "Don't you?" David persisted, leaning forward in his chair.

She nodded and then raised her head, looking straight at David, her eyes intent and sincere. "Yes, David. I do love Jerry. I love him very much, but I do not know if his great love for Roxanne can ever be moved to make a place for me in his heart. Several times I thought it could, but now I am doubtful. I have sometimes had glimpses into the deepest places in his heart, but he holds them carefully guarded. It is Roxanne, and other sorrows, or maybe other fears, that hold him captive in those dark places. I cannot get in to help him. Only Danny could, and now Danny is gone. If only she had come when he still had Danny, maybe—"

David remembered how he and Jan had struggled to reach Jerry after Doug Young's death. It was Jerry's love and compassion for Jan that had drawn him out. She had cradled the big, sixteen-year-old boy in her lap and had cried and pleaded for him to understand her fears for him. That was the key! The need of someone else! That was what unlocked the very place Rachel was talking about. "That was Danny's secret," David said almost to himself.

"What?" Rachel asked.

"Danny was an orphan, right?"

"Yes," Rachel answered. "His mother had died about six months earlier. There was no information about his father."

"Jerry was an orphan," David said almost under his breath. "And Danny was very ill?" he asked.

"He'd lost a kidney to cancer, and was receiving chemotherapy. Yes, he was very ill."

"Jerry, you old Hedgehog! All these years I've known you, known you like a brother, but I never really understood until now."

"What? David, what are you saying?"

"Danny could get in because he was already there. He already knew Jerry's pain, and likewise, Jerry already knew Danny's pain, plus Danny's desperate need. It was a given. On the surface Jerry is outgoing, kind, helpful, happy, and full of fun and mischief, an all around great guy. No one would know that he really lives inside of himself. All of his sorrows, grief, suffering, and heartache are with him everyday, locked away in the dark places, even locked away from himself. Then something happens, and the lock bursts open. It all caves back down on him, and he withdraws."

David arose, pacing the floor as he spoke with conviction. "I can see it, now. Jerry's empathy, his great compassion, and his ability to reach way beyond himself to others, as he did to me, Mom, and Danny, is a product of the unfulfilled needs from his own life. It's a gift he's developed out of his own desperate need."

David ran his hand through his short, sandy hair and walked to the window, staring out as though his new understanding was something visible. "It probably stems from his mother's death. Before that, all his needs were met through her nurturing. After that, with his father's alcoholism and abuse, none of his needs were met. He was left to go it alone. Developing compassion for his sisters, who were suffering with him, became his need. Developing compassion for his drunken father, who was suffering grief from the same loss Jerry was suffering, became his need. Man, it all makes sense now! That's why he stayed so close to his father through a living hell, and was even defensive of him. His desire to help his dad in his suffering became a passion, because he couldn't help himself in his own suffering. What a revelation! It was always right there in front of me, but I never saw it until now."

Rachel spoke softly to herself as her own personal understanding came to light. "Bezrok'wl dletsinh known by the spirits. A little boy, betlanh, knew how to walk in bekatreth. Si netl'ila. Now, to understand and help him, si must learn to walk in bekatreth. (No wonder it was made known by the spirits. A little boy, his friend, knew how to walk in his moccasins. I did not see it. Now, to understand and help him, I must learn how to walk in his moccasins.)"

✳

"Hello, Mamma Young," Jerry called, waving his crutch. Then he shuffled rapidly down the trail toward Jan. She turned and saw him, dropped her fishing pole, and propelled her wheelchair in his direction.

"Oh, my Jerry Boy, you're finally home."

Wheelchair and crutches nearly collided when Jerry dropped them mid step and bent over, throwing his arms around Jan as her chair came to a halt. He staggered on his good leg, setting his cast on the ground to keep his balance.

"My goodness, are you okay?" Jan asked, grabbing Jerry to hold him up.

"I am now." He grinned. "I'm back home with my Mamma Young. You look beautiful!"

"And you lie as you always did. I know well enough what I look like." She lifted her pink hat, smoothed her blond curls, and then replaced the hat; the same hat she had worn for years when she settled on the bank of a stream with her fishing pole. "How was your trip? Very long and uncomfortable, I would guess," she said, answering her own question. "Come, let's get you settled, and you can tell me all about it while we fish."

Kimberly and Sally laughed, enjoying Jan and Jerry's reunion; they then proceeded to the shore of the lovely woodland pond. A touch of early frost had tinted the leaves of the trees, and bright colors of red and gold reflected in the crystal blue-green waters of the pond as a skiff of fluffy clouds skimmed across the smooth surface. David's wife and Jerry's sister had become good friends during the weeks of Jerry's absence. They set up his lawn chair and pillow and then helped Jerry and Jan get comfortable so they could sit side by side and enjoy a pastime they had often shared since Jerry's boyhood. This time they would enjoy it from the grassy banks of Jan's very own fishing pond.

Kimberly and Sally wandered away. Sitting on two large rocks warmed by the early October sun near the shore of the pond, they visited, leaving Jerry and Jan to enjoy their fishing in private.

David and Rachel soon joined them.

Sally jumped up, hooking her arm through Rachel's, and excitedly introduced Rachel to Jan. Like Jerry, Jan was as dear to Sally as a second mother could be. This wonderful, caring woman had always been there for her and her sisters and brother.

David's mother took both of Rachel's hands in hers when Rachel knelt on the grass in front of her wheelchair. "Dearest Rachel, how blessed I am to finally meet you! Someone so dedicated to my Jerry Boy, in his crisis so far away from home, has secured a place of deepest respect in my heart." She placed her hand on Rachel's cheek and added, "I love you. Welcome to my home. I hope it can be your home as well." Deep gratitude in Jan's soft blue-gray eyes spoke the truth of her words as Rachel felt Jan's love soaking into her own spirit. She smiled, committing herself to the dedicated care she would give to this beautiful woman.

CHAPTER TWENTY-TWO

The evening air was growing cool as Kimberly invited Rachel and Sally to join her while she prepared a quick supper for the group in Jan's kitchen. David followed them to the cabin. He got a jacket for his mother and a lap quilt, and then he helped Rachel find one of his father's old jackets and a blanket for Jerry. Rachel excused herself from helping with supper, and she and David returned to the pond. David sat on a log facing Jan and Jerry.

Rachel held the jacket for Jerry, and then, as she tucked the blanket around his legs and across his lap, he reached out and ran his hand across her head and through her hair several times. He continued to visit with Jan and David, but took a moment to smile and tell Rachel thank you. She stood quietly beside him and ran her fingers through his hair. He relaxed, leaning into her fingers. She intentionally stopped moving her hand and waited for a moment to see what he would do. He responded, like a puppy that wants his ears rubbed more when the hand stops. She smiled as he moved his head under her hand, stretching his neck upward until he again felt the gentle caress of her fingers through his hair.

When Kimberly called them to supper, David and Rachel carried the pillow, blanket, lawn chair, fishing gear, and several nice trout to the cabin as Jerry walked beside Jan's chair with his crutches.

"He was enjoying you tonight," David said, grinning at Rachel as they followed a short distance behind Jerry and Jan.

Her smile was slightly timid as she looked over her load at the path ahead. "He was visiting. He did not even notice I was there except when I covered him up."

"Oh, he noticed! He was eating up your hand through the hair thing like a lovesick moose. And when you covered him up and he touched your hair, his expression was one of complete adoration. You may not have hooked this big sucker yet, Rachel, but never fear, you've got him nibbling hard at the bait. It's just a matter of time."

Rachel suddenly laughed, thinking of Jerry's head stretching to reach her hand.

"What?" David asked.

"Nothing," Rachel giggled as the image of a caribou straining to scratch his rack on a tree popped into her mind, along with a ray of hope. Rachel had enjoyed the evening at the pond, and Jerry's interaction with those he loved. Most memorable, though, was the later evening with Jan, David, and Jerry. The quiet visiting as the setting sun bathed the pond in its brilliant colors of orange, then pink, and then rose. The chance for Rachel to touch Jerry and to be near him as the colors faded into shadows, and the trees rested black against the horizon.

During supper, Jerry watched Rachel as she sat quietly amidst all the joy and laughter of old friends and family re-united. And David, who seemed to have appointed himself as Rachel's special envoy concerning Jerry, was most definitely watching Jerry watch Rachel. She felt a little self-conscious that David was aware of her feelings, but she also felt comforted that she had someone she could confide in who was so supportive.

After supper, the visiting and celebration of Jerry's homecoming continued late into the evening. At one point, Rachel, who was feeling a little estranged and rather tired, not knowing most of the people or incidents being discussed, quietly excused herself to unpack some of her things. Shortly, she heard the clicking and creaking of Jerry's crutches, and saw his sturdy frame in her doorway. He'd been lying in bed so long that she had forgotten how handsome he looked upright.

"Are you okay, Rachel?" he asked. "We suddenly missed you." David was standing behind Jerry, grinning and pointing at him and mouthing the words, "He suddenly missed you."

Rachel smiled as a flush of color crept across her beautiful, bronze complexion. She walked over to him. "Yes, Jerry, I am fine, thank you. I was just putting a few things away."

He placed his hand on her cheek, gently rubbing his thumb across her high cheekbone. "Okay, we just didn't want you to feel left out."

His crutches clicked and creaked back down the hall as Rachel hung her last blouse in the closet. Jerry had invited her to join them, and so she did, but there was no opportunity to be alone with him. Suddenly, she surprised herself by missing his hospital room and Jerry tied to the bed so he could not get away. She quickly shook the thought out of her head and rose to get a drink.

As the evening grew later and the din lessened, Jan excused herself. "You young people are welcome to stay, and play, and visit all night if you want to, but this lady is going to bed. I have to try to stay beautiful for my next date, so Jerry's lie will just be a little one." Jerry started to rise. "No, I'll just come to you so you don't have to get up," she said.

He arose anyway, and moved toward her on his crutches. "You are a true lady, Jan Young, and a great mother. Crutches are no excuse for me to sit when you are leaving a room." He bent and held her close for some time and then kissed her cheek. Rachel was impressed by his sweet gesture of respect, and she loved him even more.

Goodnights were said, and then Jan wheeled toward her bedroom. Rachel started to follow, but Jan smiled and patted her hand. "I think I can put myself to bed tonight, dear. You stay and visit with your friends. I'll call if I need you," she said, squeezing Rachel's hand. "Thank you for bringing him home to us. I'm so happy to have you here. Sleep well."

Kimberly arose to clear the table and cart the dishes into the kitchen. Sally and Rachel helped, rinsing dishes and loading the dishwasher while Kimberly wiped down counter tops and stove.

"Jerry, you need to marry Rachel," David said.

The deck of cards Jerry was shuffling spewed out of his hands, across the table, and some hit the floor. "Where the Sam hill did that come from?" Jerry asked, staring at David while David chuckled and collected the cards.

"Just sounded like a good idea," David said, still chuckling as he knelt down to reach a card on the other side of Jerry's propped-up cast.

"Well, keep your ideas to yourself," Jerry said, glowering as he collected the remaining cards and those that David handed him.

"Hmmm, hit a little closer to home than I expected, didn't I? I watched you with her tonight at the pond. She's perfect for you. She's tender, caring, comforting, caressing—"

"Shut up and mind your own business."

"Hey, you're my brother! Your happiness is my business. Sorry you're stuck with my nose in your life, but it's my job."

"Then, you're fired, now drop it!" Jerry's voice sounded threatening.

"You can't fire a brother. Besides, I owe you one, remember?"

"Remember what?" Jerry growled.

"You were pushing Kimberly on me," David reminded him, "and I was barely out of a coma. All you have is a busted leg. Your brain's been working, and I know you're not blind. You're not dumb, either. Look at what's right in front of you."

"These cards are right in front of me, and you're going to be picking them up again if you don't shut up!"

"Jerry, you felt it. You shared your feelings about Kim and me, and you were right. Well, so am I! Look at Kim and me," he said, patting his belly. "Have I ever looked better?"

"You'll look a lot worse any minute if you don't just drop it!"

David placed another card he had just found under Jerry's chin, and raised his head. His eyes were serious this time as he looked through the pain in Jerry's eyes, prying into the dark places.

"Why, Jerry? Why should I drop it? It's time to move on."

Suddenly, Jerry pushed the table away and his chair back at the same time. He rose and grabbed his crutches. "It's finished, David. Subject closed. It's time to go home."

"Hedgehog!"

"What?"

"I called you a hedgehog, because that's what you are." David got up and went into the kitchen, leaving Jerry standing alone with his crutches under his arms, and a puzzled look on his face.

Jerry forgot he was angry as David's unexpected response and sudden exit switched his train of thought from his inner feelings to David's meaning. "Hedgehog?" he murmured quietly. Then, feeling remorse that they hadn't even been together a full day and they'd just had an argument, Jerry groaned. He'd only seen David once at the hospital since his friend had pulled him from a deadly bog. This was a rotten payback for all David's sacrifice and grief in Jerry's behalf. He would give himself and David a few minutes to cool down and then he'd apologize when he could find a moment alone with him.

He just shouldn't have pushed it, though; Jerry had tried to warn him. It was just too soon, the memories too vivid, and the losses were too great for him to go there, now. He was fine with where Roxanne was. He hoped she and Eric would be truly happy. Suddenly, he chuckled. There was a touch of irony; after all she had put him through, she trailed a long piece of toilet paper out of his life behind her. He took a deep breath. It was all in the past, and he had found peace. He had moved on, but he wasn't ready for any commitments. In commitment lay risks and sorrows, and he didn't need anymore of that for a very long time. He shuffled to his favorite easy chair in Jan's living room and sat down, propping his cast across her coffee table. "Hedgehog?" he mumbled.

David walked beside Jerry to the car. Jerry's head was bowed. "I'm really sorry I lost my cool, David. I just can't go there right now. I do appreciate what you're trying to do for me, what you have done for me. I owe you my life. How can I ever repay you for a lifetime of friendship and care?"

"Seeing you happy will be the best payment you could ever give me," David said, embracing Jerry. Then he placed both hands on Jerry's shoulders and looked directly into his eyes. "At least think about what I said," he told him. Jerry nodded. David ruffled his curly, black hair and grinned. "Hedgehog," he repeated.

Rachel had waited in the background as the friends said good-night. David had given her a huge hug and a sincere thank you, eye to eye, and heart to heart. Sally and Kimberly had smiled warmly and waved with their goodnight wishes. Jerry had grown quiet and thoughtful. He walked past her without noticing, involved in earnest conversation with David. "Good night, Jerry," she said, but he didn't respond.

As Sally and David settled Jerry in the back seat, he looked around for her. "Where's Rachel?" he asked, but she had already closed the door and retired to her room.

He felt a strange emptiness as Sally drove away. Why hadn't she come out to the car with them? *I didn't tell her thank you*, he thought, remembering her gentle care and concern for him on the long journey home. *I didn't even get to tell her goodbye.*

The cabin was silent now; the joy and laughter hushed as Rachel flipped off the bedroom light and turned on her bedside lamp, a brilliant magenta base with a bowl-shaped, lacy, cream shade. She sat on the bed, crossing her feet in front of her and looked about the room. It was lovely and had a warm, homey feeling, but she felt cold and empty inside. All that had been dear to her in the past six weeks, Danny and his winning smile and shiny bald head, and Jerry and his strong arms and gentle hands, were gone, and she was alone with only her dream.

David believed in her dream. He wanted Jerry to come alive and realize that beautiful dream. He believed it would come true. However, David had not witnessed Jerry's reaction at seeing Roxanne that morning. Rachel had. "It's just a matter of time," David had said.

Well, at least Rachel had plenty of time, but the waiting, wondering, and wishing were so very hard. Again tonight, the closeness she felt with Jerry earlier in the evening had vanished with his smile, and he didn't even say goodnight. She had been with him every day for weeks, and he had needed her. Now, he didn't need her anymore. "I don't want you to get hurt," her father had said. She had been warned, but felt she had to believe, and she had given Jerry her heart. Rachel grasped her beaded purse from the bedside stand, hugging it to her breast. "Oh, Mother, what am I doing here among strangers in a new and different place so far from home? All for a dream that may never be realized."

Rachel arose and put on her nightgown and robe. She slipped down the hallway to Jan's door and quietly opened it. Peering into the dim room with a wisp of light from the hall touching the bed, she listened for the deep breathing of sleep, and watched the rise and fall of the bedclothes with a trained eye. She left the door slightly ajar and then returned to her own room and did the same. She settled into the fresh bed sheets, pulled the quilt over her shoulders, and switched off the lamp. Alert to her new responsibility and the precious life that laid in her guardianship, she closed her eyes, listening to the silence in the cabin even in her sleep.

CHAPTER TWENTY-THREE

Rachel arose early and was putting the rest of her things away when the phone rang. Jan, who had been reading in bed, answered it.

"Rachel, the phone is for you. It's Jerry," she called.

Rachel felt a quick flutter in her heart. "Thank you, Jan." She picked up the receiver and answered in a cheery voice, "Good morning, Jerry."

"Hi, Rachel, are you okay this morning?"

"I am, how is your leg?"

"It's sore, but I'm fine. I uh, I was just a little worried about you."

"Worried about me?"

"You didn't come out to the car last night. I wondered if something was wrong." There was a tone of hurt in his voice.

"You did not ask me to."

"I didn't get to say goodnight."

"I said goodnight, but you were talking to David."

"Oh, uh, I'm sorry. Guess I didn't hear you. You should have hit me or something."

"You were busy."

"Not that busy."

"You seemed to be."

"Well . . . hit me next time. I wanted to apologize for not saying thank you yesterday for all your help on the way home. It was just so great to see everyone, I, uh, I guess I kind of ignored you. Anyway, thank you. As always, you were wonderful."

Rachel smiled, setting aside her disappointment from the previous night. "I was glad to help you, Jerry. You know that."

"I know, but I still don't understand why."

"Jerry, I have told you why." Rachel waited for his response.

He was silent for a moment; then he cleared his throat, and Rachel could almost see him push his glasses up on his nose. "Well, I'd better go. Sally kept the shop up great, but the book work is a disaster. Guess I've got my work cut out for me for a few days. Uh," he hesitated like he wanted to say more. Rachel waited. "I, uh, I'll call you later. Bye, Rachel."

"Thank you for checking on me, Jerry. I love you."

There was a long pause before he spoke. "Uh, okay, bye."

Rachel sighed as she hung up the phone. "Well, it cannot hurt if I am truthful. At least he will know how I feel." She shrugged her shoulders and went to check on Jan.

"How is Jerry today?" Jan asked as Rachel helped her prepare breakfast.

Rachel giggled. "He is fine. He felt bad because he did not get to tell me goodnight."

"I see." Jan smiled and she stirred the orange juice while Rachel prepared to fry eggs.

"I was afraid yesterday might have been taxing on him, but he seemed so happy to be here that I didn't have the heart to send him home to bed," Jan said, smiling.

"He is much happier here with all of you, Jan. He is quite strong physically now, and although he is in some pain, he should be fine."

"And his emotional state?"

"I am not sure. His feelings are closely guarded. I think he may be struggling."

"I suppose so. You love him, don't you, Rachel?"

Rachel was startled, accidentally missing the frying pan with the egg she was cracking. "Ohoya!" she said, grabbing a paper towel and trying to catch the slimy egg as it slid under the burner.

Jan merely nodded. "I thought so." She handed Rachel another egg and smiled. "Try to get this one in the pan, dear. We'll clean the other one up after it finishes frying down there."

Rachel laughed. "Am I that obvious, Jan? David guessed it too. I can see that I will have no secrets from you or your son. Yes, I do love Jerry. I love him very much. How did you know?"

"Well, the egg told me, for one thing. Actually, I saw it in your eyes and in your care as you covered him at the pond last night. I'm sure he loves you too."

"How could you know that, Jan? He seems to make a concentrated effort to avoid any such relationship with me." Rachel put two slices of bread in the toaster. "He lives in the shadows of the past."

"Yes, I see that too, but I know Jerry. He is just fearful, Rachel."

"And I am so frightening?"

"For now, yes. Give him time."

"Must I run competition with a ghost for his love? Will he ever forget her?"

"Only Jerry can answer that, but he does love you. His eyes tell it now. In time he will know it for himself. Be patient with him, Rachel." Jan handed Rachel two plates.

"Yes, I know, I must try to walk in bekatreth."

"To walk where?"

"To walk in his moccasins, but how can I when he will not remove them from his dark place so I can put them on? How can I grow to understand his heart if he keeps it so tightly locked away?"

"But Rachel, my dear, you already know his heart, or you wouldn't love him so. You have been trying on his moccasins all these weeks. You understand him better than you realize. He doesn't know it, yet. He's afraid to face the truth. Afraid you'll just go away if he lets you in, because he won't be good enough for you to want to stay. Given time, you'll catch this stubborn fish.

The fact that you already have him in your pond is the fun part. He does love you. David and I will help. You're doing all the right things. Just keep doing what you're doing, and let David and I bait the hooks. In time he'll be yours."

Jan wheeled up to the table as Rachel placed a plate before her and sat down to her own plate. She smiled at Jan across the table.

"Basi', Jan, drana nezrunh. I am glad I have come. (Thank you, Jan, today it is good. I am glad I have come.)"

True to her promise, Jan called David and Kimberly, requesting their help. After they arrived, she phoned Jerry. "Jerry, Rachel said you are overloaded with book work that has piled up during your absence. Since I did all the book work for Doug when we had the hardware store, I'm really good at sorting out that kind of thing. Why don't you just load it all in a big box and David will drive over to get you. Bring it here and let me help you. Then we can catch a few more fish, and you can join us for trout and my potato salad for supper."

"Are you sure, Jan? I don't even know where to start myself. It's a mess."

"David's on his way. Get it all gathered together. If Sally doesn't mind, you can stay the night with David and Kim, and we can complete tomorrow whatever we don't get done tonight."

Jan hung up the phone and gave Rachel a most pleased-with-herself squinty smile.

David winked and ran his hand down the back of Rachel's head. "Wait for him, Rachel, be patient."

Kimberly came in with a large bowl of apples and gave David a quick kiss. "Stop at the store for ice cream, Honey. I'll make Jerry his favorite apple crisp. Oh, and Honey, we're almost out of toilet paper.

David nodded. He jumped into his Wrangler, and drove up the road toward the summit of Indian Pass.

Rachel drained the potatoes and eggs for the salad, and the three women visited as they prepared Jerry's favorite meal.

David and Sally helped Jerry get through the doorway and past the front seat of David's Jeep. He was finally settled across the back seat facing the driver's side.

"I'd suggest you use a can opener to get him out, David," Sally said. "I should have let you take my car."

"And leave his precious, shiny, red Jeep here for you to drive?" Jerry quipped. "He values that almost as much as Kimberly, short of sleeping with it."

David bopped Jerry on the head and then walked around and sat in the driver's seat.

Sally stuck her tongue out at Jerry and then smiled at him as she closed the door.

"I think I'll remove the seat and put you in through the back on a lawn chair pad when I bring you home," David said as he pulled away from the gallery.

David parked at the grocery store. "I'll be right back, Jerry." A few minutes later he returned with the ice cream and a large package of toilet paper.

Jerry reached into the front seat and opened the toilet paper package enough to pull out a roll. He tossed it up and caught it several times, chuckling to himself.

David glanced at him over his shoulder with a curious expression as he drove across the valley floor toward the pass. "We're so bored we're playing with toilet paper now?" he asked.

Suddenly, Jerry tossed the roll at David, hitting him in the backside of the head.

David made a slight swerve and glared at Jerry.

Jerry grinned. "Sorry, David. Danny made me do it!" Then he started to laugh as he pulled out another roll, tossing it up in the air.

David kicked the assault roll onto the other side of the Jeep and shook his head. "Bud, I don't know what happened to you in the Fairbanks hospital, but you have definitely returned home with an unstable mind."

For the rest of the journey to Indian Valley, David received a delightful memoir of a little bald-headed Indian boy named Danny Crow.

When Jerry and his crutches had finally dislodged from the

Jeep, Jerry met Rachel with a big hug, clearly glad for a chance to make up for the previous day's neglect.

Jan sat Jerry at the table and Rachel supported his cast on a pillow, making sure he was comfortable and taking every opportunity for an extra touch or caress that wasn't too obvious. Then she brought in fruit kabobs, whipped topping dip, and two tall glasses of lemonade.

David stood by grinning. Kimberly scowled at him and motioned with her head. Then she pulled him out the front door behind her. "Let's make ourselves scarce and let Rachel wile for a while," she whispered as they stepped onto the porch. She giggled, excited to be in on this wonderful scheme to submit Jerry to as much of Rachel's tender loving care as she could entice him with.

David nodded, giving Kimberly a quick kiss on the tip of her nose. "Jerry, Kim, and I are going to get the Jeep ready for easier transport," he called through the doorway. Then he put his arm around Kimberly's slender waist and pulled her against him as they walked to the Jeep. He tossed the toilet paper into the rear seat and chuckled as he threw the loose roll into the back as well. Then he helped Kimberly into the Jeep, paused, and smoothed her auburn hair over her shoulder. Stirred by the budding romance slyly being waged in his mother's cabin, he embraced Kimberly and placed a warm and thrilling kiss on her lips.

She responded, snuggling against her husband. As he stood back against the Jeep door and grinned, she giggled. "And what brought that on so suddenly? Not that I'm complaining, of course." she said. He just embraced her again and kissed her more fervently. Then he squeezed her hand and closed the Jeep door.

Rachel hovered near Jerry while he placed bills, papers, mail, and other items in piles on the table. She stooped at his side, gently placing her hand on his knee, her fingers moving ever so slightly, as she pulled items from the box and handed them to him. Then she leaned across him, her fingers resting on his shoulder or gently running her fingers across the back of his neck and ear as she handed Jan the piles he was sorting.

Jan pretended not to notice Jerry's occasional pause. His

frequent quirk of the head or slight shiver as Rachel's touch and nearness distracted him, but she smiled with a quick nod at Rachel when Jerry wasn't looking.

Rachel's presence, so near, was wearing on Jerry's reserve as her soft touch tingled through him. Her silky hair, bathed in the sweet scent of honeysuckle, repeatedly swept against his cheek and arm as she worked with the piles in front of him. As she stood near, her hand resting across his shoulder while Jan reviewed some papers, Jerry's arm raised until his hand rested ever so lightly against the small of Rachel's back. He gently rubbed his hand upward on her spine, and then back to her waist, as soft as a whisper.

In that gentle caress, tender and voluntary against her spine, was another whisper of hope to Rachel's soul. She responded by running the tips of her fingernails up and down in the hairline of Jerry's neck. The light pressure rubbing against her back became more firm and deliberate.

Later, at the pond, the lazy evening wore on, and sunset spread it's myriad of brilliant colors drifting across the surface of the pond as Jan, Jerry, David, and Kimberly visited. Rachel stood quietly beside Jerry, running her fingers gently through his hair. He moved his head under her fingers, absorbing her gentle caress while trying to pretend not to notice.

David winked at Rachel with a definitive nod, and Kimberly smiled, her beautiful eyes speaking in silent agreement. She clasped David's hand in hers and laid her head against his shoulder.

Oh, how Rachel envied the closeness she could sense between them! She was grateful to have such supportive and caring friends. "Nezruhn," she whispered to herself. "It is good."

The group returned to the cabin to prepare the freshly caught trout for supper. Kimberly and David walked with Rachel behind Jan and Jerry.

"You've got him purring tonight, Rachel," David said, grinning approvingly as he carried the lawn chairs under his arms.

Kimberly carried the fishing creel and poles, smiling and softly humming the wedding march. Roxanne was gone now from

Jerry's life. He had sent her away when she was willing to embrace him, to give herself back to him body and soul. As much as he had adored her, he had stood his ground and taught her the importance of her marriage commitment. True to the nobility Kimberly had come to admire and respect in this good and faithful friend, he had remained firm in rightness. How he deserved the joy and fulfillment that she and David shared even that very day. She prayed with all her heart that he could heal, and that he could take this lovely Indian woman who adored him into himself to become one as she and David had become one.

❉

Eric trudged home through the drizzling rain, but he didn't want to go home. He had known Roxanne would fly away while he was gone when he placed the airline ticket on the table. He didn't expect her to ever return.

As he neared the apartment, he turned and went the other way, stopping in a café for a cup of hot chocolate. His raincoat dripped onto the vinyl seat of the booth and trickled cold and wet beneath his legs and backside. He shivered, but he didn't care. He ran his brown forefinger around the rim of his cup, staring out the window at the droplets winding their strange erratic paths down the window glass. They reminded Eric of the erratic ups and downs of his unstable marriage to the dearest little wife he could have ever dreamed to call his own. Yet, she was not his own. And, but for a few precious days during the search for his father's lost mine when Eric held her near and placed his longing kisses on her willing lips, he wondered if she ever had been. The rapture of those moments had brought her here with him, but when the moments were gone, her heart belonged to another man, the man he had betrayed while taking advantage of his unselfish service. Eric didn't like himself much anymore. He had let his father down, embarrassed his sister, and offended his new friends who were, without obligation, rendering service to his family.

Yet he cared so very much for the bright, lovely, and precious

little fawn he had discovered that he had misplaced his values. With careless disregard, he had cast scruples aside to claim a treasure he had no right to. He had confused her, and then, when his deceit was discovered during one of her moments of weakness by the kiss Jerry had witnessed, she had given up, thinking all was lost. Eric had taken her to himself before her troubled guilt and confusion had time to be resolved in her anguished mind. He had brought this grief and emptiness on himself. He would go home alone eventually, but not yet. For now he would let the hot chocolate warm the inside of his stomach, but nothing could warm the inside of his aching heart.

✳

Roxanne had arrived a week earlier. She'd filled the refrigerator and pantry with all of Eric's favorite foods. She had baked desserts and planned menus for a month of meals. Then she scrubbed and polished every nook and corner of their little ocean view apartment, seeing the beauty of the wood grain molding and fireplace mantle for the first time.

Finally, she pulled Jerry's handkerchief from her purse and buried her nose and face against it, deeply breathing the mild pine and Sweet William aroma one last time. "Thank you for your kind and forgiving heart, Jerry Stone," she whispered. "I'll do as you said. I will let him be what I want. I'll give to him what you refused, and I will make him happy." Then she wiped her eyes on Jerry's handkerchief and tucked it away in a little silver jewelry box. She opened the lid of her small cedar chest that she had brought back with her to Kodiak and laid the silver box under her old childhood teddy bear in the bottom of the chest.

She had no idea when Eric might return, but she was ready for him to come home, to come home to her. Looking at the raindrops sleeting down the windowpane behind the lace curtains, she thought of Eric, out in the rain and cold, being tossed on the waves of a stormy sea. She put on her hooded raincoat and walked down the street to the rocky shore. She shivered against the ocean air, breathing the fishy smell of the sea. Feeling invigorated by the sights and smells she had never before appreciated, she gazed across the varying gray and white waves and beyond. Somewhere on the horizon the ocean met the varying gray and white hues of the sky and blended together. Sea and sky as one, like a magnificent marriage between the massive elements before her. *It really is very beautiful here*, she thought, deeply breathing the cool, misty air.

❋

Eric finally left his empty cup on the table and walked home. He entered the apartment, dim inside from the stormy weather on the outside. He didn't turn on the light. The dimness fit his mood. He hung his raincoat and hat in the closet and sat in the easy chair in front of the cold fireplace, with the stillness surrounding him for some time. Then, feeling a chill in the empty room, he arose and stooped to build a fire in the concrete firebox. He had just sat down again, still feeling cold and empty in spite of the cheery warmth from the fireplace. Suddenly, he heard the door open. Startled and expecting no one, he stood and turned toward the door.

❋

Dripping water from her raincoat, Roxanne stood staring at the burning fireplace. Then Eric arose from the chair and turned toward her, his face puzzled at first, and then disbelieving, as his eyes met Roxanne's. His eyes softened, and then brimmed with tears as she ran to him.

"Eric," she screeched, throwing her arms around his neck as cold raindrops from her hood mingled with a few run away tears on his face and dripped down his neck.

The chilling wetness of her raincoat seeping through his shirt went unnoticed as warmth filled his being. He embraced his wife with a breathless passion that made it hard for her to breathe.

"Roxanne, Roxanne!" He crushed her head against his shoulder, petting the hood of the raincoat as he looked heavenward and whispered, "Thank you!" Then he buried his face against the wet neck of her raincoat, lifting her feet from the floor, and just holding her, desperately holding her. "What—? How—? I didn't think—"

Roxanne touched his face and turned it toward hers and smiled. "Welcome home, Eric. Welcome to our home. I love you!" Her face reached toward his, with her brown eyes dancing and bright. Her lips were parted, waiting with no reserve, and her arms were tight around his neck. He smothered her lips with all the longing he had felt for the two longest months of his life. She was giving herself to him, here, and now, and forever. Promises she had made in a drab courtroom, with uncertainty and remorse, suddenly became promises of love, commitment, and desire. He lowered her to the floor and unzipped her raincoat. It slid from her shoulders and fell as he gently wrapped her slender body in his arm and slid the other arm beneath her knees. Lifting her against himself, he gazed at her, still unbelieving.

She tenderly ran her hand across his cheek and smiled.

He carried her to the bedroom. Then, caressing her lips with all the fire he felt on his own, he stepped inside and pushed the door shut with his foot.

CHAPTER TWENTY-FOUR

The rich fall colors began to fade. Crimson reds turned into shades of brown, and the bright gold lost its luster, turning a mousy yellow. The tired trees released their hold, and their leaves yielded to the autumn breezes. A thick carpet began to cover the forest floor, while leaves swirled and danced on the breeze to their final resting place, their fleeting beauty soon to be forgotten beneath the frozen snows of winter. The pond was covered with a variable quilt of colors, drifting among blue patches of sky and wispy clouds, floating on the rippling surface of the water.

Rachel's footsteps, soft and light, barely rustled the leaves as she walked beside Jan's wheelchair along the shore of the pond. In contrast with the feather lightness of the leaves, a heaviness had settled in Rachel's heart. Jerry's reservations seemed to be weakening at times, and there were special moments and touches that passed between Rachel and Jerry which assured Rachel that Jan's conviction of Jerry's love for her was truth. However, Rachel sensed that somehow time was running out.

Jerry's cast would soon be removed, and his body would be whole again. If only there was a way to cast and heal his will to commit and trust.

Soon the winter snows would cover the mountain pass between Slatersville and Indian Valley. Yet, the sixty-seven-mile drive on curving snowy roads was not the reason for the heaviness in her heart. She tried to dismiss the feeling, because it could not be validated, but it lingered, almost as a premonition, and would not go away.

A gusty breeze suddenly swirled leaves from the ground and lifted Jan's lap quilt. Rachel bent to tuck it back in place.

"You're troubled about something, Rachel," Jan said, laying her hand on Rachel's cheek. "What is it?"

"I do not know. I feel unsettled somehow, but I have no reason."

"Is it Jerry?"

"He is always in my thoughts and heart, but I have no answers. I do not understand this feeling." Hoping the uneasiness would dispel, or that reasons for her anxiety would come to light, Rachel could do nothing but go about life as normal.

She and Jan had become very close. She enjoyed giving care and help to a wonderful woman who gave so much in return. Jan's nurture and concern for Rachel was so kind and motherly that Rachel felt guilty accepting any payment beyond room and board in Jan's lovely mountain cabin. Both David and Jan insisted on a wage that far surpassed a comfortable figure for Rachel, though. When she objected, they would not listen. They both told Rachel that her dedicated care and companionship were worth far more than the meager wage they said would not be reduced.

Rachel loved working for these good people. She could be truly happy here, but somewhere in the back of her mind, the unsettled feeling hinted that she would have to go away. She kept the impression to herself, not wanting to cause concern over an unfounded qualm.

※

The Monday morning of the first week in November was the big day for Jerry. His cast was finally removed. The loose calcium had adjoined the bone, and additional calcium growth had healed the break with a firm welding of the bone.

Sally drove Jerry home from the doctor's office as Jerry rubbed and scratched the leg through his pants, moving it around for the first time in nine weeks. When he got out of the car, he put his first full weight on it and nearly fell.

"Jerry, the doctor said to use your crutches for a couple more days until your leg adjusts and gets stronger," Sally said. She had grabbed his crutches from the back seat when he got out without them. She hurried around the car as he caught his balance by clinging to the door handle and the car door. She held the crutches out in front of him.

"I don't need them, Sally, I just need to work it a little."

"The doctor said—"

"Sally, I know what the doctor said. I'm fine." He took an unsteady step forward.

"Crutches—now!" she said, stepping in front of him and blocking his path.

He glowered at her and grasped the crutches, realizing that she was right, but too proud to admit it. He'd thought the awkward cast was responsible for the weakness he now felt without it.

"Bossy sister," he grumbled, taking his disappointment out on her.

"Stubborn brother," she grumbled back, walking ahead of him and unlocking the gallery door. She pulled off the temporarily closed sign and turned the open sign around.

Jerry worked his way through the house, went into his bedroom, and closed the door. He set his crutches aside and tried to walk, bracing himself on his dresser, but lost his balance and fell on his bed. With a sigh of defeat, he reached for his crutches and began pacing back and forth across his bedroom, putting as much weight on his leg as he could. "Bossy sister," he grumbled again.

"I heard that," Sally called through his door. "You could have said thank you, instead. It's a long walk from the doctor's office."

Jerry loved his sister dearly, and she was right. She had been wonderful to him, waiting on him, and caring for the shop during his long absence, but sometimes she was too much of a big sister.

This just wasn't a good time for her to pamper him. He'd so looked forward to freedom. The cast was finally gone, and he couldn't even walk. That's what he needed—to just walk. He put on his jacket, took his crutches, and headed for the door.

"Where are you going?" Sally asked.

"Out," he said, closing the door behind him. He should apologize, but he'd do it when he came home. Right now he was irritated, and it wasn't her fault. He'd do better when his mind was calm.

Sally opened the door. "Jerry, what's wrong?" she called after him. "Don't go. It's too soon."

"I'll be back, I just need to walk." He turned at the corner of his shop and walked down the sidewalk. Without thinking about the direction he was taking, he suddenly realized he was walking past the Slater mansion where Roxanne had lived. She had been here a month earlier to visit her parents before returning to her husband in Kodiak. Jerry paused for a moment with his memories. Suddenly, he heard barking. Spooks ran toward him, yapping ferociously, ready to defend his territory—that is, as long as the intruder was on the other side of the fence.

"Shut up, Spooks," Jerry said. The little yellow dog halted and stared at Jerry, recognizing him. Then, as Jerry walked with his crutches clicking on the sidewalk, Spooks resumed his ferocious barking, as if challenging the crutches. Jerry walked on, chuckling, and he felt at peace in his heart. Roxanne was gone, and so was the pain.

"So, just what is bugging me?" Jerry said aloud. "Too many weeks of confinement, I guess," he answered himself. He put some weight on his leg as he walked, relieved to feel the numbness disappearing. This was good. The more he moved his leg, applying pressure between his foot and the ground, the more alive his leg began to feel. He walked and worked his leg for a long time, not realizing how long he had been gone.

He heard a car horn behind him. Sally glared at him as she pulled alongside. "Get in Jerry, it's going to rain. Just what do you think you're doing, anyway?"

He had planned to apologize, but the tone of her voice grated on him, and he felt his big sister irritation returning. "Well, what does it look like I'm doing? I said I was going for a walk."

"You've been gone for more than two hours. I've been driving all over town looking for you. Now, get in."

He was tired and his leg was aching, so he opened the car door and climbed in beside her. He could see that she had been crying, but he didn't say anything because he still didn't know what had triggered his frustration in the first place.

She drove in silence, pouting like she used to when she didn't get her way.

"Hey, you missed the turn," he said.

"We're not going home. Jan wants to see you."

"You called her?"

Sally nodded.

"About this?"

Sally nodded again.

"Oh, that's great! I get a little discouraged and irritated so I go for a walk, and you go off the deep end, calling and getting everyone worried and excited. Sally, I'm a big boy, in case you haven't noticed. I can take care of myself."

"Then maybe I should just pack up and leave," she said, brushing a tear from her cheek and staring at the road ahead.

"Sally, that's not what I'm saying. I don't want you to leave. Let's just turn around and go home. There's no sense in taking a little disagreement and turning it into a major production."

"I don't do major productions, Jerry, you do! Only you do it inside your head so no one can get in and help you. You just get silent and brood for days. The only difference between you and Dad is that you don't drink yourself into oblivion, and you don't blow up, and rant, and yell, and hit people. But you hide just like he did!"

"That's about as cruel a thing as you can say. I'm nothing like Dad. Sometimes I just don't like to talk."

"Or face reality, either. As long as you're in your comfort zone, you're fine. But life doesn't happen in comfort zones, Jerry. So you're missing life, just like Daddy did."

"What in the Sam hill are you talking about? I was frustrated. I went for a walk! And, now, I'm like my father?"

"Let her go, Jerry! It's over. Let Roxanne go. Rachel loves you! Can't you see that? Stop hiding behind your broken heart and give life a chance."

"Hush up, Sally! You're so far out in space that an asteroid could hit you, and you'd think it was a bus. You don't have a clue what you're talking about."

"And you do? You don't even know what you want when it's right in front of your nose."

Jerry pushed his glasses up on his nose and folded his arms across his chest. He stared at the forest landscape as they wound up the pass to Indian Valley. He had changed his mind about going home. The only thing there was Sally, silence, troubling words about him and his father, and his irritation. Sally had no right to assume that he was still clinging to Roxanne when he had put her to rest. Roxanne had nothing to do with Rachel.

He knew Rachel loved him. He could see it in her eyes and feel it in her touch. He had felt it throughout his whole body and soul as he yielded to a kiss one day, holding her, and kissing her like he had never kissed anyone. But it was too soon too fast. His heart just couldn't go there, yet. He needed time. Lots of it.

Jerry wondered how Sally knew of Rachel's love for him. Then he recalled David's off-the-wall comment about him marrying Rachel. Suddenly, Jerry began to see a stark reality. He had been the object of a conspiracy. His book work dilemma, lots of invitations, and not to David and Kimberly's house, but to Jan's, with Rachel always seated next to him. And Rachel's attentiveness and the way everyone just disappeared at opportune moments leaving Rachel and him alone—it had all been a ploy. His closest friends, and probably Sally too, had been meddling with him, playing on his feelings, and setting him up. Rachel was in on it too. He had trusted her, and she had made him a spectacle. He was embarrassed and offended.

By the time they reached Indian Valley, Jerry didn't want

to see anyone. He got out of the car, grabbed his crutches, and walked to the far side of the pond, feeling irked and used. He sat on a log, out of sight, as Sally's words returned and echoed in his mind. He had forgiven his father. He had tried to understand his father. He had stayed with him, and cared for him, and cleaned up after him. He loved him deeply for the good man he used to be, for the happy memories from his earlier childhood, but he didn't like who his father became. Did Sally really believe her own words? Jerry believed that she must.

The rain Sally had worried about finally began to fall. Jerry pulled his jacket around him and settled on the ground against the trunk of a large tree, but soon the rain was seeping through his jacket and running down his neck. The chill finally forced him to seek shelter. He stepped onto the covered porch of Jan's cabin and sat on a log bench. A moment later, Rachel came outside with David's father's jacket.

"My goodness, Jerry, you are drenched. Here, put this on and let me take your wet jacket to the dryer."

He was shivering, so he stood up and gladly accepted the dry jacket. "Thank you, Rachel."

She started to brush the rain from his curly hair, but he moved away and shook his head, brushing his own hand against the wetness.

"I'm fine, thanks."

"Jerry, you are shivering. Let us go inside." She started to smooth the collar of the jacket, but he walked around her outstretched hand and sat on the bench again.

"No, I like the rain."

"Jerry, is something wrong?" She reached out to touch the back of his neck, but he caught her hand, held it for a brief moment, and let it go.

"I'm not in the mood for company, right now. I'd rather be alone."

"Very well, Jerry, I will go back inside. Would you like a drink? We have some hot chocolate warming."

"No, I said I'm fine!"

Rachel left Jerry alone, put his jacket in the dryer, and went straight to her room and closed the door.

David saw the hurt on her face as she passed, but she tried to smile as though nothing was wrong and pretended to go to her room to hang up her jacket. She closed her door behind her, though. Sally had told the group that she and Jerry had an argument and that he was grumpy, but that was no excuse for him to hurt Rachel's feelings.

David stepped onto the porch. "What's up, Jerry?" he asked.

"Nothing," Jerry muttered.

"What's wrong with Rachel?"

"How would I know? I just told her I'd rather be alone."

"What's eating you besides an argument with Sally?"

"Nothing," he grumbled.

"Jerry, this is me, David. Come clean."

"Okay, since you insist, it's you, Sally, and everyone else trying to push me into something I'm not ready for. I know what you've all been up to. Rachel too. Everyone just needs to back off and give me some time and space."

"What makes you think—"

"David, this conspiracy of yours is about as obvious as a cow in a pig pen. I don't need to be smothered by everyone trying to help me find happiness. I'll do what I need to do when I'm ready. It's my life, and I'm not an idiot."

"That's debatable," David mumbled.

"What?"

"Jerry, since earliest childhood I've looked up to you. You were always the noblest, the strongest, the kindest, and the bravest. This is the first time in your life I've ever seen you be unkind, the first time I've ever seen you playing the coward."

Jerry was so shocked that he couldn't speak at first. Then he glared at David. "You don't have a clue what I've been through, do you?"

"No, Jerry, I don't, but I know there's a wonderful woman in there who loves you, and you're pushing her away so you can wallow in the past. It's time to move on. You're a Hedgehog, Jerry!

That's all I have to say. Come in when you're ready. Supper is on."

There was an unusual quiet at the meal as casual conversation about nothing in general bypassed the feelings and concerns on everyone's mind. Jerry and Sally left shortly after the meal, and David and Kimberly left as soon as the dishes were done. Rachel had excused herself from the meal, due to a headache. She didn't come out of her room until time to help Jan prepare for bed.

Just before ten o'clock the phone rang. Jan answered it while Rachel hung her clothes in the closet. "Rachel, it's for you." She handed Rachel the phone.

"Hello, Connie! How wonderful to hear from—what? They are certain? When is it scheduled? He is? Tell him I will come. Yes, soon. Thank you for calling me. Good-bye."

Jan took the phone from Rachel and hung it up as Rachel sank to her knees. Jan placed her hand on Rachel's head, smoothing her long black hair. "The reason for your premonition has been revealed, hasn't it?" she asked lovingly. "I know you have to leave me, my dear. I will miss you very much. Tomorrow we'll make arrangements. Try to get some sleep tonight."

CHAPTER TWENTY-FIVE

Fighting tears of disappointment, Rachel sat on the magenta colored cushions of the oak rocking chair, hurt and confused by Jerry's cold and almost hostile response to her. She looked through the lace curtains. Little droplets of rain trickled down the window as though coaxing her tears to join them. She dried her eyes instead. Time had run out. Rachel could feel it as her longing for Jerry merged with the worrisome nagging she felt inside. Maybe in time Jerry would have given himself to her, as she was ready and willing to give herself to him, but his cold reaction to her a few moments earlier had spilled her hopes onto the porch beneath his feet and crutches. She had given him all she had to give, and it was not enough to reach into his dark places and draw him into the light.

She hugged her empty arms against her breast, lowered her head, and rocked as though trying to comfort a missing child. "Doddhineh sidraya, enshuya. Xenesyayh ixu. Bedraya, still edli, nedoth. Si can be betlanh, but nejejet si 'etodel bech'o'. Nejejet si will never learn to walk in bekatreth. (Be quiet my heart; leave it be. I talk for nothing. His heart, still it is cold; it is heavy. I can be his friend, but I am afraid I will go away from him. I am afraid I will never learn to walk in his moccasins.)"

She realized she had fallen asleep when she noticed it was

dark outside. Everyone had gone, and the house was silent. She quickly rose from the chair to check on Jan, who was already preparing for bed.

When Rachel answered the phone Jan handed her, she was glad to hear her friend's voice. However, the sad news Connie shared with her was crushing. Growing rapidly around Danny's remaining kidney, another tumor had been discovered. It was cancer. However, because it was encapsulated, it had not spread. He would be operated on a week from today, his remaining kidney removed, and he would immediately be started on dialysis. His name and studies had been placed on a waiting list for a kidney transplant. Danny was frightened, and he was asking for Rachel.

The first thing in the morning, Rachel called to make flight reservations. She would fly to Fairbanks, take a one-day helicopter trip to visit her father, and then return to Fairbanks to be with Danny.

She remembered that night in the hospital when she had tucked Danny in bed and placed his stocking cap on his shiny bald head. She had kissed his cheek and squeezed his hand. In his sleep, his little fingers had closed around hers and held on tightly until deeper sleep had relaxed his small, brown hand. "Oh, Danny, how I wish—" she had whispered, never completing the thought that was forming in her heart. She had dismissed it, only as a sweet thought that was not possible. Now, with a tremendous warmth swelling inside her, she wondered if she might be able to adopt Danny. Although she was single, she was a nurse and had the skill and training to care for him. She had been seeking a purpose in her life, someone she could give herself and all of her love to. Why not this precious, little boy who already held a treasured place in her heart? Why couldn't she be Danny's Mamma?"

Tears began to flow as the warmth continued to swell, and a breathless thrill passed from her head to her toes. Goose bumps rose on her arms as she saw in her mind a beautiful, young Indian mother, dressed in glowing white caribou skins, smiling and reaching out to her, to give her little boy to another mother. Rachel fell to her knees beside her bed, weeping into the magenta

quilt. "Thank you, thank you," she prayed, knowing more strongly than words, or time, or distance that this precious gift, a child heaven sent, was meant to be her own little son. She made the call immediately to the Children's Services in Fairbanks. Fearful of his frightening illness, the kind Birchwoods had declined to keep Danny, and he had no home. Rachel called a lawyer, requesting that immediate adoption procedures be started and expedited due to Danny's serious illness. The hospital and Danny's doctors would support her. Rachel had no doubt it would happen, and soon, for the spirits had whispered truth to her heart.

Jan called David and Kimberly as Rachel packed, and they quickly came to help.

"I have one request," Rachel asked of them. "Jerry must not know why I am leaving. He would come for Danny. He must not. If Jerry is ever to be truly happy, he must search his own heart, and he must come for himself."

David hugged Rachel with all the care he would for a dear sister. "I agree, Rachel. I promise we'll take care of Jerry. You worry about Danny. He needs you. We'll honor your request. We will greatly miss you. You've made a lasting impression on all of our lives, and especially Jerry's. We'll never forget you."

David carried Rachel's trunk and bags to the Jeep as Kimberly and Jan escorted Rachel outside. Kimberly embraced Rachel. "I was so enjoying having a sister I always wished for, just across the valley." She struggled to hold back tears, then she said, "Oh phooey, I don't care if I get you wet. Please write to us. We love you, Rachel. I miss you terribly already."

Rachel knelt at Jan's knees. "I am so sorry to leave you. I could have gladly stayed with you always. You blessed me more than I ever helped you. I have long missed my dear mother. You have been that to me." She held Jan's hands against her cheeks.

Jan nodded quietly and then took a deep breath and spoke. "Like the beauty of the sunsets we have shared beside our lovely little pond, the sun rises in glory in another place, and in other lives also precious to God. May he go with you and your little Danny Boy, and bless you always with his great love." She kissed

Rachel's cheek, embraced her, and then quickly turned her chair around and drove up the ramp and into the cabin.

✳

David parked his Wrangler in front of Jerry's shop and opened the passenger door for Rachel. She clenched her fists, breathing deeply, fighting for courage and control as she went to bid farewell to her beloved Jerry.

Jerry's response to David and Rachel was cordial, but somewhat formal. His hearty grin and sense of humor seemed to have lost their source. "Well, for what purpose are we honored with this visit? I didn't know you were coming, or Sally and I would have saved some waffles for you."

David stood quietly by as Rachel spoke. "Jerry, Sally, I have come to tell you goodbye. Something has come up, and I am needed at home. I will be leaving within the hour. I am sorry for the short notice, but I just found out last night."

A dead silence filled the room as Sally sat down suddenly. Jerry, who was already sitting, just stared at Rachel as though he had not heard a word she said. Then his eyes grew wide, not believing.

"When will you be coming back?" Sally asked.

"I will not be coming back. I will stay in Alaska."

Jerry finally found his voice. "But Rachel, Jan needs you. David and Kimberly need you. How will they ever get along without you?" His voice carried a note of alarm that David realized wasn't about him, or Kimberly, or Jan.

"Jerry, I am only a nurse. They got along without me before I came. There are many nurses. I am certain they will find a replacement. Jan understands that I must go."

"Is it your father? Is he ill?"

"No Jerry, it is personal business, but I am needed."

"But you're needed here."

"By whom? You are well and about now. You and Sally have each other, and David and Kim are wonderful to Jan, and she to them." Her soft, hazel eyes looked steadily into his deep, blue eyes, and she spoke from her heart. "No Jerry, I am not needed here."

Her words, stated as a simple matter of fact, felt like a slap in the face to Jerry. David could see in Jerry's eyes what he couldn't put into words. This seemed a good time to leave him and Rachel alone. He motioned to Sally and she and David went into the kitchen. They sat at the table and Sally handed David a soda.

"Wow," Sally said. "This will be a double whammy for Jerry. I know he can be an obstinate fool, but I'm sure Rachel means far more to him than he will ever admit. First Roxanne, and now Rachel. I'm worried about him already, David."

"You and me both," David said, taking a drink of his soda. "You and me both."

Jerry was stunned, and his legs felt weak, so he didn't try to stand. Could this really be happening? Rachel, going away, far away? Suddenly, he felt horrible for his abrupt attitude toward her yesterday. Was that why she was leaving? He had been angry. He had been incensed. He had been a jerk. She had taken his cold response to her kindness graciously and had said nothing. Even through his pride and indignation, he had sensed her confusion and hurt, but he let her go, feeling he was justified. He had not seen her again last night. Now she was leaving in less than an hour, and he couldn't make it up to her.

Jerry reached for her hand. "Rachel, I'm deeply sorry about last night. I don't have any reasons. I was irritated and discouraged, and you got dumped on. I was terribly rude and insensitive. I'm so deeply sorry." He kissed her hand, but she did not step close.

She smiled and nodded. "It is in the past, Jerry. It does not matter now."

"Will you be in Fairbanks again?" Jerry asked, continuing to hold her hand.

"Things are uncertain. Probably for a while, at least."

"Will you write to me?"

"I . . . I do not know." She lowered her head.

"I understand, I know I let you down." Then he grasped her

hand in both of his, his eyes pleading. "Is there anything I might say or do that would persuade you to stay?"

She raised her head. The love was still bright in her eyes, that, and great sadness, but there was also a new look of strength and conviction. "Not now, I have to go."

Jerry bowed his head, blinking hard against unwanted tears. "I will miss you, sweet Rachel, my precious friend. May the angels smile on you always as they smiled on me when they sent you to me." He found his strength and stood, pulling her to him and looking deeply into her eyes. "I owe you my life, and I can never repay you for your kindness and devoted care. You'll never be far from me," he swallowed hard struggling to speak, "because you'll always be in my heart."

Rachel's eyes were brimming with tears now, her resolve for courage wearing thin. She longed to throw her arms around his neck as she had once before, and never let go. But she could not go into the dark places of Jerry's heart, nor could she remove shadows from the past, and Danny needed her. She took a deep breath and smiled through her tears. "Goodbye, Jerry. I will always love you."

Jerry crushed her to him and buried his face in her silky, black hair, breathing deeply the soft aroma of honeysuckle. He tucked her sweet smell, her softness in his arms, deep into his memories where he would never forget. His body shook from the emotion welling up inside him.

Then she gently pulled free and walked to the door. Without looking back, she said, "Tell Sally goodbye, and tell David I am ready."

"Would you like me to go to the airport with you?" Jerry asked as he swallowed the lump in his throat.

"No . . . I love you, Jerry." She opened the door and was gone.

After David left for the airport with Rachel, Jerry, his jaw set and his lips drawn in a tight line, limped to his bedroom and closed the door. Sally sighed and sat down to finish her soda.

Jerry sat on his bed, staring at the closed door. She was gone. His Rachel, the one who had dedicated herself, her time, and her

means to him in his great need, had found him lacking in hers. His Rachel who had openly and honestly declared her love for him, who had drawn fire from his soul in just one kiss, was gone. Rachel, who had nursed, guarded, helped, and even lectured him when he was brooding, leaving Danny alone in his needs. "What can you do about it, hibernate in here like some growling old bear?" Rachel had scolded. "You told me once that you were glad you still have your life. What life? To lay in here day after day, feeling sorry for yourself while a little boy down the hall suffers with a broken heart?" Last night he had rejected Rachel's gentle touch when she was sincerely caring and attentive. Last night he had left her alone to suffer with a broken heart, even though he had seen it in her eyes. He was too self-absorbed and brooding, just like Sally had said.

Now, Rachel was gone, and so was his anger. The conspiracy looked different in the light of a new day. True friends and a worried sister had all cared enough to try to help a beautiful, patient woman reach with love inside his closed and brooding heart.

Suddenly, Jerry saw his father sitting in a dark room, staring at nothing, hiding from his pain, and Jerry hung his head. Rachel had offered her love to him without reservation. "So you're missing life, just like Daddy did," Sally had said. Jerry felt sick as a heavy emptiness grew in his heart where he realized Rachel had been and would always belong. Now, there would be no more tender moments and gentle caresses. No more beautiful smiles like the one when she pushed Danny's bike into the room. No more scent of honeysuckle in her silky strands of hair. No more, Rachel. He thought he had time, time to know her better, to be close, to just watch her. He loved to just watch her, to bask in her presence and warmth, to stroll by the pond and just hold her hand. He'd never even been able to do that. He could have last night after the rain stopped. He could have stood with his arms around her waist, her body backed against his as they watched the sunset's brilliant colors on the pond. But it was too late, now. He had let her slip through his fingers.

Suddenly, Jerry wanted to be back in Fairbanks, back in the

hospital, his leg in traction, laughing at Rachel as a strand of toilet paper drifted from the curtain and fell across her face. That had been the happiest time in his life, and he hadn't even known it until now. Jerry's mind took him back there, seeing things in a new light, a bright light of clearness and understanding that he had never before noticed. He pulled the box of Danny's things from the shelf and opened it. He thumbed through the drawings, smiling as he saw Danny in his mind's eye. He gazed at the simple beauty of a little boys carving and felt wonder at the courage of the child. Then his eyes fell upon the menu. He picked it up and turned it over, reading Rachel's message. "He starts chemotherapy again tomorrow. It is hard on him. He is brave, but he does not like to talk about it. He will be glad to have your company today. It will take his mind off his fears. Thank you. You're wonderful! With all my love, Rachel."

With all her love, even way back then, Jerry thought, tucking the menu in his shirt pocket. He looked again at the carving. Then he remembered Danny, proudly modeling his caribou skins the day he was discharged, and his great courage as he bravely stepped across the hospital door threshold into a new and uncertain life with strangers he had barely met. Danny was no coward!

After Danny was gone and after Rachel's long walk to grieve for the child, with emotions close to the surface, she had thrown her arms around Jerry's neck and held onto him, almost desperately. "Just hold me," she had whispered. "Just hold me." Then she had turned her face to him, her fingers brushing across his chin and cheek. Her eyes, her beautiful eyes, held so much love and warmth in them. Why hadn't he noticed the depth of yearning and love in her eyes? Then her thick dark lashes fluttering shut, and the kiss. He felt the kiss, again, now, burning through his heart, consuming him. He had yielded to her for that moment, and felt all the joy and fulfillment he had ever desired. Why, only for that moment? Why not forever? He remembered so vividly her softness in his arms, the fire burning on his lips.

He had been afraid to commit, afraid to trust what his heart and this most beloved and precious woman were trying to tell him. David was right. He had been a coward. *Damn my father for wasting his life!* he thought. *Damn me, for being like my father!* Jerry burst through his bedroom door, slamming it behind him with force. Sally jumped, nearly spilling her soda and stared at Jerry.

"Take me to the airport, NOW!" he demanded, grabbing his jacket and limping too fast to the front door. Sally grabbed her jacket and keys and then snatched his crutches from the corner as she locked the door behind her. She handed the crutches to Jerry.

He flung them into the back seat. I don't need crutches anymore, not any crutches ever! He sat in the seat, his arms folded across his chest and his face set and firm with determination. "Hurry!" he commanded.

David was walking to his Jeep when they arrived. Jerry thrust himself from the car. "Where is she?"

David pointed at the airplane just lifting off from the ground.

Jerry bolted into the tiny airport. "You've got to cancel that flight that just took off. It's an emergency. They have to turn around!"

"I'm sorry, Sir, we can't do that. We can send a message to deal with your emergency when they touch down. What is the problem?"

David was pulling at Jerry's sleeve. "We'll decide what to do and then let you know," he told the agent.

Jerry followed David out the door and limped to the fence. Clutching the wire in his hands, he stared at the plane growing smaller and smaller while his Rachel flew out of his arms forever. He kicked the fence hard with his good leg and then laid his face on the back of his hands, shaking his head and moaning.

David and Sally exchanged concerned expressions and quietly waited until Jerry finally turned around. Without saying a word, he limped to the car and got in.

"David, I don't want to take him home like this. Can we come over?"

"Of course, Sally. You know you don't ever have to ask."

"I just know we won't be good company today. I'll put the "be back tomorrow" sign in the door, and then will you follow us to Indian Valley? He's terribly upset."

"Sure, I'll follow you."

Jerry insisted on going in at the gallery. He came back out, hugging a cardboard box in his arms. In addition to Danny's treasures in the box was a package of pictures Rachel had given him when she had them developed. They were pictures of Danny's farewell, pictures of Jerry's "little hospital family," as Rachel had called them. Jerry laid his head against the back of the seat and closed his eyes, hugging the box tightly against his chest. He was silent all the way to Indian Valley.

CHAPTER TWENTY-SIX

Sitting at the table in Jan's dining area adjoining her comfortable living room, Kimberly, David, and Sally conversed in quiet tones.

Jerry limped beside Jan's wheelchair toward the pond.

Jerry was silent, so Jan left him to his thoughts. When they reached the pond, she drove close to the log so Jerry would have a place to sit. Instead, he clumsily sat on the ground next to her and laid his head in her lap as he had often done when he was young. She blinked back tears, aching for her Jerry Boy. Why had life dealt such a fine young man so many heavy blows? She understood him better than anyone, his fears, and heartaches. Now she understood his grief. She had sensed the depth of his love that he had been afraid to believe in. Her gentle hand softly patted his shoulder while she ran the fingers of her other hand through his hair like she had the night his father had taken his life. Comforted by a mother's touch, Jerry wrapped his arms around her knees and snuggled close. They sat in silence, watching fish darting after each other and pushing the leaves with their noses as they played in the crystal water of the pond.

"Thank you Mamma Young, for being such a wonderful mother to me. I miss mom when I'm with you because you are so much like her."

"She was a beautiful mother, Jerry, but I'm sure her love always has, and does, surround you. Doug is always near. Sometimes, I know he is right beside me. Love is stronger than death."

"Why was I so blind, Jan? Rachel is everything I ever wanted—all my dreams—little Danny-like kids running around under foot, a family filled with laughter and love. Why didn't I even once see that when it was right in my grasp?"

"I can only guess, Jerry, but it makes sense to me. Every time you had a family or the promise of one, you lost that family—your own parents, your father's tragic death. You blamed yourself, but it wasn't your fault. You tried so hard to get your real father back, but he'd disappeared in the alcohol. Then we lost Doug." She sighed, still missing her husband after eleven years. "Because you couldn't stop your father from drinking, you took responsibility for the drunk driver who caused our accident, blaming yourself, and we almost lost you too. You dared to dream again when Roxanne came into your life, and that didn't work out. I think that deep inside you've thought you were the cause. You were afraid to love Rachel, afraid you would lose her too."

"And now I've lost her."

"Are you so certain" She wanted to understand your needs, Jerry. She said she wanted to try to walk in your moccasins, but you wouldn't open up and let her help you."

"See, that's what I mean. How could she want me now? She gave me every chance possible to open up, to talk to her, and to make a commitment. How can a person, like me, lock himself in fear inside his stupid head when the key to unlock that fear is in his own hands?" He removed his arms from around Jan's knees and sat up, looking directly at her. He held his hands in front of him. "Do you know how many times I held that beautiful girl, right here, in these hands, and that's where she wanted to be?" He shook his head, gazing off in the distance. "I kept my moccasins and my heart locked away. I never let her in."

"Go after her, Jerry."

"I don't deserve her, even if I could bring her back."

"Why don't you let her decide? Alaska is far away, but it's not on another planet."

"I don't know how she could want me after I was such an insensitive and heartless jerk."

"You won't know unless you try. Where is your heart, now, my Jerry Boy?

"With her, wherever she is."

"Then put yourself where your heart is. Go after her."

They returned to the house, and Jan gave Jerry the list of names and phone numbers Rachel had given her when she first came. He located the number for Sam Duncan and placed the call. There was no answer.

Jerry was anxious, pacing back and forth, calling every few minutes with still no answer.

"David, find him something to do before he wears out my hardwood floor," Jan said when Jerry stepped onto the porch.

"Jerry, let's prune Mom's lilac bush. She'll keep trying to call."

"You were right about me, David," Jerry said, clipping off dead branches with pruning sheers. "I was everything you said I was, and an idiot besides. I'm really sorry. I was rude and surly with all of you. I know I was blind stupid, and you had it right. Yet, here you all are, helping and supporting me when I'm the one who messed up my life." He stooped to collect some branches. "I don't deserve friends like you, but I'm grateful for you."

David's big grin and slap on Jerry's shoulder told him all was forgiven, but Jerry knew his grief and concerns were not forgotten by his friends.

Jerry grew more and more unsettled as the hours passed. Jan and David tried to keep him occupied, but with the leg cast removed so recently, they didn't want him to overdo. It was evening when Jerry finally got an answer.

"Is this Sam Duncan?" he asked. Jerry was pacing rapidly now.

"Yes, this is Sam."

"Sam, this is Jerry Stone. Sir, I love your daughter. I've hurt her deeply, and I'm terribly sorry. I've got a hard head, and I'm stubborn, but I promise I will love and cherish her always. Sir, may I have your permission to—"

"Jerry, I'm sorry, this isn't a good time."

"Is Rachel there? If I could just talk to her for—"

"Jerry . . . she never arrived. The helicopter called in a mayday and then went dead," Sam said, choking. "I'm so sorry, Jerry, I know she loves you, but we don't know—"

Jerry froze in mid step and then staggered to the couch. The receiver fell to the floor as he turned pale and his legs gave out under him. He dropped onto the cushions, pulled his glasses off, and buried his face in his hands.

Silence had filled the room when Jerry started to talk. Now expressions of alarm were exchanged as David grabbed the phone and Sally ran to Jerry's side.

"I'm sorry, Sam. This is David, we lost you for a second, what—" David spoke in quiet tones for a few minutes, and then he hung up and faced Kimberly and Jan. "Her helicopter went down. She never made it home. They have an air search going on, but nothing yet. Sam said he will call if he has any news."

Jan wheeled onto the porch and burst into tears. "Dear God in heaven, please, this can't be true. Bless our dear, sweet Rachel. And please comfort my Jerry Boy in his anguish. He must not blame himself for this."

David wrapped Kimberly in his arms, blinking hard as she wept, and Sally threw her arms around Jerry's hunched shoulders. She kissed his head repeatedly, stroking his hair. "I'm sorry, Jerry. Oh, Honey, I'm so sorry."

Jan came back in later drying her eyes, calm and composed. "Kimberly, will you please help me fix a bite of supper? Sally and Jerry will be staying here with me tonight. David, will you please prepare the daybed for Jerry in the guest room? Sally can stay in Rachel's room. You and Kim are welcome to the hide-a-bed if you want to stay here until we hear more."

David hugged his mother. "You're the best, Mom. Thank you for your strength. Jerry will need you now more than ever."

"And you, my dear son. I just hope they find her alive."

Jan offered a sweet prayer as they gathered to eat, asking for protection for Rachel and her pilot, for comfort for Rachel's family, for the group gathered at her table, and especially for Jerry.

Jerry made it to the table and then excused himself right after the prayer. He was too numb with shock to eat or even think. His strength was returning, so he slipped out doors and just walked and walked.

David grew concerned and went to look for him as the ladies cleaned up the supper dishes. David heard Jerry's voice, remarkably calm, pleading with the throne of heaven. He could see him through the trees, kneeling beside the log by the pond.

"Dear God, I know I've been a big pain to you all these years, but I know you were there for David when he needed you, and I know you were there for me when I needed you. You sent Rachel to me. Then when I forgot I needed you, Danny remembered that I needed you. Now every day I ask you to remember Danny. Today, I have a very special request. The treasure and love of my life is lost somewhere in the wilderness of Alaska. It's probably my fault, because I didn't take the gift of her love when it was offered to me, but she is the most beautiful, compassionate, and giving daughter you have. So, please watch over her because this world can't get along without her. I don't deserve her, but for some reason she sure loves me. If I can please have another chance to love and cherish her, I promise I will treat her like your daughter should be treated. I'm so sorry I didn't see your beautiful gift, my beloved Rachel. I'm so sorry, I'm so sorry, I'm so sorry." Jerry hunched over the log and wept.

David longed to embrace his friend, his brother, to try to comfort him and ease his suffering, but somehow he knew Jerry was not alone, so he quietly slipped away, touched by his friend's deep humility and simple prayer.

The phone call from Sam came just after ten in the morning. The helicopter had still not been spotted. A ground search was being organized as they spoke.

"I'm coming Sam, I'll be there today," Jerry said. Then he hung up the phone. "I'm sorry, Sally. I know this was not in your plan, but please, can you take care of the shop for me again? I promise I'll make it up to you somehow."

"Jerry, you barely got out of a cast three days ago from your last trip through the Alaskan wilderness. You can hardly walk yet," Sally objected. "I want her found as much as anyone, but they have searchers who know the country, who are strong in body. Please don't go."

"I'll go with him and keep him in line, Sally," David said. "You'll never talk him out of it. I think you've lost your first argument with your little brother. Besides, look what he's been like yesterday and this morning. He'd drive you crazy." He hugged her and whispered, "I'll watch out for him. I promise, but in his heart he has to go."

She nodded and then went into the bedroom and closed the door.

Kimberly sat quietly listening. She had experienced enough during their search for the lost mine to know how rugged and dangerous the Alaskan terrain could be in the summer. Surely a ground search at this time of year could be bitter cold and extremely dangerous, but her friend was out there, the same friend who had, without a moment's hesitation, gone alone in search for David and Jerry in their time of crisis. Jerry would be dead if it wasn't for her, and possibly David too. She would stay and care for Jan while they were gone.

Chapter Twenty-seven

It was late in the evening when the helicopter touched down in the clearing near the large, peak-roofed cabin. Sam hurried out to meet Jerry and David. He shook hands with them, giving Jerry's hand an extra squeeze with his other hand as well.

"Thank you, thank you for coming to help us. We still have no news, and the ground search today was unsuccessful. We're packed and ready to go again as soon as we get you both geared up. We'll head out first thing in the morning."

"Then, let's get moving," Jerry said grabbing his bags and limping toward the house.

"When did he get his cast off?" Sam asked.

"Three days ago," David answered.

In the light from the flood lamp, David could see Sam's concern. "Only three days?" Sam replied. "This is bound to be tough, even on a sturdy man. Are you sure he should try it?"

"Try and stop him if you can, but it won't work. He's had a hard time getting through all this emotionally, but he's on top of it now. He's deeply in love with Rachel, and he intends to find her even if he has to do it alone. Nothing will hold him back."

"When she told me she was coming, she said things hadn't worked out for her and Jerry. He surprised me on the phone last night when he told me he loves her."

"He was leery after the incident with Roxanne, but Rachel had him hooked long before she left. He just didn't realize it. He got hit with a bombshell when she said goodbye. He's been a wreck ever since. Take my word for it, he loves her, and he won't let you go without him."

Suddenly, Roxanne burst out of the cabin door. "Jerry," she shrieked, running toward him.

David stopped mid step and stared as Jerry dropped his bags and embraced her.

"What's this?" he said stepping away from her as his eyes were drawn to the slight bulge in her tummy that he had felt when she hugged him. "You're going to have a baby? That's wonderful news!" He hugged her again as Eric appeared on the doorstep. Eric looked on quietly, his head lowered until Jerry saw him. "Eric, good to see you," Jerry said, limping toward him with his hand outstretched.

Eric was a little taken aback by Jerry's friendly gesture. He took Jerry's hand and nodded, looking rather stunned.

"Congratulations, I see you're going to be a daddy."

Eric smiled slightly and nodded, still surprised by Jerry's warm response to the news.

Roxanne slipped her shoulder under Eric's arm and wrapped her arms around his waist. His arm encircled her shoulder and pulled her near as she smiled at Jerry. "The baby's due in June."

"Well, I couldn't be more happy for both of you." Jerry shook Eric's hand again and squeezed Roxanne's hand with his other one. Then he turned to Eric. "Tell me what I need to do to get ready to go. We're finding your sister tomorrow!"

Eric, still looking a little stunned, led Jerry into the house.

David and Sam watched the reunion in silent surprise. Then Sam smiled and shook his head, shrugged his shoulders, and started walking toward the house with David following him.

Inside, David politely shook hands with Roxanne and Eric and then proceeded to prepare for the search while trying to sort out his feelings. Due to the family crisis, he figured he would probably see Eric but planned to just ignore him for Jerry's sake.

However, the resentful feelings he had harbored against these two people, who had betrayed his friend and caused such deep suffering, now seemed unfounded in light of Jerry's exuberant greeting. It certainly wasn't an act or show on Jerry's part. He was most sincere. Oh, well, who was David to judge if Jerry had such complete forgiveness? He felt great admiration for his friend, his brother, making note of the powerful lesson he had just learned from Jerry's example.

Eric stood before the search party in the morning dawn. "Thank you all very much for your help. The air search is continuing, but without success thus far. They have repeatedly flown over the general area where they think the helicopter went down but have made no sightings. We've been informed that ground searchers from Fairbanks are covering an area northwest from the Elliott Highway this direction. We'll cover the area from Tolovana south until we meet up with them. I understand the snowfall has been pretty heavy this year, so a lot of the area should be accessible by the snow machines. The area where the helicopter was last reported is quite vast, though, with lots of Black Spruce and some Birch, so some searching by snowshoes will be necessary off the trails. Jack, here, has planned out the search areas. You can pick them up from him. Those who don't know the area need to go with someone who is familiar with the terrain and landmarks. We'll have about seven and a half hours from sunrise to sunset to search, so use dawn and dusk to get to and from your areas as much as possible. However, head back early enough that we don't have anyone getting lost in the dark. Thank you again for donating your time to help us. We are very grateful. Please stay safe."

"Jerry, if you don't mind, I'd like to take you with me. Dad will take David with him," Eric said. His expression was solemn, his head bowed.

"Sure, Eric, let's go find her."

Eric secured the tow behind, carrying extra fuel, snowshoes, emergency supplies, and extra clothing. Then the two men mounted the snow machine and started down the mining road toward the highway. David and Sam followed behind them.

As they cleared the thick stands of Black spruce, they turned from the road and skimmed the lower windswept slope of the dome. Then they cut cross-country wherever they could avoid the heavy forests of scrubby Black Spruce. Throughout the day, they skirted the forest and followed the rolling hills where they could find or make trails. Then when they found a valley or dip they couldn't reach by machine, they donned snowshoes and found their way into the more forested areas.

On foot, the travel was difficult and Jerry's leg was aching, but he didn't slow down. Eric watched him, feeling guilty about his injury, and appreciating his determination to find Rachel. He remained quiet for some time, studying this unusual man who had so warmly greeted him and his pregnant wife.

Finally, during one snowshoe expedition, he spoke. "I'm sorry about your leg, Jerry, and all I put you through. It was a rotten deal. I can't make amends, but I am truly sorry."

"What's past is past, Eric. Forget it. You and Roxanne seem happy. That's all that matters."

"She came to visit you, didn't she?"

Jerry remained silent.

"I knew she would when I left the ticket for her to fly home. I didn't get her a ticket to Fairbanks though. I felt that had to be her choice, but I know she did."

"What makes you so sure, Eric?"

"The change in her when I came home. You sent her back to me, Jerry, didn't you?"

Jerry was silent for a moment, carefully planning to say as little as possible about the incident. "She did come once, to apologize."

"And to see if you would take her back?"

"Eric, she was just carrying a load of guilt, that's all. I helped her unload. I reassured her that I was fine and happy and that it was all in the past. She went her way, and I went mine. That's all there was to it." Jerry turned and walked a few feet away, peering through some branches into more thick branches. "She loves you, Eric. Look at how she was with you last night. She's happy with you. She told me you love her and treat her well. She wants to be with you, and that's the way it should be. You're having a baby now, and you'll make a great family." He walked back to where Eric was standing and looked straight in his eyes as he spoke a truth. "She came to apologize; now, that's all. Let's go find your sister."

Eric smiled humbly and placed his hand on Jerry's shoulder in a firm grip that said he knew more than Jerry was telling. His black eyes carried a look of deep gratitude.

"Thank you, Jerry Stone. You're a good man! Dad said you asked his permission for Rachel."

"Well, kind of, my timing was bad, but—"

"I'd be proud to have you as a brother," Eric said as he turned and walked toward the snowmobile.

Jerry took a deep breath and smiled, feeling that a dark chapter of his life had just closed and a new chapter had just opened. He looked heavenward. "Please make it a good one. Please help us find Rachel alive," he whispered.

The searchers continued through the rest of the week, with no success. Sunday dawned warmer, and it was snowing. It was harder to see, the progress was slower, and there was still no success. On Monday, the weather cleared, turning crisp and bitter cold. The ten to twenty degrees Fahrenheit temperature plummeted to twenty below zero, and the chill factor of the wind added another minus twenty. Jerry was covered from head to toe in layers of clothing and still felt the fierce sting of the wind through his clothing. He jumped at the occasional loud cracking of frozen trees, sounding like rifle shots in the arctic air.

Eric warned Jerry to cover his mouth with his scarf and to slow his pace to avoid labored breathing so he didn't freeze his lungs.

Jerry felt panic for Rachel, out in this treacherous weather, possibly injured, and maybe freezing to death. It would be a week tomorrow since he had watched her plane shrink to a dot in the sky and then disappear. He hated himself for letting her go. He'd tried to focus on hopeful possibilities, but fear and not knowing bore him down. He would never give up until she was safe in his arms, but with each empty search, cut short by fleeting days and long dark nights, he couldn't fight a growing dread that his arms may never again feel her softness against them. He had been sleeping fitfully at night, haunted by disturbing dreams.

Eric was still hopeful. He told Jerry how he and Rachel had learned to set snares for rabbits when they were children. He told him she could build a shelter with Birch boughs and pack snow around it for insulation. The boughs could also make warm, dry beds. She could boil snow and spruce boughs and make a warm tea, or make broth from a rabbit, boiling it so that none of it went to waste. He told Jerry how they used to gather natural food from trees and lay it out as bait for the willow ptarmigans. They'd make a noose with string or rawhide, hang it on a long willow branch, and then snare the bird by slipping the noose over its head and quickly jerking upward. If she was not seriously injured, she knew how to survive, even in this bitter cold.

They returned to the house Monday night without success. Jerry felt especially discouraged. His prayers had been in earnest, but he was struggling to have faith. The wind had stopped blowing, but the temperature was still below zero. He slipped out of the cabin into the icy night. "Please, God, help us. This land is so vast, with so many areas impenetrable. How will we ever find her?" He looked into the night sky, twinkling with a million stars. Suddenly, he stood spellbound as a magnificent band of green phosphorescent light rippled across the sky. It pulsated, swirled, and waved as multiple shades appeared and blended together in pink, purple, greenish-blue, and yellow, flowing and dancing like a brilliant symphony of light across the blackness of the sky.

Jerry caught his breath and gazed in wonder. David joined him, laying his arm across Jerry's shoulders. They stood in awe and silence beneath the celestial display.

A glowing warmth started in Jerry's chest and spread throughout his body, sweeping over his being with a whispered promise that a greater hand was at work in his life. A feeling of love washed over him, and he knew that he and David were not alone. He staggered as his knees went weak, and David caught him in his arms,

helping to lower him to the steps beneath his feet.

"Jerry, you've been pushing yourself way to hard. Are you all right?" David asked, sitting beside him. Jerry only nodded, still gazing at the glorious colors in the heavens, for there were no words to describe what he had just experienced.

CHAPTER TWENTY-EIGHT

Danny huddled in his hospital bed, frightened and alone. He held the covers against his face, whimpering quietly to himself.

Connie slipped into his room. "Danny, Sarah said you are having a really hard day today. How can we help you?"

"I want Rachel. She said she'd be here today. Why didn't she come?"

Connie had just received a call from Sam Duncan, informing her of the downed helicopter the previous day. Her heart ached as she sought to comfort a little boy when the news she had just received would be devastating to him. *We won't worry him until we know if she's alive,* Connie thought. *We'll let him hold onto the hope that she's still coming until we know otherwise.*

"Danny, sometimes airplanes are held up because of storms or mechanical problems. Planes are sometimes delayed for several days, and maybe even a week. Rachel loves you. She will get here as soon as she possibly can."

"No, something is wrong. Rachel would make them bring her here. She wouldn't let them make her wait. I want her here, now."

Connie rubbed the black fuzz growing on his bald head. "I know it's hard to wait when you want to see someone you love so badly. Just remember that she loves you too, so she will come as soon as she can." Connie turned on the TV to a cartoon station,

hoping to ease Danny's worries by switching his focus to something light hearted and funny.

Instead, Danny stared at the poster he and Jerry had made that Connie had taped near his bed. His rainbow award sat on his bedside table nearby.

"When did Jerry go home?" he asked.

"He went home a month ago, Danny."

"Did they untie him from his bed so he could get up?"

"Yes, and they put a big cast on his leg so it would keep getting better."

"Did he go to his home far away?"

"Yes, Danny."

"And Rachel went with him to take care of his cast?"

"Yes, Danny."

"That's good 'cause he needed her." He was thoughtful for a moment and then voiced a new concern. "If she's coming back to take care of me, who's gonna take care of Jerry's cast now?"

"He probably doesn't have a cast anymore, Danny. He's probably up and walking around now."

"On his broken leg?" Danny sounded worried.

Connie chuckled. "Well, it isn't broken anymore. It's healed."

"I hope so. He's really gonna miss Rachel, though, when she comes here. She's his girlfriend. I saw them kissing."

Connie was glad to get his mind off his worries. She led the conversation further away from his fears. "When did you see them kissing?"

"Lots of times. He really likes her." Danny's eyes were bright now as he enjoyed his happy memories.

"Let's play a game of checkers, and you can tell me all the fun things you remember."

Danny sat up and pulled his bedside table in front of him while Connie got the checkers. They played and talked and laughed until a doctor came, and Connie had to leave.

Danny fretted and worried every day that week, but the nurses followed Connie's suggestion to encourage him to talk about his happy memories, and that seemed to comfort him.

Connie had hoped Rachel would be there for Danny's surgery, but there was still no word Sunday night. It was Connie's day off, but she felt especially worried about Danny, so she stopped by the hospital on her way home from an evening meeting. Danny was in tears and had been crying for several hours. Nothing the nurses said or did could comfort him.

"Danny, what's troubling you?"

"Rachel is supposed to be here for my surgery tomorrow. I don't want to get my kidney out if she can't be here. Something really bad has happened to her. I know it has. Maybe she's gonna die like my Mamma did." He gathered his covers in his face and sobbed.

Connie took a deep, long breath and then gathered Danny in her arms and cuddled him in her lap. She had hoped she wouldn't have to tell him, especially before his surgery, but he was prepared for the news, and waiting was only making him more worried and anxious.

"Danny, can you be brave and still go to surgery tomorrow if I tell you something really important? The sickness on your kidney is very bad, and it has to come out. Rachel would want you to do it, even though she can't be here with you."

"Okay," Danny said. He sat upright, looked into her eyes, and dried his tears on the backs of his hands.

Connie took a tissue and dabbed at his eyes, and then she dabbed at her own. "Danny, we didn't want you to worry, so we were waiting to tell you, but you're way ahead of us. When Rachel was in the helicopter something happened and the helicopter fell from the sky."

Danny's eyes were wide and pleading. "Did she die?"

"We don't know. People have been searching for the helicopter every day, but they haven't been able to find it. They're still searching. We're all praying that she'll be all right."

Danny gazed into Connie's eyes that were welling up in tears. Then he settled against her and put his arm around her. "Then she'll be okay," he replied. "I'm glad you told me 'cause I was getting really scared, but now I can pray too, so they will find her. I'll get my kidney out tomorrow. Rachel would want me to do that." He patted his hand on Connie's broad hip. "I'm okay now, but you have to go, because I have to pray for Rachel."

Connie couldn't speak. She kissed Danny's head and sat him on the bed. She looked back through her tears as she closed the door behind her. Her view was blurry, but she saw the most beautiful sight she had ever seen. A skinny, little boy kneeling on his bed, folding his arms across the bed rail, looked right through the windows of heaven, and his pure and simple prayer ascended past the angels and straight into the loving hands of God.

Danny's surgery was long, with the doctors taking great care to extract all of the deadly cells from his small form. With no living, working kidney in his little body, they closed his incision and sent him to the recovery room. He slept for most of the day, rousing at times as Sarah frequently took his vital signs and sat near his bed. He was pale and so small against his white sheets as fluids ran through needles in his little arms. Sometimes he stirred and whimpered, then settled again into deep sleep.

That night he awakened. His night nurse had stepped out for a moment, and he was alone. He gazed out the window at the dark sky, folding his arms carefully across his chest so he didn't disturb the IV tubing, and again sent his sleepy prayer heavenward.

"Thank you for taking my kidney away so I can get better, and please bless Rachel. Keep her warm and safe so the wolves don't eat her. Help the people to find her so she can come and see me tomorrow." He closed his humble prayer and gazed out the window as myriads of soft, yet brilliant colors drifted and swirled through the sky. "It's Yoyekoyh (the Northern Lights)," he said, leaning his head forward to bring the bright colors closer. "Rachel will see them. That will make her feel better." He smiled and nestled his head against his pillow, watching the lights dancing in the sky. "I know, Mamma," he whispered as he drifted off to sleep.

✳

Jerry and Eric worked their way through a stand of Black Spruce toward a drop off they had seen from the hill above them. Several large Birch trees and a bunch of willows were also clustered on the edge of the slope. Jerry was breathing rapidly, not so much from exertion as from stress. It seemed that daylight began fading into shadows almost as soon as it dawned. There was little time left again today and still no sign of the missing helicopter and his beloved.

Eric had noticed that Jerry was unusually quiet today and seemed deep in thought. He respected Jerry's need for silence, so he kept it. He was glad to have this good man alongside him as they searched for Rachel. He had come to know Jerry better each day, and he had no doubt that Jerry's love for his sister was deep and dedicated. Thanks to Jerry's sacrifice and unselfishness, Eric was happier than he had ever been. Now, this man whom he had offended and deeply hurt, searched beside him as a brother, with no bitterness or malice.

Jerry stepped close to a birch tree heading for a small clearing. Suddenly, a willow ptarmigan, its dark summer feathers now as white as the snow it was nestled in, was startled by Jerry. It flew up with a frantic flapping of wings right in front of him. He leaped backward, tripping over his snowshoes, and fell into a clump of willows and disappeared.

"Jerry!" Eric yelled. "Jerry!" He pulled his radio from his pocket, gave his father his location and said, "Get here fast! I've just lost Jerry over a bank or something. He's not responding." Eric moved toward the willow clump, testing his footing, and then threw himself to his stomach, crawling through the willow to look for Jerry. He could see nothing but a blanket of white, but he felt empty space as far down as he could reach. "Jerry," he called again, but there was no answer.

Eric floundered his way back to the snow machine and was frantically unwinding a rope from the emergency gear in the toboggan when his father and David arrived. "We've got to rope

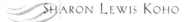

down and see if we can find him," Eric shouted. "I think it's a narrow ravine. I can see the other side, but visibility down there is zero."

"I'll go," David said, anxious and fearful as he hurried to Eric's side.

"No," Eric said, pushing past him and leading the way while he tied the rope to a harness. Eric cinched the knot as Sam fastened the harness around Eric's waist. Eric handed the other end of the rope to David. "Secure the rope around that tree and lower me down here so I don't crash into him. I've got to find him."

David quickly complied, whipping the rope around the tree and bracing himself as Sam helped Eric lower himself over the edge into the thick, white emptiness below. Sam hurried over to David, gripping the rope behind him. "We're dealing with ice fog down there. He can't see a thing. Be ready to pull up quick if he calls."

Eric was blindly descending a considerable distance, with only occasional glimpses of the scarp line he was rappelling down. He could hear swiftly moving water drawing near as he stretched for something besides space beneath his feet. "There's water down here," he called. "I can't tell where it is, but it's close." Then his feet landed on rocky ground as the sound of water swept past just inches away. Straining to see the size of the stream in front of him, he took a step backward, bumping his head into something solid. He turned, seeing a large gray form looming in front of him. He reached out and touched something hard and smooth.

"I found something," he yelled. Suddenly, to his left, he heard a squeal, and saw swift movement toward him as a form thrust out of the fog and grabbed him around the neck. He gasped, stepping backward and nearly falling into the rushing stream. He caught his balance and grasped the form clinging to him, soft and clothed. Before he could register what was happening, he felt his face covered with wetness and kisses. He jerked his head backward, peering through the thick fog and could see the outline of a woman. He rubbed the ice particles away from his eyes with his glove and peered into the lovely face of his sister.

"Oh, Eric, Eric! I knew it was you! I heard yelling from the cave and recognized your voice. I hurried out and followed the sounds, and here you are." She squeezed her arms so tightly around his neck he could barely breath as he wrapped his arms around her and carried her, feet dangling, a safe distance from the stream.

"Rachel, thank God! Are you all right?"

"Yes, I am fine, now." He set her down and gathered her to him, rocking her in his arms like he had when she was frightened, hurt, or sad—a little girl, just six years younger than himself. Suddenly, he remembered David and his father and Jerry. Where was Jerry? He looked frantically around, but could see nothing.

"Call Father and David. Tell them to rope down."

"David's here?"

"Yes, go now," he said, unfastening the harness and handing it to her. He didn't want to alarm her about Jerry, so he scanned the scarp line, peering deeply into the fog in the location where he fell, hoping to see a glimpse of him somewhere along the cliff. He hadn't heard a splash so he didn't think he had fallen into the stream. Eric could see now that the large gray form he had bumped into was the helicopter's tail. The main body of the machine seemed to be lodged in the stream and mostly submerged directly under where Jerry fell. What if he'd fallen on the helicopter and slipped off into the water? With all his heavy clothing he would have been sucked under and drowned. But Eric hadn't heard any sounds. He hadn't heard Jerry land.

Now, he could hear Sam on the ground, his father's emotional greeting, and Rachel weeping as Sam embraced his daughter. Their shapes were vaguely discernible. Eric saw the shadow that was David nearing the bottom, and quickly pulled him aside.

"She doesn't know about Jerry, yet. I didn't want to upset her, but it's too foggy, and I can't see him." He led David to the helicopter. "Jerry fell just above there." Eric pointed to the fog-covered cliff above the main body of the helicopter. "But I never heard him hit bottom. Rachel said something about staying in a cave. I'll alert Father, and he can go with her to her shelter while we try to find Jerry."

Eric whispered something to Sam, who nodded. Sam had Rachel lead him to the cave where her pilot was stretched out on tree boughs. He was alive, but in pain from broken ribs and a fractured leg.

"She's the best little nurse in the world, as well as search and rescue," the pilot said. "She managed to get me free of the helicopter before it sank. Then at the risk of drowning, she salvaged the first aid kit and blankets. Everything else went underwater, including the flare gun. She's kept us warm and fed."

Rachel started out to get David and Eric. "They're just getting supplies together up top and alerting the rescue teams," Sam said. "I twisted my ankle pretty good though, Honey, can you check it out for me?"

"Have you heard anything from Jerry?" she asked, rolling up her father's pant leg.

"Not recently," he lied.

"Well, it was nice of David to come all this way for me," she said, unlacing Sam's boot.

David and Eric searched the rocky ground from the rope to the stream on hand and knee, but Jerry was not on the ground. They decided the only thing to do was to climb up the rope, move it to where Jerry fell through, and then carefully feel their way down in case he was unconscious on a ledge. They both realized he possibly could have slipped into the stream. If that were true, there was nothing they could do.

Eric secured a second rope from his father's toboggan and rappelled down about eight feet parallel from David. They moved slowly downward, feeling the frozen cliff and peering deeply into the ice particles making up the fog in the cold air. About half way down, David bumped into something behind him. He pushed away from the cliff enough to turn around, and gasped as he came face to face with Jerry. His eyes were closed and his face looked rather gray in the thick fog. He was dangling in the air, his hands and feet hanging free.

CHAPTER TWENTY-NINE

David threw his arm under Jerry's arm to help support his weight, not certain what he was hanging from. "Eric, I have him. Move over here." David ripped his glove off with his teeth and felt around Jerry's throat to make certain he wasn't being strangled, and then he frantically felt with his fingers what he couldn't see to make sure that Jerry wouldn't fall from his arms. He gasped, whispering a silent prayer of thanks. Some guardian angel had been watching over Jerry. Had he fallen all the way down, he would have landed on the helicopter and slid off into the swift, icy water. But the helicopter blade, jammed against the earth on one end, had remained strong and solid, reaching skyward. As he fell, Jerry's backpack had slipped over the blade, suspending him in the air. David wrapped both arms tightly around him to wait for help. He could hear Jerry's breathing. He was alive.

"What the . . . what's he hanging from?" Eric asked when he'd worked his way over to David.

"His back pack hung up on the helicopter blade. He's alive, but we've got to get him down from here. It might not hold. We'd better pull him up since the stream is directly below us. Do you have another rope?"

"No, but I sent a call to the searchers. Some of them should be arriving. I'll go topside and lower my rope and harness down so

you can put it on him before something tears loose." Eric squeezed David's shoulder, climbed up the side of the cliff, and lowered his harness to David.

Holding Jerry with one arm, David stretched to grasp the harness dangling nearby. Eric moved it closer as David called out directions until it was firm in his hand. Then, praying the backpack would continue to support Jerry's weight, he carefully maneuvered the harness under Jerry's arms. Fumbling and awkward with his other glove, David pulled it off with his teeth and quickly secured the harness with his hands.

He sighed with relief. "It's on, pull it tight!" All David could do now was hold onto Jerry and try to keep him warm. It was starting to grow dark and the bitter cold was biting at David's hands. Both of his gloves had fallen when he took them off. He remembered with a chuckle how his mom used to put a string through the sleeves of his coat and fasten it to his gloves so he couldn't lose them. "Where were you today when I needed you, Mom? It's cold here!"

Shortly, Jack came with another rope. Eric rappelled down and helped David move Jerry up a few feet at a time as Jack and his partner pulled on the rope from above. They finally had Jerry safely on the top of the cliff. By that time David's hands were seriously frost bitten. Eric wrapped Jerry in blankets and then wrapped David's hands in a scarf to warm them up.

"I'm not going to tell Rachel about Jerry until we know how seriously he's hurt. I've called for two helicopters to fly all four of you to the hospital. You go with Jerry on the first one and get your hands taken care of. We'll call you later to see how you both are." Eric hesitated for a moment and then wrapped his arms around David in a hug. "Thank you, David, for coming to our rescue a second time. Thanks for helping us find my sister." He hung his head. "I'm deeply sorry for all the misery I put you and Jerry through last August. It was intolerable."

David shrugged. "Where would Jerry and Rachel be if you hadn't?"

Eric shook his head. "It's a pretty dirty deal that both times he

helped us he had to be air-lifted to a hospital. I just hope he's—"
He shook his head sadly and squeezed David's shoulder again.
"I'm sorry."

❋

At the Fairbanks hospital, Rachel was treated and released
with a splint on her broken finger. She was unaware that David
and Jerry were in the same emergency room.

She went to the nurses' lounge and took a wonderfully warm
shower, and then she dressed in a scrub uniform and hurried to
pediatrics. She tiptoed into Danny's room, with her heart over-
flowing, and gazed down on the child that was soon to be her own.
She longed to touch him but didn't want to disturb his sleep. Bone
weary and aching from sore muscles and bruising, she sat quietly
in the chair beside his bed. She saw Jerry and Danny's poster
on the wall and remembered how special their time had been
together. Now, Jerry was a bittersweet memory from the past. She
missed him terribly, but she had Danny to care for, and she was
content. Her ordeal was over. The injured pilot was resting peacefully somewhere in the hospital, and she was back home in Alaska.
Back home to stay. She rested her head against the back of the
chair, and instantly fell into a deep and exhausted sleep.

She didn't notice the slight movement in the bed as the child
opened his eyes and stirred. She didn't see the pain on his face as
he pulled himself upright in bed and then the happy, trusting smile
as he saw that his prayer had been answered. He carefully climbed
over the bed rail, biting his lip against the pain until he was safely
on the floor. Watching to not tangle his IV tubing, he pulled
his bedspread off his bed, dragging it to the chair. He reached
his small, brown hand to her face and slid his fingers across her
cheek. She was sleeping and didn't feel his knobby knees crawl
onto her lap. She didn't hear the faint whimper of pain as he settled there, or the happy sigh as he snuggled against her breast. He
pulled the covers over her lap and around his small shoulders. She
didn't know that a humble child's prayer ascended from her lap to

heaven, thanking God for her safe return. She didn't even feel her own stirring as her arms moved from her sides and encircled the little boy snuggled next to her heart. But somehow, all of her pain went away, and her sleep was much sweeter.

❋

David's throbbing hands were soaking in a pan of warm water as he watched a nurse place a blanket from the warmer over his unconscious friend. Then Jerry was wheeled on a stretcher to the x-ray department for a CT scan. Mild hypothermia and a concussion was the diagnosis. He and David were admitted to the same room that Jerry had been in for just over a month, just across the hall from the nurses' desk.

David's hands were wrapped now in soothing bandages, but the pain was still severe. He took several pain pills through the night, but his rest was patchy. Besides, he couldn't sleep because his friend wouldn't wake up. Jerry's silence made him nervous. He could recall the heavy-headed, groggy feeling he gradually awakened to when he suffered a serious head injury, and he was worried.

During the long and painful night, David overheard nurses reminiscing about Danny and Jerry. He soon became aware that he was sharing a hospital room with a celebrity. More than that, he was given a glimpse from the eyes of strangers into the compassionate and caring heart of his own true friend. This man they were speaking of was not a hedgehog. Well, not usually. And he was most definitely not a coward. David knew that better than anyone. As he listened, there were stories of others being helped and lifted by his friend and Jerry's little friend when they were both down, and one very sad and suffering lady being healed and sent home when no one thought she would, because she got licked by a pillow puppy. David shook his head and grinned.

Then he got out of bed, holding his bundled hands in front of him, and moved to his friend's bedside. He looked at Jerry's silent form and gently ran his bandaged hand across his forehead. With the other bandaged hand he wiped a tear from the corner of his own eye. He was proud to be Jerry's friend and brother.

✳

Rachel felt a wonderful sense of calm and peace before she awakened. When she finally stirred and opened her eyes, she was surprised to find Danny snuggled in her lap. She smiled and petted his fuzzy head in a gentle, caressing motion.

Eventually he squirmed and awakened. He looked up at Rachel with bright eyes full of faith. "I knew you would come last night. I prayed for you to come. Did you get hurt, Rachel?" he suddenly asked with deep concern.

"Just my pinky, Danny, but they fixed it last night."

He stared at her hand, and gently touched the splint as though his fingers could help make it better. Then he looked up at her with great sincerity in his black eyes.

"I saw my Mamma dancing in the Yoyekoyh. She was happy. She said you would come and take care of me." He snuggled deeper into Rachel's lap, wrapping his arm around her waist and tenderly patting her. The patting gradually slowed down, his fingers touching as light as a feather, and then ceased as he drifted off to sleep again.

Rachel sighed, knowing this was where she belonged.

Connie quietly entered the room. Rachel smiled and reached toward her. "Connie, it's so good to see you. Thank you for calling me. I'm going to adopt Danny." She said as Connie squeezed her hand. "They started proceedings last week. Due to the circumstances, they're going to hurry it as fast as possible."

Connie wrapped her arms around Rachel's shoulders. "And that surprises me? Oh, Rachel, we were so worried! I'm glad you're home safe! I just came on duty a few minutes ago, and they told me you had come in last night. They told me about the rescue and Jerry's accident. I checked on him before I came in here. He's still unconscious, but he's in stable condition. They admitted him and his friend to the same room he was in before."

Rachel stiffened, her eyes wide, and her head whirled to face Connie. "What? Jerry? He's here? He's hurt? What happened?"

"You didn't know? He was injured during the search and rescue. He fell over the cliff near your helicopter. That's how they found you. I thought you knew last night when they brought him in. They said you were all in the emergency room together."

"No, no one told me. They just treated my finger, and I hurried up here. How badly is he hurt?"

"It's a concussion, but they don't think it's serious. They expect he'll be regaining consciousness any time."

"Why didn't Dad tell me last night?" Rachel asked, slumping in the chair. She was talking more to herself than to Connie as she began to understand the circumstances of the previous night. "That's why he kept me in the cave, and why David and Eric never came in. That's why Dad didn't even tell me Jerry was here. I heard two helicopters. I thought the first one probably just helped to locate us, but it was for Jerry. They didn't want me to know he got hurt."

Rachel shook her head as the events of her rescue unfolded in her mind, and she realized she had carefully been kept in the dark about the drama being waged in the dense fog outside the cave. She looked puzzled. "But David was fine. Then I didn't see him when I got in the helicopter, just Eric and Father. "David was admitted too?" she asked Connie. "What happened to him?"

"Oh, my goodness, Honey! I'm sorry. You didn't know any of this, did you? Jerry's friend had lost his gloves. His hands were badly frost bitten during Jerry's rescue. Here, let me take Danny. You go to Jerry. I'll tell Danny where you are when he awakens."

Rachel's heart pounded as she ran down the hall to Jerry's room. She rushed through the doorway and then halted, gripping the door handle. David was standing beside Jerry's bed.

"Rachel, I didn't know Eric had called you yet!"

"He didn't!" Rachel exclaimed.

"How did you know we were here?" David walked over and wrapped his arms around her. "They didn't want to tell you until they knew Jerry was all right."

"I used to work here; I have friends." She sounded irked.

"Are you all right? Did you get injured at all?"

She held up her splint. "Not nearly as hurt as I am that Jerry was here all night, and I didn't even know it."

She moved to Jerry's bedside and gently took his hand as tears welled up in her eyes. She gently stroked his face with her other hand and kissed his cheek. "He did come after me, David," she choked.

David grinned. "He's in love with you Rachel—madly in love! He was on his way before your plane left the ground in Slaterville. He tried to make them turn your plane around. Sally and I had to drag him away from the airport. He was frantic, calling and calling trying to find out where you were going. When your father told him about the crash, he was devastated. We were here the next night, and he's searched side by side with Eric everyday."

"How? He could hardly walk!"

"He'd limp to the North Star for you, Honey, and that's just what he's been doing. He could limp as fast on snowshoes as any of us, and he wouldn't quit. One night his leg gave out, and he was the first one ready to go the next day."

The tears had tumbled over her lashes now and were trickling down her face. She bent over his bed. "I love you, Jerry Stone," she whispered, and she kissed his lips, hers softly lingering, while a cascade of silky hair bathed his cheek and neck.

The sweet scent of honeysuckle penetrated Jerry's senses, and the soft caress of her lips on his stirred him in his unconsciousness. He softly moaned and then sighed deeply and was silent.

Moments later, Connie wheeled Danny into Jerry's room. "We got permission," she said, smiling. "Danny knows Jerry's in a heavy sleep and that he can't wake up right now, but he couldn't wait to see him."

"Thank you, Connie," Rachel said, giving her a hug as she left.

Danny winced as he stood up and left the wheelchair. His IV tubing had been disconnected, and the needles were taped to his arms. He stood beside Rachel, her arm wrapped around his shoulder. He petted Jerry's hand and arm. "It's okay, Jerry. You can sleep until your head doesn't hurt anymore. We'll take good care of you, and we'll be right here when you wake up."

The little Indian boy Jerry loved so much and had talked about with great passion, suddenly became very real to David. The extremely tender care in his small hand, and the gentle cooing in his most sincere, childish promise, nearly overcame David. He caught his voice in a choke and sat on his bed, biting his lip as he regained control.

Danny looked up and noticed David for the first time. "Who are you?" he asked.

"Danny, this is Jerry's good friend, David," Rachel said. "He hurt his hands trying to help Jerry, so he's sharing Jerry's room."

Danny's eyes went from David's face, to his bandaged hands, and then back again to his face. Wonder and concern filled his eyes. He walked over to David's bed and climbed onto it. Wincing again, he crossed his feet in front of him as his long gown swept over his knees. "You're David?" he asked, as though he had just met a great hero. David barely had time to nod, and too little time to respond when Danny spoke again. "Wow, I hoped I could meet you. Do your hands hurt real bad?"

"Not too bad, Danny. I'm so glad to meet you. Jerry told me all about you." David smiled, deeply touched by this wonderful child.

"Jerry loves you a lot." Danny said. "He and Rachel gave me a shiny, red bike, just like the one you gave Jerry when his got stolen. He said you are his brother. You can't show me your scar where you became blood brothers 'cause it's all wrapped up, but do you wanna see mine?"

"Sure," David nodded.

Suddenly Rachel remembered the chocolate pudding and strawberry war paint that Danny and Jerry wore all afternoon and evening the day she found blood on Jerry's washcloth. She had sensed an unusual, almost sacred atmosphere in the room that day, and Jerry had said it had been a very important day for them both. Rachel moved closer as Danny pulled up the sleeve of his gown and held his arm out toward David. He pointed just below a small scar left from his old IV needle. She shook her head in amazement.

Jerry had wanted so badly to give Danny something of value. Only now did Rachel realize the depth of his and Danny's relationship, and the wonderful gift of love that Jerry had bestowed upon a lonely little orphan boy. He had given himself to Danny in a very real way, a gift of priceless value to her Danny so he would never feel alone.

Rachel turned toward Jerry and hugged his limp hand close to her heart as her heart swelled with love and adoration for this humble and compassionate man. *How could I have doubted him?* she thought as Danny proudly continued his story.

"We couldn't do it right where the scar is 'cause my needle was in the way," Danny said. "So Jerry just dropped my blood right here and poked his finger and mixed his blood with my blood. Since Jerry and me are brothers, now, like you and him, does that mean you and me are brothers too?"

"I'd be very honored to be your brother, Danny," David answered as goose bumps tingled up his arms and down his spine.

"Wow, cool!" Danny exclaimed. He carefully moved closer to David and put his arms around his waist. "Now we have a bond too."

David wrapped his arm around Danny and hugged his skinny little shoulders. "No wonder Jerry loves you so much. You're an awesome kid."

"Thank you, David." He patted David's knee and then carefully climbed down from the bed. "Well, I've gotta go take care of Jerry, now. I hope your hands get better." He paused for a thoughtful moment and then looked directly into David's eyes with an all-knowing expression. He smiled brightly and said, "I know why you let your hands get hurt, though, because of the bond. You would die for Jerry if he needed you to, wouldn't you?"

David was totally taken aback by the depth of understanding this little boy had of true friendship. "Yes, I would, Danny, and he

would do the same for me."

"I know, he told me he would. He would die for me too if I needed him to."

CHAPTER THIRTY

Danny was resting in Rachel's arms beside Jerry's bed, and David was finally catching some sleep when Jerry began to stir. Rachel laid Danny beside Jerry and covered him up. She stood and held Jerry's hand, softly running her fingers across his forehead. He closed his big hand around her small brown one and moaned, turning toward her in his bed. He moved his arm and wrapped it around Danny as though he knew he was beside him.

He quieted again for a few minutes. Gradually his fingers began to move against Rachel's hand, lightly at first, with little jerking motions, and then more and more deliberately. A slight frown wrinkled his forehead. His eyelids fluttered and finally opened. He blinked several times and focused on Rachel's hand in his own. His eyes followed her arm and rested on her smile. She was slightly hazy to his view, so he raised his other hand to push his glasses up on his nose. They weren't there. It didn't matter; he could see her clearly enough to dream. His arm wrapped again around Danny, snuggling him close as he sighed and closed his eyes. He was quiet for a few more minutes, but continued to move his fingers on Rachel's hand. Suddenly, he stopped and gripped her hand tightly. He gave a slight gasp and opened his eyes. They grew wide. "Rachel? Rachel!" he cried, reaching to touch her cheek.

"You came after me, Jerry!" she said, holding his hand against her lips and kissing it repeatedly. "You got hurt searching for me. Are you all right?"

"Only now," he whispered. "Only now. I . . . thought I was dreaming, but you're really here!" He blinked hard, trying to see more clearly, trying to clear his cloudy brain. Her beautiful smile and gentle eyes forced his mind to focus. "Oh, my precious Rachel." He reached for her and pulled her to him, pressing her face against his neck. "Are you okay, Honey? Are you hurt?"

"I am fine, Jerry," she said, returning his embrace. "I am fine."

He smoothed her long strands of hair, breathing deeply of the sweet fragrance of honeysuckle. She became more vivid to his cloudy mind. She was real, beautiful, alive, and in his arms. "Thank you," he prayed, holding her tightly. He would never let her slip out of his arms again. "Thank you!"

Rachel felt Danny stirring and gently pulled away.

Jerry gazed into her eyes then cradled her head in his hands and drew her near again. The door to his dark places fell open, and all the fears and anguish of the past poured out of his heart. He could feel them leave, while light, hope, and joy filled his soul. "I love you! I love you!" he whispered as he found her lips, softly, wonderfully, caressing them with his own. He yielded willingly this time, giving himself to her with this kiss, giving all of himself with the deepest commitment—completely and eternally.

David awakened as Jerry cried out Rachel's name. He opened his eyes and saw all of his hopes fulfilled as his friend embraced this lovely woman. He hugged her to him and kissed her with the passion of a man whose hopelessly unreachable dreams have finally come true. David smiled and closed his eyes, leaving this sacred moment to them.

A little chuckle followed by a gasp for air shattered the transcendent moment of the kiss, and Rachel drew back, smiling. It was Danny's turn to surprise Jerry.

Jerry looked down into two shining black eyes and the same, happy smile that had buoyed him up on many long, lonely days. "Danny," he practically shouted, about to throw his arms around the child.

"Careful, careful," Rachel cried a warning.

Jerry saw Danny flinch and the tight line of his lips as his sudden movement jolted the child. He halted, shocked to see the little boy's pain. Jerry carefully raised up in bed. Feeling a little lightheaded, he shook it off as Rachel quickly raised the head of the bed higher to support him. Jerry reached for Danny, gently placing him in his lap and cradling him in his arms as the child's hospital gown revealed a dark truth he didn't want to know. Danny was a patient, in pain, with needles in both of his little arms. He had some black, fuzzy hair growing on his head, but he was more frail than Jerry had ever seen him.

His eyes met Rachel's, filled with alarm. She nodded, and Jerry buried his face in Danny's fuzzy hair, fighting bitter tears. Why this suffering for a little child?

"I'm sorry, Danny," he said, gently rocking the boy in his arms. "I didn't mean to hurt you. I was just so happy to see you, but I didn't know. Where is your pain so I can be careful?"

"It's okay, Jerry. It just hurt a little." He lifted his gown, revealing a fresh surgical dressing on the opposite side of the previous scar.

"What happened?" Jerry asked.

"The cancer came back. It grew on my other kidney, so they had to take that one out and throw it away too."

Now, Jerry's eyes were wide with fear and panic. He stared at Rachel. "Is this why you came back?" he asked.

She nodded.

"Why didn't you tell me?" his voice was incredulous and accusing.

David had remained quiet, deeply touched by the entire scene he had witnessed, but now he needed to speak. "Later, Jerry. There'll be a better time."

Jerry looked at David, stunned to see him in a hospital gown with both hands bandaged. He hadn't noticed him until now.

"What happened to you?"

"Just a little frost bite. Nothing serious."

"What am I doing in here?" he asked, fully conscious now and very confused. Suddenly, thoughts began churning in his head as he remembered being with Eric and being startled by a bird. Everything was blank after that, until now.

Connie stepped in the doorway. "Rachel, it's time for Danny's dialysis. Do you want to come with him?"

"Surely, come on Danny, we will let Jerry rest for a while."

Danny's arms circled Jerry's neck, and the child planted a sloppy kiss on his cheek. Jerry forced himself to smile. "Hurry back, little brother," he said. "I've missed you!"

Rachel gently lifted Danny into the wheelchair, covered him up, and wheeled him from the room. Jerry's unbelieving gaze, his questioning and even accusing gaze, had shaken her. She was grateful for a quick escape. His question was ringing in her ears. Why had she not told him about Danny? Was it, in reality, a selfish desire on her part for Jerry to prove his love for her? He had done that! He had endured untold pain and hardship in his committed effort to find her. Rachel felt ashamed that she had doubted his love. Jan had repeatedly told her that Jerry loved her. In her wisdom, she had asked Rachel to be patient. She had not been patient enough.

Rachel asked herself more troubling questions. Had she considered Danny's feelings in her decision? How could she have thought to raise Danny by herself, when Jerry had repeatedly shown her the great compassion he was capable of? Had she not longed to give this little boy to Jerry? Then, when she had the chance, she had abandoned her dream. She had left Jerry, and she had left him in the dark. Yet Jerry had been more committed to Danny than she had. He had become his brother. Rachel felt heartsick, finding it hard to pretend, but she must be light hearted for Danny. She and Jerry could talk after Danny was asleep.

Jerry's head was reeling now, and he felt nauseated. He grasped for an emesis basin and dumped the contents of his stomach. He had eaten very little for days, so there wasn't much there.

David hurried to his side. "You okay, Bud?" he asked, and Jerry nodded. "I'll get a nurse." David walked to the door and asked for help.

Kelly was working that day and had asked to have Jerry on her list of patients.

Her familiar presence and cheery ways were comforting. After she left, Jerry asked David to sit near.

"David, you understand this mass confusion in my head, you were there once. I'm not going to try to figure out what happened. Somehow I got hurt, and you got hurt. Someone found Rachel, and—"

"You found Rachel, Jerry. You fell off a cliff she was under. We'd still be hunting and never find her. So while you're trying to think straight, which won't happen for a while, and while your head is splitting with a headache, just remember she's here because of you."

"No, not because of me. The feeling I had, that night watching the Northern Lights . . . that stupid bird . . . it was that stupid bird!"

"What?" David said. "You're off the deep end, Jerry. Try to rest for a while." David used his wrists to cover Jerry up as he obediently laid his head back on the pillow.

"No, not because of me, because of him. That stupid bird was a miracle!"

David didn't hear the last word, for it was only a mumbled whisper as Jerry fell asleep. "Wow!" David said aloud. "I've got myself in the middle of some heavy stuff."

He strolled in the hall for a while, recalling Jerry's amazing and tender response to Danny, his great concern for the little guy when he himself was still very ill and barely conscious. And then there was Rachel and that kiss. Jerry was so upset at her for not telling him about Danny that David hoped that in his delirium Jerry wouldn't forget that kiss.

Danny was very tired after his exciting and trying day. He didn't like dialysis, and he was upset that he had to leave Jerry, but he was weak and needed to rest. Rachel tucked him in bed early after he'd fallen asleep in her lap. She kissed him goodnight and slipped out to call Eric while they put a cot for her in Danny's room.

Eric was going to call her that morning after he talked to David and tell her about Jerry, but David said she had already been with Jerry.

"I'm not a little girl anymore, Eric," she gently scolded. "You don't have to protect me. You and Father should have told me." He apologized.

She asked him if he could get to the airport and pick up her bags. She had left all her luggage there under security since she had planned to be back that evening to find an apartment. She was grateful for the scrub outfit, but her own clothes would be nice.

Eric told her how much respect he had for Jerry. He repeated what David had also said about Jerry's great efforts in the search, and Eric told her that he knew Jerry loved her.

Everyone could see it but me, she thought, more angry at herself than ever.

Then she sat back and let go of her worries about Eric as she listened to him talk. He excitedly told her that they were moving to help his father in the mine. He wasn't going out to sea anymore. He wanted to be home with Roxanne. They had plans to build their own cabin nearby. He told her how happy he and Roxanne had become, and about the baby, and about his new friend and brother.

Rachel was surprised when he included Jerry in a conversation about his happy marriage. "Eric, aren't you jumping to conclusions?" she asked when he called Jerry his brother. "He hasn't been conscious long enough to make that kind of commitment." Well, maybe he had. That wonderful and thrilling kiss he had so voluntarily given her and the deep emotion she felt in it certainly felt like a commitment to her. She could still taste it sweet on her lips.

"Did you know he saved my marriage, Rachel?" Eric's question brought Rachel back to a telephone conversation she had forgotten she was having.

"What?"

"Jerry saved my marriage, and he probably saved Roxanne's life as well. I'd have lost her one way or the other. I was terribly worried to leave her alone. I thought she might even throw herself off a pier. That's why I sent her home while I was gone. I thought she'd be safer with family, but I didn't expect her to ever come home. She went to see Jerry."

Rachel knew that, but she kept it to herself.

"He forgave her, us, both of us, and he sent her back to me. I don't know what or how. I don't know what he said or did, but she came back because she wanted to. She's really happy now. I will be forever in his debt.

Rachel finally understood Jerry's response when he saw Roxanne in the Seattle airport—he was not grieving; he was letting go! She had been wrong about Jerry in many ways. What other surprises were awaiting her from inside this humble man's moccasins?

Feeling happiness for Eric and hoping that Roxanne would prove herself to be true and faithful, Rachel swallowed her bitterness, giving seeds of forgiveness a chance to grow. After all, Roxanne was family now.

Rachel checked on Danny and found him resting peacefully. Hoping that Jerry could find it in his heart to forgive her for the inexcusable wrong she had done him, she returned to his room. She needed to apologize, but she could not find the words. She honestly could no longer understand her own reasons for not telling Jerry about Danny. She had wronged them both. What if she had died when the helicopter engine stalled? Jerry would have never known, and Danny would have had no one. She had learned a powerful lesson about how fleeting life can be. She still did not know how to answer Jerry's pointed and accusing question as she took a deep breath and opened the door.

When she entered the room, David and Jerry were visiting. She slipped in quietly and sat in the chair beside Jerry's bed. He reached down, still visiting with David, and felt for her hand. She put it where he could find it, and he did. He lifted it onto his bed and held it in his own. When the conversation ended, he turned to her and smiled.

"How is our Danny boy?"

"He was very tired, so I put him to bed. I was in trouble because he wanted to come back, but I will bring him tomorrow." Rachel paused, staring down at her knees, and felt Jerry's eyes watching her. She took a deep breath and looked into his blue eyes. "Jerry," she said, "I am so sincerely sorry that I did not tell you about Danny. I have no good reason. It was unfair to you, and it was unfair to him. I won't ask your forgiveness because you may not want to forgive such an uncharitable act, but I do want you to know that I am truly sorry." She stared at her knees again.

He remained quiet for some time, still holding her hand. Then he spoke, and his voice was kind, without blame. "David and I have been talking about hedgehogs," he said.

Rachel looked up questioningly.

David said nothing. He sat in bed, his arms across his chest and a wide grin on his face.

Jerry continued. "They are most unusual creatures. They make great pets, but only for certain people. They can be very trusting when you've proven yourself to them, but are often more likely to huff and roll away into a prickly ball where they feel safer. You can gain their trust by softly talking to them, touching them, petting them, and even putting something you've had near you, or on you, where they sleep. That way they get more used to you." He paused, and gazed into Rachel's eyes.

She looked confused. "Jerry, what does this have to do—?"

He put his finger up to his mouth, and she fell silent. "Now, David, here, knows a lot about a certain hedgehog. He's a really stubborn one; it is hard to win his trust, even with the kindest of efforts, or the most tender touch, or even the most dedicated and unselfish care. You can stay with him and be close to him, but he still curls up and is slow to respond. Yet, he's really very lonely and his life is incomplete. He longs to be like other hedgehogs, to get married and have lots of little baby hedgehogs, and he will never be happy unless he can give his master his full heart. David and I are in total agreement that the best master that this difficult, obstinate, prickly, and balled-up hedgehog could ever have, is you."

Jerry turned toward Rachel, took her other hand in his other hand, and pulled her closer. "My precious and enormously patient Rachel, will you take this difficult and impossible hedgehog into your heart? Will you own me, and pet me, and trust me as I have learned to trust you with all that is dear and precious to me? Will you live with me, and sleep with me, and give me a whole bunch of little baby hedgehogs to love?

"I'm asking you here and now, because I might be discharged tomorrow, and this is the cage where I fell in love with you. My kind, compassionate, and beautiful Rachel, will you marry me? And if you say yes, I promise with all my stubborn, hedgehog heart, that I will never again curl into myself and shut you out. I will give myself to you, completely, now and forever." His eyes were soft and pleading and so very blue and sincere.

Rachel squeezed his hands and raised from the chair. She sat on the edge of his hospital bed and leaned toward him, caressing his lips with hers. She remembered the first kiss she gave him in this very same hospital room, and the compassion and care that inspired it.

"Basi', Jerry, Si draya' dadhk'wn' it is on kwn'. Si 'etodel into your neshuli. I will walk in your moccasins. I will be your tr'axa. (Thank you, Jerry, my heart, it is burning, it is on fire. I will go into your mountain teepee. I will walk in your moccasins. I will be your woman.)"

"Does that mean yes?" Jerry asked, placing his hands on either side of her face and pulling her closer.

"Yes," she whispered, slipping her arms around his neck. Their lips met in sublime sweetness, burning, consuming, and melting the two into one as with eternal promise. He dropped his hand from her face to her waist, drawing her to him. This is what he had dreamed about all those years. His beautiful Rachel, with her soft, black hair bathed in the sweet scent of honeysuckle, brushing against his face, her arms hot and tight around his neck, her lips warm and sweet. She was his dream, the dream that would mother all of his other dreams. For the first time in his life, Jerry felt complete. And he was home in her arms.

CHAPTER THIRTY-ONE

Rachel snuggled in Jerry's lap, her head resting on his shoulder as they sat in the chair in his room. She gently ran her fingers down the side of his face, blinking hard, and trying to control her emotions. Finally she spoke.

"Jerry, I have started proceedings to adopt Danny. I called from Indian Valley to get it going the morning that I left."

Jerry was silent for a moment, a look of hurt in his eyes. "You've been thinking about this for a while then, haven't you?"

"Only since that day. I just had a very strong impression that I am supposed to. It feels so right."

"Then you'd better go for it. If it's right, it's right."

"Oh, Jerry, I am just so sorry that I did not include you in the first place. I know how very much you love him." She hung her head, fighting tears.

"Rachel, I was pretty upset when I found out you didn't tell me about Danny, but David explained your reasons to me."

"They don't even make sense to me now, Jerry. It was very wrong."

"I am hurt, Rachel, that you didn't tell me. But what really hurts is that you couldn't trust me enough to tell me."

A tear squeezed its way onto her cheek and trickled across her face, dripping off her nose. "I am truly sorry, Jerry."

"No, Honey, I'm sorry. I hadn't given you a reason to trust me. That's what hurts. You were honest with me from day one, but I gave you a rough ride. David told me what you said when you asked him not to tell me about Danny, and you were right. The answer to my own happiness is in my own heart. I only had to open it up and let you in. I failed you, Rachel, and left you to face it all alone. You must have been heartbroken when you heard about Danny. You should have been able to call me and share your pain. But I wasn't there for you. I let you fly away without ever admitting to you or myself that I would be lost without you. I didn't come for Danny, and I didn't come because your helicopter went down, Rachel. I came for me, because you are my happiness. I need you desperately." He sighed and wrapped his arms more tightly around her.

"I know a young woman who was living in the anguish of the past. She was tormented and miserable. I was blessed with the opportunity to help her on one occasion. I told her that the past is gone, and that she needs to let it go. She had everything she could ever want to make her happy, but she was confused. I told her to make what she already had become what she really wanted, and then commit to it with all of her heart. I think she did; I hope she did. I didn't, and I nearly lost you. Can you ever forgive me?" Her gentle kiss mingled with her tears told Jerry that he was forgiven.

David had drawn the curtain between the beds to give his friends some privacy, but he heard every word spoken. He breathed a deep sigh of relief. He and Jan had worried about Jerry for seventeen years. Finally, Jerry had found his heart by giving it away.

In the quiet hospital, Jerry held Rachel in his arms and dreamed of his own family. An overwhelming feeling of joy and peace flooded through him as the full impact sank in. How he had longed for his own little son as he held and comforted a stranger's child. He had loved Danny as dearly as his own. Now Danny would be his own, and all the memories were theirs to keep. Suddenly, Jerry let out a war whoop he'd learned from Danny. Rachel jumped, nearly falling off his lap.

David threw open the curtain and stared at Jerry with much

the same expression that Rachel was staring at him.

Before either of them could speak, he yelled, "This is great! I'm gonna be a daddy!" He lifted Rachel as he stood up and took hold of her hand. "Come on, Mommy, I wanna go see our little boy."

David laughed out loud as they left the room. He laughed until he cried, but the tears weren't all from laughing. He had never seen Jerry so happy. With his menu pencil gripped painfully between two bandages, he dialed the phone to tell his mother and his wife the wonderful news.

Jerry stood in the darkened room with his arm around his cherished wife-to-be. They looked together upon the sleeping child who would be their own, and Jerry stroked his hand across the boy's fuzzy head.

"How long can he go on dialysis without kidneys?" Jerry asked with deep concern.

"Some people get along for years, but I am worried. Danny is very weak right now. He seems more fragile than I am comfortable with."

"Will he need more chemotherapy?"

"No, the tumor was encapsulated. It hadn't spread. He's not a good candidate, anyway. He's not strong enough."

"Well, at least it didn't spread. That's one piece of good news for the little guy. How soon can they do a kidney transplant?"

"Jerry, it can take months, even years to find a match."

"Then, we'll just have to find us a miracle, won't we?"

"There's your little miracle worker, right in front of you. Did you know he prayed me here? Connie said she's sure of it. She heard his humble little prayer right after they told him my helicopter had gone down, and he told me he prayed I would be found the day I was found. He wasn't surprised to see me, Jerry. He knew I would be here."

Jerry recalled the overwhelming feeling he had the night he saw the Northern Lights. The next day they had found Rachel. "That stupid bird was the answer to Danny's prayer," Jerry mumbled. "I knew it was a miracle, but I didn't know it was his miracle."

Rachel looked at Jerry questioningly, but Jerry just hugged her as he touched Danny's knobby knees through the covers.

❋

Danny sat next to David on his bed, both of them facing Jerry. Jerry had pushed his bed a few feet from David's and the bedside table was between them. He held a handful of cards, and Danny proudly held David's handful for him. Jerry was grinning smugly, and Danny and David were looking perturbed.

"Okay now, Danny, hold our hand below the table and hide her really good so he won't know where she is," David coached, looking over Danny's shoulder.

Danny's tongue helped him move the cards about like it had helped him move his pocketknife when he was carving. Jerry savored the memory. Soon Danny proudly held his bulging hand of cards across the table.

"Betcha get her back," he said, moving the cards under Jerry's fingers so the old maid was always in line for him to draw. David winked at Jerry, and Jerry pretended to be upset when he drew the old maid again. Danny laughed, thinking he'd been very sly.

Finally, Danny tired of the game, so they put it away.

"Hey, Danny, if you take a nap right now, maybe Rachel won't make you go to your room when she gets back," Jerry said.

"Where is she?" David asked.

"Her brother's bringing her some clothes this afternoon, so she's probably taking a shower in the nurses lounge again. I think they'll just let her kind of live here for a while." Jerry nodded his head toward Danny.

David understood. "So we're gonna take naps, huh?" he said, helping Jerry's plan.

"Why don't you lie down beside me and we'll at least pretend," Jerry said. He was worried and hoped Danny would sleep for a while. He had noticed how unsteady Danny's hands were while he held the cards, and how often he had leaned against David for support.

"Can I take a nap with David this time? He never got to share a nap with me before like you and me have."

"Sure," David said, scooting over to make room for Danny. Jerry leaned across and held the covers up for Danny to crawl under. Then David wrapped his arm around the little boy, enjoying his delightful company. Danny took special care not to bump David's bandaged hand resting against his leg, but he kept looking at it.

"You were helping Jerry when your hands got frozen, weren't you?" Danny asked.

"Nah, I was just being careless."

"No, I heard Rachel talking to someone on the phone when she thought I was sleeping. And she said she didn't know Jerry was hanging in the air and David was hanging onto him so he didn't fall, 'cause if he fell he'd drown. Then she said that's why he took his gloves off." He looked up at David and smiled. "I'm glad you didn't let Jerry fall. You helped him and froze your hands because of the bond, I know."

Jerry was staring at David. "So the truth comes from the mouths of babes, huh? You saved my skin again! How did you get frost bite, David?"

David shrugged. "Ah, I just dropped my gloves, that's all."

"When you took them off to tie something around me so I wouldn't fall. What was I hanging from?"

"Your backpack caught on the helicopter blade."

"Holy cow! Your prayer must have been protecting me too, Danny."

"I know," Danny said in simple faith. "See, David, you were helping Jerry. He told me you do that lots of times."

"He helps me just as much," David said, grinning. "That's what brothers do."

Jerry reached across and grasped David's shoulder in a firm grip, his eyes grateful and earnest. "Thanks brother," he said.

"Wow, you told me about it, Jerry, but I never really saw the bond work like this. It's so cool. Will I ever have to die for our bond?"

Jerry and David looked at each other with stunned expressions.

"No, of course not. Why did you ask that, Danny? Very few people have to die for a bond," Jerry answered.

"I just wondered, because I wouldn't be afraid to die if David or you ever need me to. You're my brothers." He yawned and snuggled deeper into the covers and closer to David, who tightened his arm around the child and swallowed hard to move the lump from his throat.

Both men sat in silent awe, side by side in their hospital beds, looking with admiration at a little brown Indian boy who had greater courage than many men. Jerry folded his hands behind his head and settled against his pillow, deep in thought. David knew him well, and watched him for some time while they waited to speak until Danny was soundly sleeping.

"Okay, what's running through that brain of yours, Bud? I can see the wheels turning, and you're not thinking small stuff." David's voice was soft so as not to wake the child, but it carried a serious tone.

"I'm gonna do it, David. With God as my witness and begging him that this will work, I'm gonna do it."

David knew Jerry had something big in his mind, but now, as goose bumps crawled up his back, he felt it. "Jerry, you're making me nervous. This isn't just big, is it? This is really big. What are you going to do, or would I rather not ask?"

"I'm going to donate a kidney to Danny. How long can a little boy live without one, and I've got two. He's going to be my son, and I don't want to lose him. You saw his little hands trembling. He's so weak it's hard for him to sit up. You heard him. We've got a bond, and you and I both know he meant what he said a minute ago about dying for you or me. I've got to do this. God, please help me, I have to do it for my little son." Jerry pulled his glasses off and buried his face in his hands as an indescribable feeling swept through him, much like he had felt under the majesty of the Northern Lights. He was overcome and remained unmoved for some time.

David sat in silence, feeling pride and esteem for his friend's noble desire. Then he ran his free bandaged hand through his hair and blew his breath out through pursed lips. He leaned his head against his pillow, glancing at Jerry frequently, but not wanting to disturb him. Besides, he was too moved to speak.

※

David's hands were still painful but were healing slowly. They looked better with each dressing change. He and Jerry were ready for discharge. Since Jerry was going through extensive blood and kidney tests, and David was laid up anyway, Jan and Kimberly suggested that David stay with Jerry until he either went to Seattle for the transplant, or came home. They rented a room at a boarding house near the hospital.

News about the adoption and news about the kidney transplant came the same day. Both were approved. Rachel, who was wearing a beautiful diamond ring, and Jerry were holding hands when they walked into Danny's hospital room just after lunch. On insisted invitation, David followed them with a wheelchair.

Danny had been lightly dozing and awoke immediately when Rachel placed a soft kiss on his forehead. Before she could raise up, his arms circled her neck and hugged her.

"Danny we have some wonderful news to tell you. It's very special news, so the hospital gave us a cozy family room so we can all sit together."

Danny's eyes were wide and bright. "Are we going to have another party?"

"Not today Danny, but soon we'll have the best party ever!" Jerry promised. "Come on little Buddy, let's go for a ride with Uncle David."

"Uncle David?" Danny asked, twisting his face into a strange little question mark.

Jerry just lifted him over the bed rail and settled him in the chair. David made the ride fun, pretending to run over nurses who got in the way. In the room, Rachel sat on a soft couch. Jerry sat

Danny between him and Rachel, and David sat nearby with a grin so large that it could break his face.

Jerry held Rachel's ring in front of Danny's face. "See that ring? It's like a bond—a different kind of bond, but just as special. It's a promise that two people make when they love each other."

Danny's mouth dropped open. "Are you and Rachel gonna get married?" he asked, and then, without waiting for an answer, he continued, "I knew it when you started doing all that kissing." Danny flashed a happy smile that said he was going to take credit for the whole courtship.

"That's only part of the happy news, Danny." Rachel took the letter from her purse approving the adoption. "Danny, this paper gives permission for me to adopt you as my own little boy. Then, when we get married, Jerry can adopt you too."

Danny just stared at Rachel with a confused furrow on his brow. "You mean you and Jerry will be my mom and dad?" he asked. Rachel nodded. "Really?" This time Jerry nodded. "I can live with you and be your kid?" They both nodded.

Wincing with pain but too excited to care, he turned around on the couch, kneeling between them, and threw his arms around their necks, pulling them both close and hugging them as tightly as his little arms could hug. When he turned, big tears were rolling down his cheeks.

"Look Jerry, I'm crying happy tears."

"So are we, Danny," Rachel said, laughing and wiping her eyes as Jerry lifted his glasses, brushed his handkerchief across his eyes, and then blew his nose. "We are going to be a family."

"Wow, a family! Is that why David is Uncle David now?" David nodded.

"This is so cool!" Danny said, sitting back down, almost like a rag doll, his energy spent from the excitement. "What about the party?" he asked, leaning weakly against Rachel.

"It's called a wedding. When we get married you'll get to meet all your aunts, uncles, and cousins," she said supporting him with her arm.

"I'm gonna have cousins?"

"Nine of them—no, ten," Jerry said, remembering Roxanne and Eric's baby.

"Where will we live?

"We'll build a home near Uncle David and Aunt Kimberly's Mom so she can be your Grandma. Then Rachel—I mean Mom, can take care of her. Aunt Sally said I've left her alone in the shop so long it should be hers, anyway." Jerry chuckled.

"We will miss Alaska, Danny, but we will come back often to visit our family here. We will be happy in Indian Valley. It will be our home, and we will be a family. That is most important." Rachel hugged Danny and smiled. "We can keep Alaska with us forever in our hearts. It will always be a part of us because you and I will always be Athabaskan and Alaskan.

CHAPTER THIRTY-TWO

"Wow, I get to ride on a real airplane!" Danny said, as he, Jerry, Rachel, and David waited to board the plane to Seattle for the kidney transplant. Rachel, who was now Danny's legal mother, and Jerry had decided to keep the news from Danny until the night before the surgery. They didn't want him to worry. Besides, Jerry was worrying enough for all four of them.

When they arrived, the hospital personnel honored their request to admit Danny and Jerry to the same room because Rachel was a nurse and a mom, and they would soon be a family. Danny was used to hospitals, but he began to have questions and some growing apprehension when he and Jerry were admitted. He was with his new mamma and his "almost Daddy," as he called Jerry, so he wasn't afraid, but he pressed for answers.

"If your head isn't hurt anymore, then why are they dressing you in a hospital gown?" Danny asked suspiciously.

"They are going to help you get better, and I didn't want you to feel lonesome so I asked for one too," Jerry said.

"Huh uh, 'cause they gave you a regular bed, and not a cot like they gave Rachel. What's goin' on?"

"The doctors think they have found you a kidney so you can get well," Rachel said, realizing he knew a lot more than they supposed.

"Where are they getting it from?" he asked.

"Some nice person who didn't need two kidneys wanted you to have it, Danny, so you can get strong and healthy again," Rachel answered, tucking him in bed so the lab technician could draw some blood. He flinched and gritted his teeth when the needle came near, but he didn't move. He watched warily as the technician moved to Jerry's bed. He drew the curtain, but Danny was sure he drew Jerry's blood as well.

David tried to play games with Danny, or tell him stories about him and Jerry. Danny loved to hear the stories, but today, Danny remained solemn and watchful, especially if any hospital staff approached Jerry.

"Can people die if they don't have kidneys?" Danny asked.

"Well, you don't have any, and you're not dead," Jerry answered, watching Danny's unusually solemn expression and suspicious eyes. "Come on, Danny, lighten up. You and I know how to have lots of fun in hospitals, don't we?"

"This hospital's different. They're up to something!"

Jerry, David, and Rachel exchanged surprised glances.

David covered a smile that he couldn't wipe off his face. He knew this was serious business, but he was frequently surprised and delighted by Danny's wit and insight. Danny, he believed, would keep Jerry on his toes. It would be a joy to watch his friend being a daddy to this charming youngster.

Jerry watched Danny, trying to listen to the thoughts behind Danny's words.

"Someone could die without a kidney, though, couldn't they?" Danny asked.

"Not very often anymore, Danny," Rachel said, rubbing his skinny little shoulders and casting Jerry a questioning gaze. "Dialysis helps many people live without them."

"I need to know who's giving me a kidney," Danny said emphatically, folding his arms and sitting against the raised head of his bed. He was looking intently at Jerry.

Jerry wrinkled his brow and looked at Rachel, who was looking back at Jerry in amazement. Maybe it was time to tell him, but they didn't get the chance.

"It's our bond, Jerry, isn't it? I've been really sick, so you're going to give me your kidney." His dark eyes were steady and sure.

Jerry left his bed and picked Danny up in his arms. He carried him to his bed and sat him beside him. "Okay, you guessed it. We didn't want you to worry."

"I've been worrying all along, 'cause they're doing things to you like they do to me. I don't want you to get stuck by needles and get your side cut open like me." He raised his gown revealing the newest scar on his side.

"Danny, I asked if I could give you a kidney. I prayed really hard that the doctors would say yes. I wanted a miracle for you. I need to do this." He gathered Danny in his arms and held him close. "I want you to play, and have fun, and be a kid. I love you very much, and I want to see you well and strong."

"But if you die, I can't see you. I only saw my mamma once, in the Yoyekoyh (Northern Lights). I want you here with me. I'm finally gonna have a dad, like other kids. I don't like the bond anymore." He threw his arms around Jerry's waist and clung to him desperately as big tears rolled down his cheeks.

Rachel went to Jerry's bedside and wrapped her arms around her family, soothing and comforting Danny, while Jerry's eyes met with David's, pleading for help.

David nodded and then arose, staring out the window at the Seattle lights, wondering at the depth, heart, and soul of one little brown Indian. He ran his sore hands through his hair and blew out a long breath, then looked at his hands. He remembered Danny's concern when he saw the bandages, and his almost reverent pride in David, because he had been true to his bond to Jerry.

For the first time in Danny and Jerry's relationship, Jerry could think of nothing he could say to help. His commitment and deep desire to help his child had come off as a betrayal. He quietly asked David to sit with Danny while he and Rachel went for a walk to discuss the situation.

Danny was pouting, but the pain in his eyes verified that his fears were very real.

David picked Danny up and put him in his lap, wincing from the pain in his hands. Danny immediately noticed, gently touching David's red and swollen fingers.

"These hands are what it's all about, Danny. If you had been there instead of me and seen Jerry hanging where he could fall and drown, what would you have done?"

"I'd have grabbed him and held onto him like you did."

"I couldn't fasten Jerry's safety harness because my gloves were in the way. I knew my hands could freeze. I'm an artist. I paint beautiful pictures with these hands. That's one of my favorite things in the whole world to do. But if I didn't secure Jerry's harness, he might fall, and I would lose my brother. What was more important, Danny, my hands and my painting, or my brother?"

"Jerry is more important. He would have died."

"You told me you aren't afraid to die for Jerry. What if he was sick and needed a kidney, and you had two good ones?"

Danny dropped his head. "I'd give him one."

"How do you think I would have felt if Jerry woke up and told me he didn't want me to rescue him, and I just had to let him hang there, knowing he might fall?"

"That would make you sad, because you love him."

"Danny, Jerry sees you kind of hanging from your IV tubes. He's afraid that if you don't get a kidney, you might fall."

"You mean he's afraid I might die?"

David nodded. "His kidney is your safety harness, Danny. He knows he'll hurt. He knows he might get really sick like you have been, but he is making this sacrifice because you're more important than his pain, just like his safety harness was more important than my hands."

Danny looked at David's hands, and then he looked into David's kind, blue-gray eyes as tears brimmed in his own. "Okay," he said.

David grinned and ruffled his short black hair. "I understand wonderful things happen when you pray, like Rachel getting found. So let Jerry take care of you, and you ask God to take care of Jerry. Then everyone gets taken care of, deal?" He held his hand up.

Danny smiled and gently slapped David's hand. "Deal," he said, and then looked worried when David winced with pain. David grinned, and Danny grinned back.

David had gone to his hotel room, and Rachel was sleeping on a cot on the other side of Danny's bed. Danny snuggled in Jerry's arms in the quiet darkness of the hospital room. He sniffled, wiping tears from his eyes with the back of his hands, trying hard to be brave.

"Are you scared?" Jerry whispered. Danny nodded in the darkness, and Jerry felt his head move. "You're going to be fine, Danny. You'll be able to run and play and ride your new bike all over the mountains."

"I know, but I don't want you to die for me, so I can do all that stuff."

"Hey, cut that out! I'm not going to die!"

"But you might, and I wanna grow up with you for my dad."

Jerry took a long, deep breath. Hoping to ease Danny's mind, he faced the fact that Danny well understood how fragile life is. "Danny, hundreds and thousands of people have surgery and don't die. You've had two, yourself, and you're still kicking around. I know that on rare occasions someone might die, and if that were to happen, hey, that's just part of the deal. That's why our bond is so important. But now, it'll even be stronger."

"Even if you die?"

"Sure, instead of us just mixing our blood, we're mixing our insides too. Wherever you go, part of me, really, part of me will always be with you, and I'd want you to do all the fun and happy things for me too that we like to do. I took you home with me when I left Alaska, and I know you took me home with you to the Birchwoods." He felt Danny nodding. "See, no matter where we are, we'll always be with each other in our hearts."

"Like my mamma," Danny said as he patted Jerry's cheek.

"And mine," Jerry said, kissing his small hand. "Now, say our prayer for us so we can go to sleep. We've got a big day tomorrow."

Jerry had never known heaven was so near as he listened to

the humble pleading, and felt the great faith of this child's prayer. It surrounded and encompassed them. Then Danny snuggled beside Jerry. As he wrapped his strong arms around the skinny little boy, a memory warmed him, a dream far away in a hospital bed in Alaska. He and Danny were fishing together, and Danny was his own little boy. His tears dampened the short hair on the head pressed against his cheek as he realized that dreams really can come true.

※

David stood beside Rachel, his comforting arm resting on her shoulder as they stood by the bedside in the Intensive Care Unit. The surgery had been long and had encountered some difficulties, but the prognosis was good for Danny and Jerry.

They had been in separate beds in the room. However, Danny was restless, thrashing about, whimpering, and getting tangled in his IV tubing. Jerry, though groggy and disoriented, was also restless and kept trying to reach out to comfort Danny. Rachel suggested that they put them together. Fearing that Danny might get hurt as both patients lay in the irrational sleep induced by anesthesia, the nurses were reluctant to follow her advice. Finally, they decided to try her suggestion. Danny calmed the instant he felt Jerry's arm around him. And Jerry, gently holding the child, knew that he was there, even in his sleep. They were both resting peacefully, now.

"Thank you for your wonderful friendship and support, David," Rachel said, leaning against him as she slipped her arm around his back. "Everything has happened so fast. Just a few months ago, I had never met you, or Danny, or Jerry. I keep pinching myself to make certain that I am not dreaming this wonderful family. When you call Kimberly tonight, please tell her how deeply grateful I am to have a friend with me through this ordeal. I am certain she misses you very much."

"David hugged her shoulder and drew her closer. "Where would Jerry or Danny be without you, Rachel? For the first time in years I feel complete peace when I think of Jerry. Since you and I pulled him out of that bog together, we've been a team. With you on my team there was no way we could lose this one, even though we felt we might a few times. This is all so right." He kissed the top of her head and then chuckled. "For someone he didn't know he loved, you could sure get his stubborn hedgehog's heart pounding. Are you sure you don't want me to stay? What if you need help?"

"Thank you, no. The nurses are here and attentive. You call Kimberly and then get some rest. I may need you more tomorrow so I can rest. Please tell Jan that I miss her greatly."

Rachel sat in the chair near the bed and watched over Danny and Jerry. She was very tired, but felt at peace. As she studied Jerry's handsome face, minus his ever-familiar glasses, she longed to be in his arms and feel his kiss on her lips, but that would come soon enough. Right now, he was the most unselfish, tender, noble, and compassionate daddy in the world. Even in his great pain, voluntarily suffered for the child in his arms, his first response any time he roused, or Danny stirred, was to touch or comfort the boy.

Suddenly, Rachel remembered a powerful premonition, from a time past when she sat in another hospital room watching this man and this child. It had touched her then, and it touched her now, washing over her, and tingling through her. *What am I feeling?* She had asked herself back then, sensing something far greater than she knew. The feeling returned now, as sublime fulfillment of those impressions. How could she have ever imagined the promise that lay hidden in that premonition? She gazed with a joyful heart at her future husband and her very own son. Enlightened by blessings beyond measure, she finally understood the quiet whisperings of the spirits that had directed her to take a sad and lonely little boy to visit a discouraged and heart-broken man.

"Ehe', drana nezrunh. Betlanh has become be ele'a. Si draya' it is full. Much happiness I have from Belo' in the yo. (Yes, today it is good. His friend has become his daddy. My heart, it is full. Much happiness I have from His hand in the sky.) Basi' (thank you)," she whispered, bowing her head and smiling. Then she gazed through

the dim light at the sleeping man and boy in the hospital bed. Danny was snuggled under Jerry's arm, his hand resting softly against Jerry's cheek. She sighed deeply and relaxed, settling herself in the chair to guard her precious family through the night.

Chapter Thirty-three

Lilac and chokecherry bushes were in full bloom, and wild roses displayed their delicate pastel color near the shore of the pond. The rich aromas blended and mingled with the scent of evergreens and the earth washed clean by recent thunderclouds.

The pond lay shimmering beneath the bright, spring sunlight, as fluffy clouds drifted lazily across the smooth surface of the lovely woodland pool.

Kimberly and Sally were busying themselves with last minute table settings and floral arrangements on the rented tables. The tables were draped in brilliant Magenta coverings with a skiff of pale pink chiffon, and accents of mint green flowers scalloped along the edges of the tables located near the pond. Jane and Stephanie, Jerry's two older sisters, were hustling about in Jan's kitchen, mixing punch and placing hors d'oeuvres on plates. Their older children helped set up chairs, while the younger ones played hide-and-seek among the bushes near the pond.

Jan and Roxanne had just met, and visited in the living room about the new baby. Roxanne was smiling, happy, and extremely excited.

David watched her, sitting cross-legged on her feet in his mother's chair, softly rubbing and patting the large bulge in her tummy. She laughed, and her laugh was enchanting like he remembered her in times past. The bitterness and anger were all gone, now. He was glad to have her back among friends.

"David," Eric said, placing his hand firmly on David's shoulder, "Jerry's sister, Jane, I think it is, said they need some strong men to move a wedding cake. Shall we brave it? Dad said he'll supervise, but he won't touch it." Eric chuckled and added, "After his two last mining accidents, the old miner said every time he touches anything, he either breaks something, or it caves in on him. He said he doesn't want to show up at his daughter's wedding reception wearing her cake."

"Sure," David replied, following Eric to the cake. "Man, you should have seen Jerry this morning," he chuckled as they carefully moved the cake toward the edge of the pond where Jane and Stephanie were nervously waiting for it. Their husbands who had been supervising the children's play kept the children out of their pathway.

"What did he do?" Eric asked.

"Wait, I'll start at the beginning. Sally said he's been impossible to live with ever since he came home from Alaska. He's moaned and groaned around the house, forgets where he's going, forgets what he's doing, and last month the phone bill took all the grocery money. They've eaten canned soup for a month. She said she'd have booted him out, but he paid the rent through today so she couldn't." They reached the cake table and carefully set it in place. Then they strolled around the pond as David continued his story.

"This morning I went to load his van with the rest of his things to bring to his new house. He was rushing around, getting ready to pick Rachel up from the motel. He couldn't find his shoes, and he couldn't find his glasses. He'd put them up on his head while looking for his shoes. He's been that way for four months. He finally left the apartment to go get her, but came back about fifteen minutes later, embarrassed and burned. She'd pointed out that he had on his tie and tux jacket, but he'd forgotten his shirt."

Eric laughed. "Rachel's been pretty cool. She's had Danny to keep her occupied. She helped Dad a lot with his business, and she and Roxy have gotten really close. They made an entire layette for little Jerry."

"Who?" David asked.

"Our baby," Eric said, grinning proudly. "There was only one name we could rightfully give him. So, when he's born, his birth certificate will read Jerry Samuel Duncan. Think Uncle Jerry will mind?"

"Not in a million years, Eric. He'll be honored." David answered, feeling that life was pretty darn good after all.

Jerry and Rachel had chosen to have a very private, short ceremony just between themselves. Then they would drive to Indian Valley where everyone was eagerly awaiting their arrival for a special ring ceremony and reception. Jerry had promised Danny a big party, and everyone was here to make sure that he was not disappointed as he met all of his new family and friends for the first time.

As Jerry knelt with Rachel at the altar in the small, but beautiful marriage room, he took her soft, brown hand in his. The feelings surrounding them were incredible. He smiled, gazing deeply into her hazel-green eyes, as he committed to the sweet and sacred promises of marriage. He had never seen her more beautiful, and he knew that to love, cherish, and adore her forever just wouldn't be long enough. They exchanged promises and then shared a tender kiss across the altar—not one of passion but one of promise, a promise that meant forever. As the officiator concluded the ceremony, they stood facing each other holding hands. Then they looked at their images reflected in gold-framed mirrors on both walls. Rachel's image, so lovely with her long flowing black hair, stretched before Jerry's view forever, and ever, and ever.

He gently pulled her to him and embraced her, smelling the sweet honeysuckle fragrance of her hair, and kissed her warmly and tenderly. They were separate beings, and yet together they made one, and they were whole.

❊

"They're here, they're here!" Sally squealed with her strange little jumping dance. She had been standing as a sentry, just as happy for her brother as David was.

Jerry, looking sharp and dashingly handsome in his white tux, strolled around his new family van and opened Rachel's door. Her gown was floor length, made of simple, white lace. A matching waist-length veil was wound into her hair with strands of fireweed, covering only the crown of her head.

The crowd lined the pathway to the pond, applauding and cheering as they walked toward the celebration. Danny walked proudly behind them in his white tux. His bronze skin looked striking against his white clothes. His full and healthy head of jet-black hair was cropped loose around his ears, with just a little touching his neck. He was slightly taken aback at the large crowd of strangers, quickly picking out cousins closest to his age, but he knew he belonged here.

After everyone was gathered near the cake table, Sam Duncan proudly announced the marriage. "I'm proud to introduce my lovely daughter, Rachel, and my great, new son, Jerry Stone, as husband and wife, to all you fine people. Jerry and Rachel, may you live in each other's hearts so deeply that you are as much in love when you are old and wrinkled as you are today." He nodded at Jerry and smiled, releasing his Rachel into her new husband's loving care. Jerry acknowledged Sam's tribute, returning a nod with a promise that he would cherish her always. "This couple has been blessed with a very special gift. Rachel and Jerry are the proud parents of my handsome new grandson, Danny Crow Stone." Everyone applauded, and Danny stood as tall and proud as he could beside his mother and his almost—no—his father. Each of them placed a loving hand on his shoulder.

"And now the couple will exchange rings," Sam said, smiling and backing away.

As Jerry took Rachel's small, brown hand in his and slipped the wedding band on her slender finger, he was stirred by a memory from his past. She flashed him the beautiful smile he had come to love so much, her hazel-green eyes gazing deeply into his with her love shinning through. She slipped the ring on his finger. Suddenly, he was overcome with the memory, now profound, from deep within his heart. He saw her hands, like his mother's, covered with flour, and her wonderful smile, like his mother's, as she stood watching him, like his father, playing with his—Jerry's eyes swept to Danny—his own son. The empty dream, crying for so many years from the depths of Jerry's soul had finally been filled. Jerry's heart was bursting with joy, light, and love, exquisite beyond anything he had ever imagined. Time, distance, place, and people all disappeared as he grasped his precious wife and son and gathered them to his heart. Tears ran down his face as he turned his face toward God.

"Thank you for the difficult journey," he whispered. "You knew all along it would be worth it. I had forgotten that your Son has already walked in my moccasins."

✳

A mild wind stirred the leaves and blossoms, whispering across the pond, but the water remained smooth, crystal clear, and translucent. Wispy clouds, the rustling leaves and blossoms bowing in the breeze, became frozen on the surface. An iridescent glow, more brilliant than the sun, fell upon the mirrored surface of the water. Three images grew out of the brightness and became as light. Three beautiful mothers smiled, two dressed in white caribou skins and braided hair, and one in a white gown, fair skinned with soft brunette curls. Reaching out of the brilliance, they touched the little family embracing on the shore. Their love, surpassing the space between life and death, surrounded and encompassed their children. Then the breeze stirred the surface of the water, and the vision disappeared into the sparkling ripples on the pond.

About the Author

Sharon Lewis Koho grew up on a small ranch near the town of Inkom, Idaho. Her beloved father died when she was five years old, and she and her siblings were reared in humble circumstances by a hardworking and courageous mother.

In her youth, Sharon discovered she could create any world she wanted to visit or any story she wanted to be a part of by climbing high trees bordering her cherished ranch. Her daydreaming amid the songs of birds, the rustling of leaves, and the babbling of the nearby creek inspired many wonderful stories.

Sharon married Bill Koho from Nampa, Idaho, in 1967. They were married thirty years until his death in 1997. She is the proud mother of six children.

Although she is a licensed practical nurse by profession, she has had much more experience in creating and telling stories. Her favorite thing to do is to spend time with her children and grandchildren. She also enjoys visiting, traveling, camping, reading, writing, swimming, and any adventurous idea that pops into her head.